D0838192

"I want to see the child,"

Colter insisted.

"I consider that unwise," Elizabeth began. "I'm sorry that you have wasted your time to come out here in such foul weather—"

"Elizabeth," Colter interrupted softly, almost too softly, "don't think to put me off. If she is my daughter, I have a right to see her."

"You must never say that! She cannot be claimed as yours."

"Are you now denying my paternity?" he queried in barely concealed anger. "Or have you some ploy in mind?"

"I want nothing from you."

Colter stood, watching her, his gaze shifting from the soft undulation of her hips to the lush swell of her breasts and then, with calculated assessment, to her lips. "I see you've donned armor." Her look begged an explanation. "The widow's weeds."

"Perhaps you should have worn your saber, Colonel. The cuts would be cleaner by far."

Dear Reader,

December is a busy time for most of you, and we at Harlequin Historicals would like to thank you for taking a moment to find out what we have to offer this month.

From author Marianne Willman, we bring you *Thomasina,* the continuing story of a character from *Vixen,* Ms. Willman's first book for Harlequin Historicals. Set in the Mexican countryside, the heroine lives out her dream of becoming a doctor and discovers love along the way.

In *A Corner of Heaven,* newcomer Theresa Michaels has written the touching story of a woman reunited with the father of her child amidst the danger and hardships of the Civil War.

Isabel Whitfield's *Silver Fury* takes place in a California silver town where a stubborn washerwoman and a rebellious blue blood manage to overcome their differences and find happiness. Caryn Cameron's *King's Man* takes the reader to Tudor England where a lady smuggler and a loyal soldier outwit their common enemies.

We hope that you will enjoy our December titles. From all of us at Harlequin Historicals, our best wishes for the holidays and the year ahead.

Sincerely,

The Editors

A Corner of Heaven

Theresa Michaels

Harlequin Books

TORONTO • NEW YORK • LONDON
AMSTERDAM • PARIS • SYDNEY • HAMBURG
STOCKHOLM • ATHENS • TOKYO • MILAN

Harlequin Historicals first edition December 1991

ISBN 0-373-28704-6

A CORNER OF HEAVEN

Copyright © 1991 by Theresa DiBenedetto.
All rights reserved. Except for use in any review, the reproduction or utilization of this work in whole or in part in any form by any electronic, mechanical or other means, now known or hereafter invented, including xerography, photocopying and recording, or in any information storage or retrieval system, is forbidden without the permission of the publisher, Harlequin Historicals, 300 E. 42nd St., New York, N.Y. 10017

All the characters in this book have no existence outside the imagination of the author and have no relation whatsoever to anyone bearing the same name or names. They are not even distantly inspired by any individual known or unknown to the author, and all incidents are pure invention.

®: Trademark registered in the United States Patent and Trademark Office and in other countries.

Printed in the U.S.A.

THERESA MICHAELS

is the pseudonym for an award-winning historical romance author. Avid reader turned writer, Theresa collects old Western newspapers and antique books on Western lore and Victorian Americana. A former New Yorker, she writes full-time and lives with her family and one cat in Florida.

To Elizabeth Cavanaugh,
for always being in my corner

Chapter One

Richmond, Virginia
November, 1862

"Elizabeth." Colonel Colter Wade Saxton whispered the name, rubbing his eyes. By the press of his knee he instantly brought his bay hunter to a halt and dismounted, half-believing that he had seen an apparition. Two loaded supply wagons rumbled past before he caught a glimpse of the woman's slender back. There was something... Ignoring his fellow officers' warnings that they were late for their meeting at the War Office, Colter dodged the carriages and wagons congesting the street and crossed to the building that the woman had disappeared into.

He quickly mounted the steps, compelled by an inner urgency. Once inside, he was jostled by the ebb and flow of people in the reception room belonging to Christopher Memminger, the Confederate secretary of the treasury.

Colter used his considerable height and lithe body to wedge a path through the crowd, absently begging the pardon of several matrons whose belled skirts he crushed in his progress. Coming to an abrupt stop, he searched for sight of his quarry. Spying the light gray mantle draped over a plum-colored skirt that the woman had been wearing, Colter shouted her name, disregarding the attention he brought to both of them. When she turned toward him, Colter tried to conceal his shock. Her face was pale, her eyes bruised with shadows. She silently mouthed his name, her gaze clouded with disbelief.

Caught at the far end of the room, hemmed in by the press of bodies, Elizabeth had no avenue of escape. She stood perfectly still, feeling time stop in the moments that it took him to move with a deadly, almost pantherlike agility to her side.

Colter swept her along to a small clear space against the back wall. "Dear Lord, Elizabeth, it's been so long." Silently cursing her bell hoop and crinoline, he took her into his arms and muffled her cry with his lips. Colter wasn't thinking; three hours of sleep in as many days had robbed him of that ability. The room, the shocked gasps, the war, all of it receded in those precious moments when he held her. His hand spanned the small of her back, pulling her closer to his body. He wanted to plunder her mouth with all the feverish intensity that gripped him, but her lips were soft and he gentled his kiss.

Elizabeth had had no time to marshal her defenses. Colter was here, alive, holding her and kissing her as if it were still his right.

And she was letting him.

No. Innate honesty demanded that she acknowledge she was desperate for his kiss, drowning again in the memory of her first taste of a man's passion. She gripped his arms and arched her head back, giving him her mouth with the hunger of a love too long denied.

As he held her against the hard warmth of his body, her senses blossomed to life, drawing in the well-remembered masculine scent that was Colter's alone, so that desire sharpened into consuming need.

Lovers...once, but no more. Her passion wasn't Colter's right to take, or hers to give.

The moist, smooth glide of his tongue skimming the seam of her lips forced her to pull away. Summon outrage for this breach of impropriety, she commanded herself. But she simply could not. For a few moments she stole the comfort of his arms, pressing her cheek to the soft wool of his uniform frock coat, and listened to the wild thud of his heart that kept cadence with her own.

Colter, both dream and nightmare from the past.

Colter pressed his lips to her temple, felt the frantic pulse beat and knew that another would beat in the hollow of her throat. He drew deep breaths that brought to life the delicate scent of peach blossoms. The scent was hers. A scent that had haunted his nights.

"I won't apologize, Elizabeth."

She jerked her head back, staring up at him with dismay. "You must. I—"

"Of course, how remiss of me." A cynical smile broke the sensuous curve of his mouth. His eyes glinted with fury as he stepped back and released her. "Our gallant code of honor demands that I be the one to apologize for *taking* liberties from a married woman."

"And you, sir? Would your wife not object?"

"Wife? One near chance to enjoy the married state was enough to cure me of the desire."

He had no right to cast his bitterness on her, Elizabeth thought. She bit her lower lip, wondering what he had meant by his pointed words, but she would not ask. Glancing down to where she twisted the cord of her reticule, she prayed that no one she knew had been witness to her indiscretion. Fear of what could result made her attempt to step forward.

Colter quickly raised his arm and braced his hand against the wall, using his body as both a shield and an imprisoning force. He was certain she had no wish to create a scene.

Elizabeth gazed up at him. Colter was dangerous, but at heart he was still a Southern gentleman. His words dashed her hope that he would step aside.

"No. You're not running off. Surely, you can be gracious enough to spare a few minutes to renew your acquaintance with an old friend?"

Elizabeth flinched under the relentless bite of his words. Although he had waited years for this confrontation, Colter found he took little satisfaction in seeing the pleading look in Elizabeth's eyes. Her face whitened until he feared she would faint.

"Please, let me pass, Colter. We have nothing to say to each other." Elizabeth could feel the powerful tension from his body surround her. She did not want to remember how his clean-shaven cheeks and jaw felt beneath her lips, or how the neatly clipped sideburns felt against her skin. She did not want to notice that he appeared exhausted. She was not going to allow even a tiny ember of compassion to interfere with sane reason, which begged her to get away from him quickly. Now, while she could still summon the will.

"What are you doing in Richmond, Elizabeth? Has James managed to get himself a desk job to sit out the war? Is that why you're afraid to talk to me? Is James here?"

"Have mercy, Colter," she whispered. "Don't you know?" His frown and puzzled look answered her. "He was declared missing after the fighting at Shiloh."

"The Hornet's Nest? With Johnston?"

"Yes."

"But that was over seven months ago."

"Were you there, Colter?"

"No. But I know we lost almost a third of our men in that battle, along with any hope for a quick and bloodless end to the war. Surely in all this time you've had some word of James?"

She closed her eyes, shaking her head slowly, trying but failing to regain her composure.

"Are you certain, Elizabeth? So many men have similar names. There could have been a mistake. When we first heard that General Johnston was killed there, no one realized that it was Albert and not Joseph who died."

She opened her eyes and looked up briefly. "There were no Warings listed among the dead, wounded or the prisoners taken by the Union forces." She hoped that Colter would credit the start of tears to the news of her husband. She must never let him know how betrayed she felt, first by Colter and then by James. She could never tell him that her marriage to James had been a terrible mistake, or explain that James's status of missing left her exposed to the viciousness of her mother-in-law, Alma Waring. Her stomach began to churn with nausea. She would never let Alma succeed with her plan.

Meeting Colter was a complication she didn't want or need. He was part of her past, and, heaven help her, she had to keep him there.

Without thinking, she raised her fingertips to her lips. She could feel the lingering heat of Colter's mouth, just as the tip of her tongue could still taste him.

"Don't."

His tortured whisper nearly undid her. Her gaze locked with his, and she had to force herself not to plead. "You must excuse me, Colter."

He sensed her desperation to get away from him, but he didn't move. There had been too many nights when he had longed to see her again, despite the bitterness he harbored. But he puzzled over why she appeared to be afraid of him. That wasn't a trait of the Elizabeth he knew.

With considerable effort, he buried the questions he wanted answers to, stifled the roil of emotions she raised inside him and offered her a smile.

"I won't hurt you, Elizabeth. Can't you tell me why you're here? I can assure you, the secretary won't be able to give you any information regarding James."

The soft, coaxing drawl of his voice soothed her. Colter, at his charming best, was difficult to resist. She sighed, releasing some of her tension.

"I'm here to apply for a job." As she said the words, she prayed that Colter was not quartered in or near

Richmond. She would not survive being forced to see him again.

"I don't understand."

"Ever since the Confederate congress passed the Conscription Act to recruit more men to fight, women have been allowed to fill the vacant positions in government bureaus."

"But what does that matter to you? Why would you need a job?" Colter couldn't stop himself from teasing her. "Ever the rebel, little fox?"

A wicked grin creased his lips, beckoning her once again to share her innermost feelings. Despite the past, Elizabeth was tempted to open her heart to him. She stared up at his eyes, watching as their green color darkened, splintering the gold flecks into bright shards of desire.

Colter gazed at her, then murmured, "You haven't forgotten when I first called you that, have you?"

A flood of warm memories assailed her. One by one, she fought them down. "Stop this, Colter. Don't say anything that you will regret. And do not call me that again. I've left all my childhood indulgences behind."

"Childhood indulgences?" he repeated with scorn. "Is that what I was to you?" He leaned closer, forcing her back to the wall. "Tell me, Mrs. Waring, do you greet all the ghosts from your past with such ardor?"

She searched his features, as familiar as her own, and found no softening in them. With a lift of her rounded chin, she summoned courage. "I am quite sure that you have other important business to tend to, as I do."

"Nothing," he grated from between clenched teeth, "could possibly tear me from your side."

An inner door opened, and the crowd surged toward the under secretary, who stood, list in hand, calling out names. Colter glared at a couple that shoved him from behind, almost causing him to crush Elizabeth against the wall. Yet he couldn't deny that he would seize any excuse to be close to her, and the devil could take his damn honor.

Elizabeth's head remained bowed as Colter stepped back and stared his fill. She appeared to have a deceptive air of fragility. Willow slender, delicately boned, her height barely brought the top of her head to his chin. Not that her height ever stopped him from claiming the lush fullness of her mouth. He could feel his blood grow hot, pulse and surge, all of which he forcibly subdued. His gaze shifted to the small, smoke gray bonnet perched toward the back of her head, revealing the smooth center part of her hair. The color of her hair reminded him of the warm blend of nutmeg and cinnamon spices, and he almost reached up to touch it.

Elizabeth glanced up, then away. Colter thought about feathering kisses at the slanted corners of her eyes, watching them darken to the deep richness of whiskey. Her lashes were long and straight, light at the tips. Right now, to his frustration, she used them effectively to bar his gaze from meeting hers.

"Are you finished, Colter? People are staring."

"No. I've questions that have gone begging for answers and I won't be cheated."

Elizabeth withdrew inside herself. It was the only way to cope with him.

Colter's breath caught and he released it slowly. He wanted to shake her, but at the same moment he wished he could turn back time. Four years to be exact. He should have proposed marriage to her, not given in to a damn misplaced desire to allow her time to explore and grow in her newly found freedom. He had thought her too young to marry at seventeen. *But not too young to make love,* a nagging devil reminded him.

He clenched his hand at his side. His best friend, James Waring, had had no such noble sentiments. Within months of Colter's arrival in England on family business, James wrote that Elizabeth had agreed to marry him.

It was an open wound that had never healed. He knew she had loved him. She had proved it that last night together, defying all she had been taught, all she believed in, to love him.

Elizabeth noted the change in his breathing. His eyes were closed, and she knew that Colter was lost in the past. Why didn't she bolt and run? Colter had no right to stop her. But he would. She knew that.

Hesitantly she placed her hand on his arm. "Colter, it doesn't do any good to remember the past."

His dark brown lashes lifted, revealing a look so cold that it sent shivers down her spine. He covered her hand with his, shaking his head.

"This isn't the place for us to talk. And I need—"

"No. It's over," Elizabeth said. Colter's gaze hardened, raising her anger. "Haven't you exacted enough payment? You left me, Colter, four years ago. What do you want of me now?"

It pained him to hear her agonizing plea. "Come with me."

Elizabeth swallowed. Honesty was the only weapon she had to use. "I can't leave. I told you I'm here to apply for a job. Please, Colter," she whispered, seeing the firm set of his chin. "It was difficult for me to make the arrangements to come to Richmond. Mr. Memminger has ignored every letter I've sent." She looked around the room, adding, "You can see for yourself how many are here."

Colter, too, glanced around him. "Is that what these women want from him, jobs?"

"Living in Richmond is expensive. By their dress most of them appear to be widows. The salary offered is sixty-five dollars a month, and I've been told that for every opening there are over a hundred women applying, so you see, I must stay."

"And the chatelaine of the Waring plantation is planning to live on that pittance? Your bonnet had to cost more."

"Stop mocking me. I was never the chatelaine of the plantation. James's mother wouldn't allow it."

"If fear of not seeing Memminger is all that is keeping you from accompanying me, rest assured, my dear Mrs. Waring, I'll arrange a private appointment for you." Colter took her arm and tucked it into the crook of his elbow, holding her hand firmly so that she was anchored to his side.

She tried to argue, but it was a futile exercise. Colter intended to escort her out, and he couldn't or wouldn't listen to her. She felt an unwanted stab of jealousy as women turned admiring glances his way. Colter had a commanding presence, a reputation for being a daredevil, and his rough-hewn features that hinted of an untamed virility were sure to attract female attention wherever he went. Even Elizabeth wasn't immune.

Once they stepped outside, the rising winter wind made its bite felt. Elizabeth shivered beneath the light wool mantle she wore. Colter noticed, but he was swearing softly to see the small contingent of his fellow officers waiting for him. He ignored their knowing grins, distracted for a moment. He couldn't very well take Elizabeth to his suite at the hotel. Where in the overcrowded capital was he going to find a respectable place of privacy?

"They're waiting for you, aren't they?" she asked, blushing at the young men's boldly admiring glances.

"Where are you staying?" he demanded, watching his friends dismount. Before the officers could climb the stairs, Colter had escorted Elizabeth down. He should have known that they would wait and, seeing Elizabeth, would demand introductions.

"I have rooms outside the city," she murmured, dreading the thought of meeting these men. They all appeared younger than Colter by a year or two, but as they drew closer, she could see the same fever-bright cynicism in their eyes that marked so many of the South's young men now. Elizabeth stood quietly at Colter's side, hoping that his chivalrous upbringing would make him offer her his protection.

The youngest of the three came forward, sweeping off his hat with a flourish, directing a rakish grin at Colter. "You are forgiven for making us wait on you."

"Mrs. Waring, may I present Major Brice Carroll, and don't mistake his charming looks for softness. Brice is the deadliest shot in our unit."

Elizabeth forced a smile, but she had to look away from his too-knowing eyes.

"A pity she's married, Colter. However, I would be most pleased—"

"Brice." The soft but unmistakable warning in Colter's voice captured the officer's immediate attention. "Mrs. Waring and her husband are old friends of mine. She has just informed me that James was lost at Shiloh."

The change in Brice's demeanor was startling. Elizabeth accepted his sincerely offered sympathy, but inwardly she cringed. The whole situation seemed fraudulent, somehow. As Colter introduced Lieutenant Colonel Andre Laurent, Elizabeth found her hand brought to his lips before she could refuse, and the warmth in his eyes expressed an offer she didn't dare acknowledge.

Last was Captain Hugh Morgan. She responded to both Colter's affectionate tone and the young captain's warm smile. Brice motioned Colter to his side. Elizabeth tried to murmur her excuses, wanting to escape, but Colter merely glared at her.

"I won't be long."

"Walker's gonna throw a fit seven ways to the devil if we're late, Colter. She's charming, and I fully understand your reluctance to join the secretary of war and his staff when such a young, lovely widow is in need of consoling, but she'll keep."

"You misunderstood me, Brice." Colter lowered his voice so that Elizabeth would not overhear them. "Her husband is listed as missing, not dead. Mrs. Waring has always had my utmost respect and I expect you to act accordingly." Placing his hand on the younger man's shoulder, Colter grinned. "But you can buy me a few minutes' time, can't you? I really do need to talk to her.

There seems to be some family crisis that I may be able to assist—''

''Say no more.'' Brice set his hat on his head with the wide brim tilted forward. ''Hugh, I do believe the colonel's bay has thrown a shoe. If you'll tend to it, Andre and I will make his apologies to the secretary.''

They took their leave quickly but respectfully from Elizabeth. Colter once again took her arm and led her around the corner of the building. It wasn't private, but it would have to do. He sheltered her with his body from the prying eyes of passersby.

''I want you to listen to me,'' he began. ''First, explain why you are in rooms outside the city? What happened to the Waring town house? Better still, tell me why you're not with James's family? Petersburg has been kept safe from the fighting.''

''It was Mother Waring's decision to sell all the Richmond properties.'' She was tempted to escape into the bustling street, knowing that Colter would not stop his interrogation until he had heard everything. Bowing her head, she tried to conceal the weariness that had taken its toll these past few months. Why, today of all days, did Colter have to come to Richmond? He would never accept the fact that he had no right to ask her anything. And fleetingly, Elizabeth wondered why she couldn't lie to him.

Colter leaned one shoulder against the building's wall, barely listening to the constant squeaks and rattles of lumbering wagons passing. He was, he thought, exercising a great deal of patience. It was difficult to temper his need for answers when she was so reluctant to supply them.

Removing one of his gray gauntlets and tucking it into his sash, he brushed his thumb across her cheek, then raised her chin. "Tell me what's happened to you. No judgments, Elizabeth. I care and need to know what I can do to help you."

"If you truly mean that, leave me alone."

"You request the impossible of me."

The gentleness of his touch proved almost too much. Elizabeth could fight his arrogance, his anger and his mockery, but not this. Tears formed and she blinked them back, but not before Colter caught one on his fingertip. She watched him bring that tiny bit of moisture to his lips.

The tip of his tongue licked it. His eyes narrowed all the while, staring intently into her own.

Elizabeth felt a warmth unfurl inside; she couldn't turn away.

"It isn't sweet, love. No tears from such bruised eyes could be. You remember how stubborn I am."

"Yes. Yes, I remember."

"So you'll tell me what I want to know."

Elizabeth found the decorative gold braid on his sleeve far easier to look at than the intensity of his gaze. "There isn't much to tell. I've been through no more and no less than most women in the South."

"Don't feed me that pious pap!" Her stricken look forced a barely polite apology, but it didn't stop his desire to take hold of her arms and shake the answers from her. Colter reminded himself that she was another man's wife, not his to demand anything of. Elizabeth couldn't be his.

She studied the deep creases at the corners of his eyes, the straight-bladed nose, the curve of his lips that had taught her pleasure. Her gaze lingered on the faint thin scar that marred his high-boned cheek.

Colter, as if he had sensed her thought, touched it. "A careless move against a saber. I was lucky with this one."

"There were others?" The thought of Colter being hurt...no, what was she thinking? She mustn't care about him.

"All minor. Stop distracting me. Shall I repeat—"

"No." Her voice was clipped as she cut him off. Colter was always fierce in his desire to have his demand met at the moment he expressed it. Resentment flooded her. She was a woman now, not the half-grown child he had carelessly led on and deserted. And she was quite comfortable with her independence, if not the manner in which she achieved it.

"James's mother didn't care for my conduct. It was not her idea of what befitted a grieving, proper Confederate widow. She expected me to pray for hours and refuse all condolence calls. She even attempted to lock me in my room. Her son, she claimed, deserved that much from me. When I tried—"

"She cast you out?"

"That doesn't surprise you. No, of course not. I had forgotten how well you knew the Warings. Alma then proceeded to turn the family against me."

"Elizabeth, did you love James so much—"

"Never ask me that. You truly have no right to."

The proud set of her head, the spark of fury in her eyes and the color flagging in her cheeks stopped him from debating the point. He conceded this tiny skirmish to her with a curt nod.

"I will tell you that I cannot grieve for James because I don't believe that he is dead. And if anyone is to blame for my leaving the family, it's me. The constant bickering, along with what they were trying to do to Nicole forced my decision."

"Nicole? I don't remember anyone with that name."

Drawing a shaky breath and slowly releasing it to control the urge to scream, Elizabeth paled and clutched the edges of her mantle. "I should have remembered the cruelty you're capable of, Colter." She stepped back and pivoted away from him, weariness cast aside under a surge of rage.

"What's come over you, Elizabeth? Stop backing away from me as if I were going to attack you!"

"How dare you pretend you don't know? How dare you! James relished telling me every detail of his last meeting with you."

Colter eased away from the wall slowly. Alarmed by her wild-eyed look, he stalked her.

"Colter!"

He spun around at the sound of Hugh's voice, still bewildered by Elizabeth's accusations.

"Brice sent me to find you, Colter. Walker is demanding your presence."

Torn between duty and his own need, Colter glared at him. "A few minutes more." He faced Elizabeth. "Where exactly are you staying? I must leave, but Hugh will arrange an escort for you and we'll continue this conversation later."

"That is unnecessary. I don't want anything from you, Colter. I certainly have no desire to see you again."

"But I intend to know why you've lashed out at me for no reason!"

"No reason? Will that be the needed sop to your pride? Must you hear the admission from me? Didn't you believe James when he told you about Nicole?"

"I haven't seen James in four years. Not since the day I sailed for England." His accusing voice stabbed the air between them. "If your husband told you differently, he lied. Now, who the devil is Nicole?"

"She's our child. Nicole is our daughter, Colter."

Chapter Two

"Colter," Hugh warned again, motioning to several people who stopped to stare at the shouting couple to move on.

"Christ!" Colter's voice became a strangled groan. They had a child! He turned away from her, his mind reeling. A child? His vision wavered and he had to brace himself against the wall to keep from stumbling. His shoulders heaved as he struggled to breathe.

He was grateful that Hugh came to his side and lent the strength of his shoulder for him to lean upon. Colter brushed his hand over his eyes as if to clear them. She was lying! She had to be lying! He shoved Hugh away, but when he spun around, it was to see the last of Elizabeth's skirt hem disappearing around the corner.

"Elizabeth! Damn you! Come back here!"

Hugh grabbed his arm before he could start after her. "I'll go after her, Colter. You'd best get to the meeting."

Turning to Hugh, Colter made no attempt to hide his anguish. "Find her. I don't care how you do it, just find her."

* * *

Leroy Walker, the Confederate secretary of war, sat behind his desk, his receding hairline streaked with the same gray as his beard. When Colter entered the room, Walker glanced pointedly at his mantel clock, heard Colter's brief apology for being late and offered a curt nod.

Seated beside Brice, Colter, of necessity, banished Elizabeth from his thoughts and watched the secretary scan some correspondence before placing it in his portfolio.

Brice gave him a whispered summation of the discussion he had missed. Two months before, in September, Lincoln had declared his intention of issuing a proclamation to free all slaves as of January 1, 1863. The secretary informed them of various reactions, concluding with the opinion that Lincoln's political opponents and several supporters exhibited uncommon good sense in condemning the plan.

Walker cleared his throat and set aside the last of his papers. "When you are ready, Colonel."

Andre handed Colter his map case along with a mocking smile that irritated Colter as he opened the case and spread two small but detailed maps on the clean surface of the desk.

"Sir, before I explain General Lee's intent, I would like to inform you that the rumors are confirmed. Since McClellan procrastinated so long in crossing the Potomac, Lincoln has relieved him of command of the Army of the Potomac and appointed Ambrose Burnside."

"Burnside, is it? I'm not questioning the validity of your information, Saxton. I know your reliability too well. But you are aware that Burnside refused this commission twice before."

"True, sir, he did. But this is confirmed."

"This should amuse President Davis. Lincoln set a great store by McClellan. I am given to understand that he was insulted by his fair-haired general more than once. But I digress. His background?"

"Brice," Colter ordered, and then stepped aside for him to stand at attention before the secretary.

Without embellishment, Brice reported Burnside's background. "He successfully led the expedition that captured Roanoke Island from us in January of this year. McClellan gave Burnside command of one wing of his army at South Mountain and Sharpsburg. With all due respect, sir, our forces are in agreement that due to his delay in crossing early that day, we were stopped from suffering a crushing defeat."

"Yes," Walker agreed. "I recall Lee mentioning that in his report to the president."

Brice returned to his seat and Colter motioned Andre forward.

"By all accounts," Andre stated in his softly drawled voice, "Burnside does not feel that he is competent to command such a large army. Although he spent several days being briefed by McClellan, indications are that Burnside does not agree with McClellan's plan to keep our armies separated. But Colonel Saxton will explain further."

"With our General Longstreet near Culpeper and Stonewall Jackson in the Shenandoah Valley, sir, McClellan had intended to stop them from uniting. He had a good chance to do it, too, since it would take two days of hard marching for our forces to join." Pointing to one of the maps, Colter continued.

"Our reports indicate that Burnside is marching along the north bank of Rappahannock toward Fredericksburg. He has reorganized his army into three divisions under the commands of Hooker, Sumner and Franklin."

"Yes, we have that intelligence report. One of your people, wasn't it?"

"Yes, sir."

"Excellent job, Saxton."

"Thank you, sir." Colter hid his impatience with the politeness he was forced to adhere to. He wanted to be done and gone. "Lee feels that striking at their communications would be a mistake. He'll cover the capital by crossing the path of the enemy. With his forces placed on the heights south and west of Fredericksburg, earthworks and artillery will fortify his position."

Walker studied the map. His eyes were shadowed and he seemed to be lost in thought. "Small town, isn't it? I remember fog hanging in the valley every morning, enough to hide the town."

"Yes, sir. It slopes up from the river to low hills," Colter answered. "The slopes are mostly clear, but there are woods here, sir." Once again he drew Walker's attention to his map.

"There's nearly five miles to protect," the secretary remarked.

"True." Colter smiled and gazed at him. "I have good reason to believe there will be extensive delays for the Union forces to contend with. A mishap with the pontoon train would stop an immediate crossing of the river."

Tugging his beard, the secretary grinned. "I see. Good reason, you say?"

"Yes, sir. And you must convey to President Davis General Lee's considered opinion that he will not be able to stop Burnside from crossing the river. The Union force has deployed over one hundred guns on this rise of the left bank. It gives them a command of the intermediate plain."

"Pity. Well, I must respect Lee's judgment as I know the president will."

"A survey of the area leads me to believe that Acquia Creek would be Burnside's choice for a base. I will have confirmed reports of the exact sites within three to five days."

"The president does not wish to have these blue bellies at the gates of Richmond again. Do convey that message to General Lee."

"Most assuredly, sir."

"If that is all, Saxton, the meeting is concluded."

Colter nodded, rolling the maps and replacing them in their leather case, which he handed over to Walker.

"My respects to the president, sir."

"Rest assured that I will give them, Saxton. He'll be pleased with your report. And now that the formalities can be set aside, please remember that I knew your father well. As an old family friend, I want to know what's wrong with you."

"Nothing a few days' personal leave wouldn't help."

"Are you ill?"

"No, sir. A matter requiring my immediate attention has come up and—"

"Three days. I'm sure that is all the time you can be spared without objections. You'll remain in the city where I can reach you quickly should the president wish to speak to you further?"

"The hotel—"

"Yes, yes. I suppose you'll be wanting leave for these young men of yours, too."

Colter smiled and glanced behind him to where Brice and Andre waited expectantly. Turning back to face Walker, he said, "If it could be arranged, sir. They have been across the lines with me for almost two weeks."

"I envy you your youth and stamina, gentlemen. If there is nothing else—"

"Since you've asked, sir," Colter was quick to say, "Captain Morgan would like me to secure safe passage for his wife to return from New York."

"Yankee?"

"They've been married almost five years, sir. She returned to her family almost a year ago when she suffered the loss of their child."

"Bad business, that," the secretary stated, picking up his portfolio.

"Indeed, sir," Colter agreed. "The child would have been their first."

"No. Not that. My intent is not to appear callous, but this business of having family loyalty split is bad."

"I can assure you, Mr. Secretary, that no one would dare to question the loyalty of Hugh Morgan. No one."

"Watch that rashness, Colter. We need you." Sure that he had Colter's attention, the secretary smiled to soften his reprimand. "I hope your men appreciate your quick defense of their reputations. I pray they never need to return the favor. Come, we'll have my secretary draw up the papers to reunite your young captain with his lady."

Colter carefully closed the door behind him and followed Walker. He hid his disappointment that Hugh was not waiting in the anteroom for him with news of Elizabeth.

Brice and Andre stood at attention, impatience stamped across their features. Colter couldn't blame them. He knew, as they did, how quickly the order could come to cancel their leave. He buried a stab of guilt for the resentment he momentarily felt as the safe-conduct pass for Jenna Morgan was written then signed.

Colter glanced down and silently read it. "Pass the bearer and his party, unmolested, by Government transport." Below was the secretary of war's signature.

"You'll need military passes, but I think you can secure those, Saxton."

"Yes, sir." Securing the paper inside his uniform frock coat, Colter, as well as Andre and Brice, bid Walker good day.

Once outside, the bitter wind had given way to a dreary rain. Colter swore softly and ignored the good-natured taunts between Brice and Andre over where they intended to go first. His announcement that he would return to the hotel to wait for Hugh brought him their undivided attentions.

"Whiskey and women, Colter," Brice offered in a chiding tone, holding the bridle of Colter's purebred hunter as he mounted. "Three days to forget the damn war, if we're lucky."

"Enjoy it. Both of you."

"What's gotten into you, Colter? You ain't been listening to that puritan Jackson again?"

"That's *General* Jackson, Brice, and no, I've not been listening to him."

"Tart an' snappy as the general findin' ants in his vittles."

"Leave him be, Brice," Andre said. "Colter's made other arrangements. Being a true gentleman, he has no intention of sharing. Do you?" he asked Colter, gazing up at him.

"If we were not friends, Andre, I would call you out for what you are implying."

"But you will not, *mon ami,* because I am right."

Brice quickly stepped in front of Andre. "You're entitled to satisfaction, Colter, but—"

"Leave off, Brice." Colter saw the blaze of deadly challenge in Andre's eyes, true to his quick-tempered heritage that had him ready to fight at a word or a sidelong glance. Once Colter had been the same. Wearily he shook his head. Fighting was a pastime of the South's men. Not only the young aristocrats like Andre and Brice, but even the poor whites could be ready with pistol or knife to avenge the real or imagined affront.

"Save your desire to have satisfaction for the battlefield, Andre," Colter warned. "I promise you, you'll soon have it." With the seep of chill rain crawling down his neck, he swung his horse out into the street.

"Never remember Colter refusing a chance to drink and whore with us, even if he's discreet as a parson," Brice remarked, mounting his own horse.

Andre's dark brooding gaze was targeted at Colter's retreating back. "I believe the lovely widow planted a few immoral thoughts in his mind. Thoughts another woman couldn't begin to satisfy. But she'll bring him trouble." With a rapid swing of mood, he turned to Brice. "My friend, it shall be up to you and me to fulfill the dreams of the Richmond belles."

With a laugh, Brice shrugged off Andre's dark mood, along with Colter's unexpected anger. But his thoughts turned to his first sight of Elizabeth Waring, standing beside Colter at the top of the steps. Innocent and seductive. He couldn't blame Colter. He couldn't blame any man for taking what he could. Pleasure had to be measured in hours now. Brice felt a sudden sense of desperation. The world they knew, the one they all believed in was slipping away. He turned for a last look to where Colter disappeared and hoped Andre was wrong. Colter needed someone to care for, not more trouble.

Free from duty, Colter allowed his thoughts of Elizabeth to surface. He refused to examine Andre's uncalled-for attack. Something was bothering his friend; he had never known Andre to provoke his temper in such a deliberate manner.

He would have to make time for his friend. He couldn't work with him, worrying whether or not Andre would be there when needed.

Keeping his horse to a walk through the thronged streets, Colter fought off a bone-deep tiredness. He was in need of sleep, a peaceful few hours that would ease the weariness of weeks spent behind enemy lines.

At the corners of Broad and Seventh streets, Colter remembered where his favorite saddler's shop had stood along with a hotel and the Richmond Theater. Stubble was all that remained of the buildings after a fire in January.

He waited for wagons of refugees to pass, closing his eyes briefly against the dazed looks reflected in most of their faces. He couldn't remember the city being this crowded, but then he had been gone for weeks. An ambulance wagon lurched across the street and Colter stilled his hunter. The ambulance would be heading toward the warehouses down on Eighth. Since the summer battles had brought the fighting to the threshold of the city, a flood of wounded and their families had burdened every structure until even private homes had become hospitals.

Colter guided his horse behind the hotel to a small private livery. He was about to dismount when he heard Hugh call out to him.

"You found her," Colter stated, knowing Hugh would not return unless he had. Hugh drew alongside him but didn't dismount.

"Just get finished?" Colter nodded, and Hugh, reading the signs of impatience, quickly gave him directions. He wiped the rain from his face and leaned closer. "The house belongs to Emily Perkins, a widow. Her servant wouldn't tell me much. Near as I could tell, there's no one else there. Mrs. Waring has been residing with her for almost a week." Hugh stopped and looked away from Colter. He wasn't quite sure how to continue. He didn't want to admit that he had overheard most of Colter's conversation with the lovely Elizabeth.

"Hugh?" Seeing the pained expression in the young captain's eyes, Colter understood his reluctance to say more. "It's all right. I'm sure you couldn't help but hear us. And for whatever it's worth, Hugh, I'm comfortable with your knowing about Elizabeth. As for—"

"Your secret is safe with me, Colter. I'll think of something should Andre or Brice dare to question me."

"There's no need to lie. They've drawn their own conclusions." Colter's next question was burning to be asked, yet he found the words hard. "Did you by chance discover if there is a child with her?"

"No. I'm sorry, Colter. But we're both fools for staying in the rain. I could use a warm brandy to chase this damn chill."

"Go on, Hugh." Colter stilled the restive movements of his hunter. "Here, I almost forgot this." He pulled the safe-conduct pass from inside his coat and handed it over. "You've got three days' leave. Don't wait to take this to headquarters and get your military passes."

"I've missed Jenna so," he uttered with a simple honesty. "How can I thank—"

"No thanks are needed. I can't repay you for what you did for me today."

Hugh reached over and clasped Colter's hand. "Are you going after her now?"

"I must," Colter answered, like Hugh, speaking the simple truth.

Perched on the edge of the mulberry silk horsehair sofa, Elizabeth sipped the mulled wine that Emily Perkins had asked Rutha to make for her. A fire was burning in the back parlor given over for her use. She shivered beneath the serviceable flannel wrapper she had changed into upon getting back from Richmond. She wished her pride would have allowed her to accept Emily's offer to use her carriage. The sudden rain had left both her best shoes and her spirit as sodden as the earth.

The only blessing she offered the rain was for its aid in escaping Colter.

She rubbed her aching temples. Colter. What was she going to do about him? It was another foolish mistake to have told him the truth about Nicole. How could she have forgotten Colter's relentless pursuit when he desired something? After their confrontation this afternoon, she had no reason to believe he had changed.

A cold knot of fear expanded inside her. She had lost the opportunity to talk to Mr. Memminger about a job, and she didn't have enough money to leave the city.

And even if you did, a tiny voice nagged, *where would you run to?*

She gazed at the ruby liquid in her glass and drained it quickly, praying for courage.

She would protect her daughter and, despite Alma Waring's claims and threats, provide for Nicole. Somehow she would find a way.

You can begin by not making assumptions about what Colter will or will not do.

Why should Colter care about her or Nicole, no matter what he had said? Four years had passed without his making any attempt to contact her.

She realized that not seeing Colter all those years had been a blessing. Now there was no comfort to be had in heart or mind. He was an inescapable part of her life.

From somewhere, she had to find the strength to deal with this. There was no one to confide in, no one to depend upon to act as a buffer. Not even James, weak as he had been under his mother's relentless rule, could protect her from her own feelings for Colter now.

The gloom of the day settled into the room, and it matched her mood. She had no idea how to dispel it. Sweeping her hip-length straight hair forward, she began to braid it, not caring that it was still damp.

When she was finished, Elizabeth rose, restlessly pacing over the faded Brussels carpet. Time and again she stepped to the window and watched the raindrops roll down the pane. She had no tears left. They had all been shed as she ran from Colter.

"Why?" she whispered. "Why did you leave me?" She could have asked him today, but she had been swept up in the joy and fear of seeing him.

Lost in thought, it took several minutes before she became aware that Rutha, Emily Perkins's cook and, now that the slaves had run off, housemaid, too, was talking to Nicole. Elizabeth ran to the hall door, casting aside her grief for what might have been, smiling to hear her daughter's laughter.

"Here's your mama, chil'." Rutha set the squirming little girl down.

Kneeling, Elizabeth held her arms open for Nicole. Her honey blond ringlets framed a face that had begun to lose its plumpness, giving a hint of the child's beauty to come. For a moment Elizabeth savored the baby-sweet scent of her daughter and reaffirmed the vow that no one would ever take Nicole from her again.

"Rua gave me honey cake, Mama. I was so good."

"I hope you were, precious." Above Nicole's head, Elizabeth's anxious gaze sought reassurance from Rutha.

"Miz Beth, don't be churnin' butter what's already done."

"I won't, Rutha." Elizabeth smiled up at her, admiring once again the woman's majestic height and slim, stately figure. Rutha's face, unlined and smoothly polished like the glow of rare satin wood, gave no hint of her age. Elizabeth stood and held Nicole's small hand. "Thank you again, Rutha. I know how much you have to do without the added care of her."

"Hush. With Miz Emily's misery comin' on her bones with this rain, don't have all that much to do. I don't mine that chil' none. She be a fine little lady for Rutha. An' Mister Josh, he's gonna have a swing for her in the garden real soon."

"You both spoil her."

"'Pears to me it's 'bout time. An' her mama could do with some spoilin', too."

"I'm all right, Rutha. We're safe here." Elizabeth turned away from Rutha's arched gaze that said she recalled opening the door to a bedraggled woman who could not catch her breath for the stitch in her side from running. "Really, I am," she repeated, leading the way to the parlor.

"Sure, an' I picked cotton today," she said coming into the room. "We'll be needin' the lamps lit. Don't wanna be in the dark."

"I don't like the dark, Mama."

"I know you dislike the dark, honey. I'm sorry I didn't light them myself."

Rutha finished lighting the second lamp, replaced the glass chimney and blew out the match. Walking to the fireplace, shé tossed a piece of wood onto the fire and picked up the empty wineglass. "Jus' nice and cozy for you an' missy. Supper'll be ready soon."

"Will Miss Emily join us?"

"Don't rightly know. I was plannin' on seein' to her now that you got little missy."

"Tell Mister Josh I said thank-you," Elizabeth murmured as she settled down before the fire with her daughter. She hid her face against Nicole's hair, holding unpleasant thoughts at bay. She was thankful that she had been granted this sanctuary, the one place of refuge that Alma Waring would never think to look for her and Nicole.

Mister Josh would protect them with his life if the need arose. He was almost sixty, a tight white cap of curls attesting to his age, but his back was ramrod straight and he moved with the agility of a much younger man. Both he and Rutha bullied and hovered protectively over Emily, and now that same caring had come to include Nicole and herself.

A distant roll of thunder broke into Elizabeth's thoughts. Despite the fire, the room was chilly, and she snuggled closer to Nicole. The child seemed content for the moment to be held, as she often was after a nap. Elizabeth sighed with the pleasure of having her child to herself. It was a luxury she would never take for granted again.

"Mama, Mister Josh is gonna give me a pretty doll."

"Did he tell you that, Nicole? If he did, you can be sure that he will."

"Oh, yes," she answered, nodding her head. "He promised."

Smoothing Nicole's hair, Elizabeth asked, "Are you happy here?"

"I like it real fine. Miss Emily said I was a good girl. She doesn't yell at me. I don't wanna go—"

"Hush, love. We'll never go back there. Mama promises you that. Never."

Nicole squirmed against her tight hold. Elizabeth released her and wished she could ease the tension that held her in its grip.

Minutes later, Nicole begged a story. Elizabeth obliged, and then, to Nicole's delighted laughter, she played out parts from her daughter's favorite tale.

An hour passed, an hour without fear or worry, when crawling on all fours, laughing and growling at Nicole's pretended shrieks were all that concerned her.

She thought she heard voices from the front hallway but could not make out whose they were. Moments later Rutha came into the room, wringing her hands in a manner so unlike her that Elizabeth immediately stood, rigid with fear.

"Best get presentable. There's a gentleman come to call an' he sure don't take no for an answer. Mister Josh seen him skulkin' up the road afore he come here."

"Who, Rutha?" Elizabeth could barely get the words past the constriction in her throat.

Chapter Three

"He's mighty fine—"

"It's Colter, isn't it? Colonel Colter Saxton?" Without waiting for Rutha's confirmation, Elizabeth picked up Nicole, soothing her with whispered assurances. "Honey, you be a special angel for Mama now and go with Rutha."

"No. I wanna stay."

Elizabeth closed her eyes, praying for patience. When she opened them, Nicole's stubborn-set jaw and pouting mouth brought a sigh of exasperation.

"Please, Rutha, take Nicole and keep her out of sight. I don't think Colonel Saxton will make any trouble, but I don't want Miss Emily upset. Nicole, please let go of Mama." Handing her to Rutha, Elizabeth avoided the woman's penetrating gaze. "Colonel Colter is—"

"I ain't blind. I know who he is."

"Please give me a few minutes and then Mister Josh can show him in."

"Mama..."

"Hush, chil'. Rutha's gonna..."

Whatever Rutha promised her daughter was lost to Elizabeth as she ran into her bedroom. She sagged against the door, trying to collect herself.

There was no time to think or question his reasons. Tossing her wrapper and night rail onto the four-poster bed, she rushed to the dresser. Her meager supply of underwear was all neatly folded and starched. Elizabeth donned a fresh camisole and cotton drawers. Most of her petticoats were still damp, as was the crinoline hoop. With every intent to make this meeting as brief as possible, she tied one petticoat in place, slipped on a black watered-silk skirt and hurriedly fastened its tapes. A matching bodice had her swearing in an unladylike fashion as she tried to secure the twenty-odd buttons up the front. The material pulled snugly across her unconfined breasts, but she couldn't worry about that now. Rolling her braid, she quickly tucked it into a net. Her eyes watered when, in her haste, she jabbed herself repeatedly with hairpins.

Beyond her closed door, she heard Mister Josh in the parlor and the low murmur of Colter's voice. There was no time to put on stockings. Sliding her feet into a pair of dancing slippers, she took a deep breath and found she couldn't move toward the door.

What are you afraid of?

Losing Nicole. Myself. Colter's desire. Mine.

Colter won't harm Nicole or you.

She began to breathe more easily. She was hiding in her room like a ninny. If she could face down Alma Waring and manage to escape her with Nicole, she could certainly stand up to Colter.

Unable to rid herself entirely of tension, she eased the door open a bit.

Colter stood opposite, his back toward her, his hands braced on the edge of the mantel. With his head bowed, he appeared to be staring into the flames. A half-filled brandy snifter rested next to the silver candlestick by his right hand.

The glisten of rain had darkened his near-black, collar-length hair. Without his uniform coat, his body appeared as lithe as she remembered it, but there was a maturity to his muscular build that enhanced his pantherlike grace. His damp shirt clung to his back, delineating the straight length of his spine, and his gray wool trousers and knee-high boots revealed every line of his muscular hips and legs.

Elizabeth was seized by a wave of longing. She tamped it down quickly, ruthlessly.

Judging by the mud splattered on his clothes, Colter had ridden out after her directly from his meeting. But how had he found her?

"Are you finished inspecting me, Elizabeth?" he asked, turning to face her.

She didn't answer, but opened the door fully and stepped into the room. "Why have you come?"

Colter's laugh was bitter. "Just the right tone of arrogance. Worthy of the formidable Mrs. Waring. The elder," he clarified, making a bow.

"You are making a mockery of my thought that you were a gentleman, Colter."

"Don't count on my being a gentleman," he warned.

"How foolish of me. But pray tell me, why are you here? I can assure you that we harbor no Yankees within these walls. There are no horses left to conscript for the army's use, nor is there an overabundance of food."

He studied her with a narrowed gaze, giving away nothing of his own thoughts. "After your damn announcement, you still need to ask why I've come? You ran off like a coward, Elizabeth. I want to see the child."

"I consider that unwise. She has been unsettled with our move. I'm sorry you have wasted your time to come out here in such foul weather and—"

"Elizabeth," he interrupted softly, almost too softly. "You won't put me off. If she is my daughter, I have a right to see her."

"You must never say that! Never, do you hear me? She cannot be claimed as yours."

"Then why the devil tell me?" he demanded. "Are you now denying my paternity, Elizabeth?" he queried with barely concealed anger. "Or have you some ploy in mind? No, of course not, you're far too honest to try that old trick upon me." Colter rubbed the back of his neck, weary of their verbal fencing. "Madam, I am aware that women often choose a devious route to obtain their goal, but you should beware. I've neither the time nor the patience for it."

"I want nothing from you," she said with a haughty air.

"I see. You've simply taken the woman's out and changed your mind."

"Don't patronize me, Colter," she snapped, rushing toward him and suddenly stopping.

Colter watched her, his gaze shifting from the soft undulation of her hips to the lush swell of her breasts and then, with calculated assessment, to her lips. "I see you've donned armor." Her look begged an explanation. "The widow's weeds."

"And perhaps, Colonel, you should have worn your saber. The cuts would be cleaner by far."

Colter flashed her an exasperated look. But he couldn't help admiring her recovered spirit; this woman was more like the Elizabeth he remembered.

"I didn't come here to spar with you, Elizabeth. I admit that I questioned the truth of what you said. Upon reflection, I concede there is the possibility that she is my child."

"You are far too kind, sir," Elizabeth whispered with honeyed malice. "Pray, take a seat. I will see to some other refreshment for you, since brandy doesn't appeal."

"Oh, no, madam!" With lithe steps he was upon her, taking hold of her arm, hauling her gently but firmly to his side. "Play the belle with others, little fox, not me. Never again with me."

"You damn blackguard!"

"I've never denied that."

She looked up and stared at him. His lips tightened grimly. "Let me go, Colter. And then, I demand that you take your leave."

"I want to see her. And before you think to disabuse me of the notion, I assure you it will take more than you are capable of, madam, to stop me."

Incensed, Elizabeth could no longer hold her anger at bay. "You have no right to make any demands. I did not seduce you, Colter, and then abandon you. I was not the one who found fairer game within months of arriving in England, was I?"

"What the devil are you accusing me of? I never thought of you as game. What lies were you told? I found no other woman in England."

"James told me—"

"James! Damn his soul to hell! What did he tell you?"

"Your cousin...he said you had offered marriage to a distant cousin. That the marriage would take place immediately, and that you would bring your bride—"

"He lied, Elizabeth. James lied to you." With a sudden wrench, Colter understood. "And to me," he added, easing his grip on her.

Elizabeth pulled herself free of him. "Lied?" she repeated, swaying where she stood.

"Yes. He lied when he told you that I found someone else to marry. Just as he lied to you about telling me of Nicole." He raised his hand to touch her cheek, but Elizabeth backed away and he was forced to still his need to hold her.

"Tell me what happened," she demanded in a whisper.

"I received a letter from James nearly five months after I left you. He claimed that you had agreed to marry him and wished for no further contact between us."

"And you," she snapped, "accepted his word without a thought of writing to me? How could you believe him after what we shared? How could you—"

"Just think! James and I were the best of friends. Why would I question him?"

Elizabeth softly moaned and wrapped her arms around her waist, as if to contain the emotions inside. "You never saw or heard from him again? He never... Will you swear to me that he never told you about my daughter?"

"You have accused me of much this day, but now you dare to impugn my honor to query the truth of what I tell you?"

"Your honor means little to me! Will you swear it?"

There was a rawness to her appeal that he couldn't deny. "Yes, I swear it. James never told me about her. He never told me about any child."

"All lies." She could barely say the words.

The waste of the past four years struck Colter like a blow. Elizabeth's whispered words defused his anger. She met his gaze directly, and before Colter spoke, he saw the defeat within her eyes.

"There's more."

"No. I don't... I can't hear—"

"James knew I loved you. He knew I intended to ask you to marry me when I returned from England."

Elizabeth could not begin to measure her sense of betrayal. "You never made your intentions known. And now they do not matter. Hell, I hear, is paved with good intentions."

Colter was not going to pursue the matter now. It was enough that he had found her again; nothing she did or said would shut him out.

"I want to see my daughter."

"Be sure of what you are asking, Colter. I believe you need time. I know I do. I'll send word of my decision."

"You didn't suffer from these lies alone." He raked his hand through his hair, forcing himself to be patient.

She turned from him, then seemed to think better of the move and faced him once again. "Nicole is a sensitive child who has been uprooted from all she knew. I can't have her hurt."

Colter struck like lightning, grabbing her arms and hauling her against him. "Now. I won't leave without seeing her."

She searched the implacable set of his features and still found the courage to shake her head.

"Listen to me," he stated, shaking her. "No mercy. You've twisted my life upside down today. And I—"

"What you want doesn't matter. How can I make you understand?" she pleaded, pushing against his chest.

"Do you hate me so much, Elizabeth, that you believe I would hurt an innocent—"

"You forget, Colter, I was once an innocent, too."

"Madam," he stated coldly, releasing her as if he couldn't bear to touch her, "it is you who now wields the saber."

"Colter, I..." Elizabeth stopped herself from uttering any apology. It was better to let him remain angry than to give in to his demand. Living with Alma Waring had taught her to attack where someone was vulnerable. It wasn't a pleasant skill to put into practice, however. She turned away from him, undecided about his seeing Nicole.

Her daughter took the decision from her.

"Mama! Mama!" Nicole shouted, running down the hall. "Mister Josh made a dolly! Look, with real lace drawers." Nicole came to a sudden stop at the doorway. Clutching the doll to her chest, she stared at Colter. "He's awful big."

Elizabeth bit back a smile. She turned to share it with Colter and found him stunned at the sight of Nicole.

Elizabeth tried to see her daughter as he did, her hair bow gone, her lilac sash untied and a streak of mud on one white stocking. Nicole's eyes were rounded and Elizabeth could see the fear in them. She was about to lash out at Colter for frightening her, but his own gaze was filled with hunger and pleading.

The hunger frightened her. James had been an indifferent father at best. She never thought that Colter would care for Nicole or want more than merely to see her.

She hurried to Nicole and knelt before her. "Honey, I know he seems very big to you, but there is nothing to be frightened of. Colonel—"

"He won't take me away." Nicole wrapped her arms around her mother's neck, clinging tightly.

"No, love. He's not going to take you away." Elizabeth eased her daughter's hold until she could look at her. "Colonel Saxton is an old friend of Mama's. I would like you to meet him. I promised you that no one would ever take you away from me, didn't I?"

Nicole nodded and stole a look at Colter.

"Would you like to have some time?" Again the child nodded and Elizabeth glanced over at Colter. She forestalled his questions with a gentle shake of her head.

Colter watched while Nicole pressed her cheek to her mother's. A raw ache spread inside him. He longed to take them both within the shelter of his arms, swearing protection and making promises he had no right to. But a rage also surfaced, rage that this child, his child, was afraid of him. Being unable to have his questions answered immediately added to his turmoil.

To stand helplessly and watch while Elizabeth rubbed Nicole's back, pressing tiny kisses to her temple and murmuring soft reassurances was a torment unlike any he had known.

Elizabeth finally rose, but Nicole's face was still buried in her mother's skirt. Smoothing her child's curls, Elizabeth silently tried to convey how Colter should proceed.

Colter hunkered down so that his height would not be intimidating to Nicole. Elizabeth offered him an encouraging smile.

"If you peek, honey, you'll see he's not so big anymore," she coaxed.

Colter smiled. The little girl was a miniature of her mother. She had the same delicate features and hair that was lighter in color but just as thick and glossy as Elizabeth's. Nicole's lower lip thrust forward as she peeked shyly at him from behind Elizabeth's skirt. He couldn't stop looking at her eyes—eyes the same green color as his own.

A glint of wonder brightened his gaze. Colter's emotions churned, shimmered and coalesced into a feeling of love so new, so encompassing, that his eyes filled with the glimmer of tears. This tiny person was a part of him. In that moment she owned his heart, his soul and all that he silently vowed to give her.

Colter was overwhelmed by the need to touch her. He extended a hand toward her, a hand that shook slightly. "I've never met a princess before," he whispered huskily.

"Silly. I'm not a princess."

"To me you are. You're certainly as pretty as one."

Solemnly Nicole shook her head. "Mama is pretty. Not me."

Colter withdrew his outstretched hand and cupped his chin. Nicole was still suspicious of him. Helplessly he sought a way to earn the girl's trust. "I agree," he said softly, after giving her announcement serious thought, "that your mama is lovely. But only a little girl as special as you can be a princess."

"Special?"

"Very special."

"A real princess?"

"You'll always be a real one to me," he answered with a smile.

Colter, entranced with his daughter, didn't see Elizabeth wipe the tears from her eyes. She knew he was capable of being gentle and tender, but never had she witnessed him like this. If she had never loved him, she would now, she thought, locking this moment in time. This sensitive, patient side of him tore down all of the barriers she had carefully erected as protection. When Colter masked his disappointment that Nicole did not return his smile, Elizabeth felt his hurt as deeply as if it were her own.

She had not planned to interfere with them, but Colter deserved something from Nicole. With a gentle touch Elizabeth turned her daughter to face her. "I think a real princess would make a curtsy to a gentleman who offered her a compliment."

Nicole hesitated and then stepped out from behind her mother's skirt. Her little legs wobbled a bit, but she managed to make her curtsy. Lifting her head, she stared at Colter, then at the floor, swinging her body to and fro. "A real princess has a castle."

"Why, yes, she does. And I'll—"

"Colter," Elizabeth warned, alarmed that he was about to promise her daughter a castle.

Helplessly Colter looked at her. What did Elizabeth expect from him? He knew nothing about children and even less about his own daughter. But when he again looked at Nicole's face, she appeared to be waiting for him to finish.

"I'll...I'll find you one," he promised in a lame voice. Her crestfallen expression told him he had somehow failed her expectations. This new feeling of tenderness for his daughter was overwhelming. He held back rash, impossible promises, but only with a great deal of effort and Elizabeth's warning in mind. Glancing down to the doll Nicole still held, Colter was inspired.

"I will find you one that will be a perfect size for your doll. That way," he added in a lighter tone, "you can both be princesses."

Nicole gazed up at her mother, seeking her approval. Elizabeth managed a nod. She turned back to Colter and took several hesitant steps forward.

He held his breath, anticipation over the reception of his promise making his chest feel tight. That he would appear foolish to anyone who really knew him never entered his mind.

Timidly Nicole extended her hand to him. "My doll and me are pleased to be your princesses."

Colter enclosed her tiny hand within his own and gently raised it to his lips. He closed his eyes, silently praying that he was worthy of this child, and savored the first touch of his daughter.

When he looked at her, she seemed oblivious to the emotional turmoil he was going through.

"You honor me, my dear."

Elizabeth felt her heart constrict, but for her daughter's sake she forced a joyful smile to match Nicole's, then offered the same smile to Colter. Nicole began to giggle.

No praise for a job well done from his superiors could have pleased him more. He was lost, enchanted and thoroughly caught up in the spell of this little minx.

"When?" the child asked.

"Tomorrow," he answered, vowing to turn Richmond upside down if need be to get her a castle.

"Nicole," Elizabeth said, well aware that her daughter was not above extracting more from him if she could, "I think you should show your new doll to Rutha."

"Ain't a need, Miz Beth," Rutha said from the doorway, startling the three of them. "I came to tell you that Miz Emily will join you." With a look that could only be called disdainful, she stared at Colter.

Alarmed, Elizabeth asked, "Can't you dissuade her?"

"Miz Emily's got her mind set like them Yankees. She's comin' to see him."

Elizabeth pushed past Rutha in the doorway to step out into the hall. Mister Josh's soft tread and the thump of Emily's cane warned her that time had run out. There would be no escape for Colter. Clasping her hands, she lifted her chin and walked back into the room, ignoring Colter's bemused look.

He rose and faced the door. Colter stared first at the ebony cane embossed with a scrolled silver design. Something familiar about the cane begged him to remember where he had seen it before. Its tip was placed firmly on the floor, its dark gleam a contrast to the soft shade of rose cloth behind it.

With a rustle of crinolines and petticoats, Emily entered the room on Mister Josh's arm.

Nicole ran toward her. "Miss Emily, he promised a castle for me! I'm a princess!"

"Not now, Nicole." Elizabeth rushed to take her daughter's hand, pulling her aside. She heard Colter's sharp intake of breath and turned to him.

"Dear Lord, Elizabeth, do you know who this woman is?"

"Quite well, Colter," she answered defiantly.

"That's Lily—"

"No," Elizabeth snapped, so angry with Colter that she forgot Nicole was in the room. "Her name is Emily and I am aware that she was my father's mistress."

Chapter Four

Colter was a soldier. He prided himself on being able to handle sudden shifts in battle, the sometimes unaccountable behavior of men under his command and the unexpected from the enemy. But this...he wasn't quite sure how to react. He opened his mouth, ready to demand further explanations, but Elizabeth's militant stance stopped him for the moment. With an audible gnashing of his teeth, he closed his mouth.

Rutha, having seen enough, took Nicole by the hand and motioned her husband, Josh, to leave. For once, Nicole left quietly with them.

"Pray be seated, Colonel," Emily offered, slowly making her way into the room.

Elizabeth moved a needlepoint armchair closer to the sofa, knowing how painful it was for Emily to sit on the low furnishing. Unobtrusively she blocked Colter's view as Emily sat down and settled herself, before she sat on the sofa nearby.

"Colter..." With a graceful gesture, Elizabeth motioned him to sit beside her.

"I'll stand, if you don't mind."

"There's no need to be snappish—"

"Elizabeth," Emily chided, "remember that your colonel has had quite a few shocks this day."

"I've had a few myself, and he is not *my* colonel."

"Be that as it may, I do believe the man is entitled to an explanation."

Elizabeth glared at Colter, then turned away to stare at the fire. "And I don't believe he is entitled to any more explanation from me than I wish him to have."

"You can't mean that, my dear."

Meeting Emily's gaze, Elizabeth knew the older woman was right but resented being obliged to reveal the sordid details of what brought her to Emily.

Colter moved to stand before Elizabeth, his legs spread, his hands clasped behind him. The look on his face was forbidding.

"If you will remember that I am not one of your soldiers, Colter, I will tell you how I came to be here."

Not trusting himself to speak, Colter nodded curtly.

"I told you a little of why I was forced to make a decision to leave the Warings and—"

"Very little, I recall."

"Let me tell this in my own way." Clasping her hands together, Elizabeth looked up at his unyielding features. Praying for Colter to find a measure of patience, she continued. "You must simply accept my word that the situation became intolerable. Alma succeeded in cutting me off from the contact with the few friends I had, and those who remained were blind to what she was attempting to do. Without family to turn to, I despaired of escaping her."

Elizabeth had to stop. She closed her eyes as if to shut out the memory of the desperation that marked those days. And the nights . . . the nights had been endless bouts with the fear that she wouldn't survive to see the morning.

Colter's need to know how his daughter came to be living with her grandfather's mistress was suddenly tempered by his sensitivity to Elizabeth's pain. He hunkered down before her, covering her hands with his. The chill of her skin alarmed him, and to his surprise, he found himself glancing at Emily for guidance.

Emily studied Colter's face for long moments, seeing the strength, sensing a deep well of protectiveness, but she knew there was a rage building inside him. Fearing it would only intensify if he was forced to wait, she took matters into her own hands and continued on Elizabeth's behalf.

"After Elizabeth's father passed on, I managed to keep apprised of her doings through a mutual acquaintance. When I heard rumors of her decline after James was reported missing, I began to query further. Some rumors added to my disquiet and after a long deliberation, I managed to have a letter smuggled to Elizabeth, offering her whatever help I could give."

"And she accepted?" Colter heard the damning tone of his words, but it was too late. Elizabeth pulled free of his hold.

"Without Emily's help, I would be locked away without my daughter, or dead."

Perhaps under other circumstances Colter would have handled the situation differently. But he lacked sleep, had found a woman he loved and believed lost to him and discovered he had a daughter. That they were living with a woman whose reputation was at best questionable was intolerable to him.

"Tell me, Elizabeth," he asked, "did you always know of Miss Emily's relationship with your father?"

Elizabeth refused to look at him, turning to the fire instead, but she did answer in a strained voice.

"I knew exactly what kind of a woman my mother was. She was cold, unfeeling and selfish. Hers was an arranged marriage she opposed. To her joy, I was conceived immediately and she turned my father out of her bed and her life. She never tried to be a mother to my older half-brothers. Two months after I was born, my mother left on an extended visit to England. She returned the day of my third birthday, which she had forgotten."

With a proud lift of her head, she continued. "Emily gave my father love, warmth and companionship. They made no secret of their relationship, and I see no reason to condemn them for seeking what we all need, Colter. After all," she stated, finally facing him and meeting his gaze with a bitter look, "who am I to cast a stone? I was not concerned with having the sanction of marriage when I gave myself to you. I didn't even have the sense to obtain a promise of marriage before you left me."

Colter stood and towered over her, his fury at hearing her mocking tone contained with a barely leashed control.

"And you couldn't be bothered to inform me of my impending fatherhood, could you, Elizabeth? No, you turned to James. You tell me not to condemn Emily and your father, yet I stand condemned in your mind."

"As I stand in yours," she snapped with a lift of her chin, her expression daring him to deny it.

Emily watched and listened, both to the words and their weighted silence. She thought to speak but held herself quiet. There could be no healing between them unless they vented the bitterness of the past four years. But she could buy Elizabeth time to compose herself, and so she turned Colter's attention on herself.

"I understand why a gentleman such as yourself, Colonel, is uncomfortable with having Elizabeth and Nicole reside with me. But I can assure you that few know of my sordid past. No taint will touch Elizabeth or her child."

"My child, too, madam," he returned stiffly. "And I resent your mockery. Despite what Elizabeth believes, I do respect honesty and answer you in kind. I am most uncomfortable with them being here." Colter gazed directly at Emily's serene face. Her eyes met his with candor, and he murmured an apology for his harshness.

With a weary sigh, he raked his fingers through his hair, forcing order to his thoughts. "Will either of you tell me the reason why Alma Waring centers in your fear?"

Emily did not answer him but directed her attention to Elizabeth. "He should be told."

"The risk—"

"Risk? What risk?" Colter asked. "Stop speaking as if I weren't here!"

"There is no need to shout, Colonel. Please remember that you are a guest in my home."

"And stop pacing like a caged animal, Colter," Elizabeth added. "You will treat Emily with all the respect due to her or you will leave. She offered me sanctuary when I had no one else. Both her home and heart are open to Nicole and myself, and I have only the highest regard for her. I will not countenance anything less from you."

Colter nodded, more pleased than he would reveal. Her statement indicated that he could return and be welcome. He wouldn't push for more now.

"Will you tell me about Alma?"

Elizabeth looked down where she had been unconsciously pleating the material of her skirt. "She swears to have Nicole at any cost."

"You will write her immediately and inform her that Nicole is my daughter and that she has no claim to her. If she wishes, I will reimburse her for any expense she incurred on your behalf."

"I cannot," Elizabeth replied softly.

Emily raised the tip of her cane, forestalling Colter's protest. "You claim to respect honesty, Colonel. So in plain talk, would you have your child branded a bastard?"

"No. I will—"

"You cannot do anything until the matter of James's whereabouts is resolved," Emily explained, knowing she was infuriating him with her calm. "Think, Colonel." And to Elizabeth, she added, "Please tell Rutha that the colonel will join us for supper. I believe we need a respite. Will you offer me your assistance, Colonel?"

Colter acceded to Emily's request. He helped her to her feet and watched as Elizabeth left the room ahead of them.

"You still love her, don't you?"

If Emily was disappointed that Colter didn't answer her, she kept it hidden as he escorted her from the room.

Elizabeth sensed the angry tension emanating from Colter while they ate. Emily had offered them a brief truce with supper, and she knew that was exactly what Colter thought it to be. Once they were done and Nicole was tucked into her bed, he would begin his interrogation again. Feeling as if she had used her last reserves of courage and strength, she prayed for a mercifully quick end to the day and to see Colter gone.

Colter had mercy in short supply. Still seething inside, he chafed at the unspoken agreement for a truce. The supper fare was plain. While the fish was plentiful, the greens were barely flavored with bacon, and the corn bread quickly disappeared before he became aware that he had had more than his share. He hadn't realized he was eyeing the last piece until Emily offered it to him.

He refused, concerned now with their food stores. The thought prompted him to survey the room. His gaze swept the shadowed walls, for the two branched candle sconces concentrated most of the light on the table. The walls were as bare as the sideboard. No silver pieces graced the highly polished wood. Colter thought for a moment that Emily might have been hiding her valuables. Times were uncertain.

But when Rutha entered the room and placed a plate with a small honey cake in front of Nicole and then set one before him, Colter reconsidered the household's situation. He waited for Rutha to return, and as the moments passed he knew she had nothing else to offer

Emily and Elizabeth. No inducement could have made him pick up his fork to taste that bit of sweet. He suddenly recalled a laughing Elizabeth's delight with a box of bonbons he had once presented to her and was forced to tease her into sharing.

Nicole obviously shared Elizabeth's craving for sweets. She had polished off the cake in short order and now, as he watched, she placed one finger on each crumb and brought it to her lips. She caught his eye, and an impish smile met his wink. Colter felt a warmth spread inside him to share this small act with his child, a warmth that left no room for darker emotions but made him promise that nothing, not even the war, would touch this precious life.

"Finish your milk, Nicole," Elizabeth said softly.

"And if you do, there's another cake for you," Colter added, hoping to bribe another smile.

"She's had two already. It's quite enough."

"But our becoming friends," Colter returned, "should allow you to bend the rules, Elizabeth. After all, she is a princess and—"

"And you will not interfere in how I raise my—"

"Elizabeth," Emily warned, cutting her off. "I am sure that the colonel means well. Perhaps half of his portion would satisfy all."

Elizabeth curtly nodded, but she shot Emily a look that clearly indicated what she thought of her defection to the enemy. To her surprise, she found her resentment of Colter's attention to Nicole gave her strength and courage. Did he intend to be a part of their lives? Or would he abandon them once again? She had trusted Colter with her young love, and he had shattered that trust. Now, by word and deed, he seemed to be asking for it again. A look at him from beneath her lowered lashes forced her to amend her thoughts; Colter wasn't asking or demanding, but simply taking his place among them as if it were his natural right.

With a forbidding reserve, she excused herself to get Nicole bathed and ready for bed.

Colter passed the next hour with Emily. He quickly discarded his plan to subtly question her, for she appeared amenable to telling him whatever he wished to hear.

"I sold most of my valuables to garner money to help Elizabeth escape Alma, with the exception of Timothy's cane. I assumed you recognized it," Emily concluded in answer to his query about their financial state. She concealed little, noting that his demeanor had softened considerably. "Elizabeth will need to work. She came away with some clothing, but little else."

Colter revised his opinion. "You care nothing that you are without resources to fall back upon?"

"I loved Timothy Hammond enough to give up all hope of respectability, and I extend that love to his daughter and grandchild. We were never blessed with a child of our own. Perhaps," she stated with a soft sigh, "it was just as well. I could not have lived with myself if I withheld anything I possessed to keep them safe."

"Elizabeth will not accept my aid."

Emily gazed at Colter, who was standing to one side of the fire. He was young, but there were shadows in his eyes that bespoke a much older man. A man of action, not patience, although she admitted that he appeared to curb his natural tendency toward exerting his will until he had enough facts to make a judgment.

"No, she will not make it easy for you."

"I thought as much."

"And that makes you angry. However, this is still my home, Colonel. If you will promise to temper your desire to command, I extend my hospitality to have you visit when you may. Should you wish to share provisions with us, I will not let pride dictate objections. I do ask that you respect Elizabeth's place as Nicole's mother and abide by her wishes before you proceed to spoil her child."

"Sage advice, madam." But while his tone held a sardonic note, his smile conveyed sincerity. "Am I then to conclude that I would find a willing accomplice in you?"

"Colonel!"

"As you stated earlier, plain talk, madam. Will you allow me to ease your lot in whatever ways I can without offending Elizabeth's pride?"

Emily nodded and matched his smile. "Do not step beyond the boundaries of propriety."

"Are there any where a man's child is concerned?" Colter stopped himself from adding *and the woman he loves.* His emotions wanted venting, and bitterness rose to the fore. "You offer me help, madam, then you tie my hands."

"And it must be Elizabeth's decision to free them. She will be down in a few minutes with Nicole. If you will once again offer me your assistance, Colonel, I will leave you."

As they reached the foot of the narrow staircase, Rutha joined them to light the way. Emily bid him good-night just as Elizabeth made her way down holding Nicole. The lamplight illuminated their faces, and Colter longed to reach out and hold them to him. A matching flush tinted their cheeks and he envied whatever whisper Elizabeth made that brought a giggle from his daughter.

Emily received a kiss and a hug from Nicole before Elizabeth, still holding the child in her arms, turned to him.

"Mama said I could kiss you," Nicole said.

Her child-sweet fragrant warmth enveloped him as he offered his cheek. The touch of her lips was far too fleeting, but to his surprise, her fingers touched and lingered on the faint scar on his cheek.

"Was it a bad hurt?"

Pressing forward to hold her touch a moment longer, Colter whispered, "Not anymore."

"Mama's kisses make hurts better. Would you like one?"

"Nicole! I think the colonel—"

"Would love one," Colter finished with a delightful grin.

Elizabeth barely pressed her lips to his cheek, earning a frown from her daughter. To her mother's surprise, Nicole added two more pecks of her own as if to ensure Colter's well-being.

"I wish you a safe journey, Colonel," Elizabeth stated in dismissal, turning away.

"May I carry her up for you?" Colter looked at Nicole, awaiting her decision, but not her mother's.

"We say prays first."

"Then I must join you, for I have much to be thankful for." He reached for his daughter, no longer content to wait.

Nicole hesitated a moment before holding out her arms.

Elizabeth's eyes flared with a furious resentment she couldn't control. Colter's desire to make his presence felt overwhelmed her, but not wanting to make a scene in front of Nicole, she turned and led the way.

"Sweet peace, precious," Elizabeth murmured as she took up one lamp and left another in her daughter's room. Colter watched his sleeping daughter for a few brief moments then followed Elizabeth out.

At the foot of the stairs, Elizabeth turned to him. "I'll show you out."

"There's no need. I'm not ready to leave." He took the lamp from her and led the way into the back parlor. The fire had already been banked for the night, but as the rain continued, the room still held a chill. Colter set the lamp upon the table near the settee and waited for Elizabeth to sit.

"Before you say a word, I want to know why Nicole is afraid of the dark."

"Alma refused to allow her a lamp. She believed it made for weak character."

The lack of emotion in her voice alerted Colter to Elizabeth's exhausted state. He sat beside her and clasped her hand. "I vow to give you all the protection that I can. Alma will not have my daughter, no matter whose name she carries. If you allow me," he whispered, bringing her hand to his lips, "I will do more."

"You'll use Nicole as a weapon, Colter."

"Never," he promised, drawing her closer. When she resisted, he added, "Let me hold you awhile, nothing more. Then I'll take leave."

With a shuddering breath, she nodded and tilted her head back to rest against his shoulder. Colter closed his eyes, savoring the absolute rightness of her being nestled against him.

Elizabeth, too, closed her eyes, sealing her mind from the turmoil of the day. Colter's heat and strength seeped into her. As his hand stroked her arm, a fragile peace overcame her.

"I have three days' leave," he murmured, easing around so that she reclined against the back of the settee. "I want to spend them here with you and Nicole."

"Are you asking or telling me, Colter?" she returned without opening her eyes.

The fire's glow cast intriguing shadows across her face, and Colter placed a kiss on her brow.

"Don't."

"I must," he answered, sliding his hand down to the small of her back and lifting her closer. His lips skimmed her cheek, touched her chin and moved softly to still the flutter of her eyelid. "Rest, Elizabeth. I won't take more."

Elizabeth's breathing kept cadence to the slowing thud of her heartbeat. She drifted into sleep, lulled by Colter's soft murmuring voice and fleeting kisses.

Once he was assured that she was deeply asleep, Colter lifted her into his arms and carried her into the adjoining bedroom. After setting her down on the soft bed with care not to wake her, he unfolded the quilt and covered her.

Returning to the parlor, he blew out the lamp and stared at the fire, debating with himself. He had promised Elizabeth he would go. Outside the wind chose that moment to gust, splattering rain against the windows.

With slow deliberation he unbuttoned his shirt.

From the doorway, Rutha whispered, "Mister Josh stabled your horse. He'll keep watch."

Colter nodded as if nothing untoward were happening. He slid the suspenders off his shoulders and removed his shirt. Rutha came forward with her hand outstretched.

"Best let me have it."

"You don't like my being here."

Rutha took his shirt. "Ain't my place to say."

"The females in this house outnumber me and they all have a say."

"But you don't hear so good," she shot back in parting.

"It depends on what a man listens with—his mind or his heart," he whispered to himself. He sat to remove his boots. It proved a struggle as he tried to be quiet and take them off without a bootjack. Setting them away from the fire, Colter noticed his half-filled glass of brandy on the mantel. He finished it and set the glass on a table outside the parlor door. Closing it softly, he crossed back to Elizabeth's bedroom.

Chapter Five

Throughout the night the rain was muted, and at dawn the clouds thinned before a freshening breeze blew them away. Since the house was set on a gently rolling plateau, the height of the land lent Colter a view of the stubbled field and forest beyond as he watched the day begin from his place beside Elizabeth.

He crossed his arms behind his head and released his breath, knowing that while the hours of his sleep were few, they were the most peaceful ones he could count in months.

In contrast, he knew that Elizabeth's restless turnings and senseless murmurs offered little of what he had found. Less than an hour before, she had turned to him, her head tucked between his neck and shoulder, one hand beneath her cheek, the other against his chest.

In an agony of desire he lay next to her, the feel of her unfettered breast burning his skin. His hungry gaze roved her parted lips and his tongue moistened his own suddenly dry ones. It took all of his considerable self-discipline not to angle his head so that their lips could meet.

As the sun rose, its light turned her hair to a bright, almost copperlike shine and revealed the sleep flush on her cheek.

Colter tried to ignore the fierce quickening in his loins, but every breath they shared, every moment beside her, only made his desire increase.

Like the first time...

He had not noticed her immediately when he had arrived late for a neighbor's house party. A country set was forming and he was content to watch until she caught his gaze. He demanded an introduction from his hostess, received a shy smile from Elizabeth and wanted her then and there.

He could recall the faint strains of the waltz that had played. They danced, but halfway through he led her out to the garden. He kissed her, passion flaring bright and hot after that first whimper of sweet agony when their lips parted. He wanted her even if it would destroy him. She was far too young...and she wanted him, too.

Elizabeth. Her lips soft, lush and hungry. Her breasts rising and falling with each unstable breath. Trembling a little in his arms, filled with bravado, so damn innocent and seductive...

He had longed to tell her to listen to her own instincts and run. She was afraid, but not enough. And he had fought for sanity and control.

One year. He almost won the battle. But each time they were together, letting her go became more agonizing, more an impossibility.

And he loved her.

"Colter?" Elizabeth's quick intake of breath brought Colter instantly back to the present.

"I hope the unspoken part of that question is what am I doing here?"

"What are you doing here?" she asked, closing her eyes to steal another minute of his warmth. Her fingers kneaded lightly against his chest, fingertips tangling in the dark swatch of chest hair. Colter's groan, soft but coming from deep inside him, made her snatch her hand away as if burned.

Before he could stop her, she twisted from him and sat up, shoving back the hair freed from her braid. "What are you doing here?"

His hand stole a long lock of her hair and he tugged gently, silently demanding that she return to her place at his side. Elizabeth's back, rigid with tension, drew his touch. "Look at me. I did no more than sleep beside you. The first peaceful sleep I've had in months."

"Colter, are you mad? Nicole could—"

"She won't." A tug on her bodice tumbled her back against the pillows. Taking instant advantage, Colter leaned over her, the shift of his weight forcing the feather tick beneath them to form a deeper nest.

"Elizabeth." He touched her throat, whispering her name again. Scattered kisses from his lips feathered her jawline, gently coaxing and lulling her to feel the same sweet heat that filled him. The need to shelter and protect her, to hold and touch her was balm to his soul. And as her sleep-flushed body softened to his, Colter believed he could desire nothing more than to remain thus for time unmeasured.

Her lush mouth drew his gaze. Her lips begged for his.

Her eyes denied him. He kissed them closed.

Elizabeth was torn. She felt as if she were betraying her deepest self to remain within his sheltering arms, wanting their warmth and their strength. Once she had belonged here, letting his heat flow over and through her, taking the chill of fear and loneliness away.

She was filled with a deep longing and trembled with the force and suddenness of it. The price of her need for Colter the first time had been high.

Panic assailed her. The skirt and petticoat were tangled around her legs, the quilt an added bond. And Colter...

Her eyes opened to meet the desire in his. She slid her hands up his arms, cupping his shoulders, her fingers eager to tangle in his hair, holding his head fast. She didn't want to think.

He molded her to his hard, warm body, his lips plundering hers again and again—elusive wisps of pleasure, soft, coaxing touches that melted what little resistance she had. When his tongue licked the corners of her mouth, his murmurs of encouragement brought a cry of arousal from her.

She craved his taste. Her body craved his passion, remembering its long abstinence from all things sexual. Elizabeth arched up against him. Her sense of shame was given a forced burial as she opened her mouth to him.

He feasted and she gloried in it. The sounds he made, male, guttural, mating sounds, gratified the lover he had taught her to be. For him. Only for him.

Colter left her mouth and swept hot kisses on her cheeks and nose, her temples and earlobes. His hands slid beneath her to secure her hips hard against his. The base of her throat enticed his mouth and he used his tongue shamelessly to excite her.

She drew his head up, meeting his lips for another kiss of fire. With wild, savage thrusts he deflowered her mouth and left no question that it was his to claim, his absolute possession.

And Elizabeth gave to him even as she pulled his lower lip into the heat he created of her mouth. Her tongue stroked the wet lush fullness, branding him hers.

He rolled to his side, freeing one hand to tense around the slimness of her waist before sliding up to mold the undercurve of her breast. Elizabeth moaned, wildly tossing her head.

Colter freed her mouth. The sharp-set glitter of desire brightened his eyes as he looked down at her. She held her own gaze to his and his hand covered her breast with a gentleness that was almost reverent.

"Did you nurse Nicole?" he whispered in a passion-rough voice. Her lips quivered, her nod barely discernible. He massaged her through the bodice, rubbing the silken material back and forth over her fevered skin until he felt the nipple bud against his palm.

Elizabeth's cry of desire turned to denial. She shoved his hand away, turning, nearly falling from the bed.

"No. I can't do this...." Pulling the quilt free, she slid off the bed. She wrapped her arms around her waist and doubled over. Almost immediately, Colter was beside her.

"Are you in pain? Dammit! Tell me what I did." He couldn't make sense of the wild shaking of her head. "You wanted me, you can't deny that. Did I hurt you?"

With deep heaving breaths, she slowly regained a measure of control. Yes, she wanted him. But she wouldn't admit it. His body heat surrounded her, his taste was melded with hers, and he towered over her, threateningly close.

Colter made an effort to soften his voice. "I have a right to know what caused you..." He paused to think, then asked, "Did I violate your sensibilities by asking about nursing Nicole?"

"No. I..." How could she tell him?

"Sit down, you're shaking like a leaf in the wind. And you will answer me or you'll not leave this room."

She sat, not at his order but because her legs would not support her. Colter stood before her, his back to the window's light, leaving his face shadowed.

"Tell me. I am not going to disappear from your life. Eventually, every ghost, every lie, anything that keeps you locked away from me is going to be shared."

"You're a man, Colter. There is nothing I can say to make you understand."

"Try me, madam." Coming to his knees before her, he took her hands in his. "I don't want to demand from you. I simply want you to share with me." The anguish in her eyes pierced him. "Elizabeth, I had four years of my daughter's life stolen from me. But the greater crime by far was the loss of the woman I loved. Would you still deny me?"

"Colter," she cried, leaning forward and welcoming the sweep of his arms that brought her against him.

"What the hell did they do to you?"

"Just hold me. I need you to hold me. I'll tell you, I promise," she pleaded in a rush before she could think. "Just give me time."

As he cradled her in his arms, Colter closed his eyes. Time was all she asked from him. Time was the one thing he couldn't freely promise to give.

He rocked her and long minutes later, her whispers nearly undid him.

"James stood up to Alma. He insisted Nicole stay with me. I wanted to nurse her, even if it is unfashionable. I had my baby for almost three weeks before Alma found an excuse to send James away. She took Nicole away from me within minutes of his leaving and gave her to a wet nurse. By the time James came back, it was too late. And you know he was no match for Alma."

He took the pain, the bitterness and the despair of each word and held them deep within himself, offering soothing, meaningless murmurs. In a sense, what she had claimed was true; he didn't understand her loss. But instinct warned him that there was more. Cautioned by her promise to tell him, he waited. And jealousy rose. He tried not to think of James with his child, with Elizabeth.... As if to stop his thoughts, Elizabeth continued.

"The pain drove me mad. I wanted and needed my baby."

"Yes, love. Yes, you would."

"Alma wouldn't let me see her. I couldn't hold her. There was no relief to be had. Alma taunted me each time she came to visit, and James said I upset him and kept away from the house."

Stroking her head, pressing her tight to his body, Colter scattered kisses against her hair.

"And you weren't there, Colter."

It was the softest of whispers. The deepest cut. He swallowed the only defense he could offer. *I didn't know.*

Inside, rage grew to fury—not the burning, white-hot fury that demanded reckless revenge, but a colder, deadly fury that made Colter vow he would live to see the Warings pay for the pain they had caused Elizabeth.

He held her while she cried. But as her sobs lessened and she grew quiet, Colter's need to hear the rest of the story grew stronger. He hated to take advantage of her vulnerable state, but he knew that once she became more calm and rational, she would try to rebuild a wall between them.

"Why did Alma hate you?"

"She didn't. Not at first." Elizabeth stroked his beard-stubbled cheek and wiped the last of the tears from her eyes. She avoided his gaze, and he sensed her reluctance to tell him more.

"Then tell me, why did you turn to James when you learned you were carrying my child?"

"Robert died a few weeks after you left for England. When they learned about my half-brother's death, Alma and James paid their respects. I kept fainting and Alma told me why."

Elizabeth, restless, moved to stand. Colter let her go, knowing she was already withdrawing from him. But his need to know more stilled his protest.

"At first," she continued in an emotionless voice, "I didn't want to believe her. Each day she came, and she was always kind. The weeks slipped by. I was alone. There was no one else I could confide in. Alma didn't judge me, but she did beg me to consider what I would do. When my half-brother Thomas was lost during a storm at sea, I no longer had any family to cling to. That's when James told me of your letter. I don't know why he lied. He offered me the protection of his name and a home for my child."

"I heard that your brothers both died and their ships were sold. But your wish that I shouldn't contact you—"

"Not mine! James's wish, remember that, Colter." Color flagged her cheeks and with a distracted air, she glanced down at herself. "Nicole will wonder where I am."

It was pointless to continue. Colter rose. "I'll return to the city, but I'm coming back, Elizabeth."

"Give me time."

"I can't. There's a war going on, much as I would like to forget it. I was granted three days' leave and need to be with you and my daughter. Before you say no, Emily has graciously offered me the hospitality of her home."

"But not my bedroom!"

"No," he agreed with a grin. "Only you have that right. But I want you and no matter what lies you tell yourself, love, you want me, too."

"I'm James's wife," she reminded him in an anguished whisper.

"For his betrayal, James is a dead man."

Four mules were loaded with provisions to send to Miss Emily's. Colter satisfied himself with securing enough foodstuffs to keep them for weeks. He had made arrangements with several merchants to supply staple goods and fresh meat when it was available, all bills to be sent to his account. He did not delay in setting up a trust fund for Nicole. He could not claim her as his, and so had named his near-brotherly friendship with James as his relation to Nicole, choking on the gall it raised.

What Colter desperately wanted was to find a castle for Nicole. While treasures of every description were available for sale as families in need parted with their possessions, nothing resembling a castle had surfaced. He had vowed to turn the city upside down, but time was against him and he began to rethink his rashness.

Aid came from an unexpected source.

Colter returned to his hotel that afternoon to change from his uniform. He dreaded finding a message that he was recalled to duty.

Needlessly, it turned out. But Andre was waiting.

One look at Colter's unshaven face and Andre knew he had not been back to the hotel since the day before. "The war is taking its toll on your skill, *mon ami,* if it took you all night to console the lovely Elizabeth."

"You court death recklessly, my friend."

"More than you know."

It took several preoccupied moments before Colter realized that Andre was serious. Silently cursing a possible added delay, he stopped stropping his razor and faced Andre.

"If you've killed a man I'll have you out of the city before anyone knows."

Helping himself to the bottle of bourbon, Andre poured a drink and sipped it. "I am thinking about it, but the deed remains undone."

"Don't be selfish with my liquor. Pour one for me. And then, tell me what's wrong."

Andre handed him a drink, topped off his own glass and asked, "How much money would you lend me? Before you answer, Colter, remember my estate is gone. My life, as yours, is uncertain at best. All told, the chance of repayment is slight."

"How much did you lose?"

The amber liquid in his glass drew Andre's gaze. "I would admit this to no man but you. What price would I put on my heart?"

"A woman? Who? Have you fallen prey to—"

"As you have to Elizabeth?"

Colter met Andre's knowing look, their emotions stripped bare for the moment before Andre looked away.

"Write out your request and I'll sign it. You can have the money immediately."

"Without questions, *mon ami?*"

Colter faced his shaving mirror. "Tell me whatever you wish. If you'd rather say nothing, I'll accept that."

"Two thousand in gold and an hour of your time," Andre intoned, only the slight tremble of the glass in his hand revealing how important this was to him.

Colter set down the razor, stripped off his uniform pants and walked to the wardrobe. Removing a shirt from the folded pile, he tossed it to Andre. "Finish packing for me."

Colter found a little problem waiting at the bank. When his demand for gold was met with vague excuses, he used his rank and hinted that government security was at stake, dropping a few prominent names after swearing the banker to secrecy.

"Now what?" he asked once they were outside.

"You risk a great deal for me. And now, we walk." Andre glanced at Colter and, without warning, said, "She is a quadroon."

Colter chose to ignore the underlying note of challenge in Andre's voice. "She must be lovely," was his only comment.

"In my city each year, there is a ball that brings men from all over the South as the *petite amours* are presented to possible patrons. They are the loveliest women of color to be found anywhere."

"And I would imagine a man's purse weighs in the consideration of his patronage."

"Without question, *mon ami.* Come, we turn down here," Andre said, leading Colter away from the center of the city. "It is not much farther. And to continue, the patron must prove that he can offer financial security, private lodgings in an acceptable area, servants, a carriage, horses and other concessions that must be carefully negotiated before he takes possession. The liaison is often long lasting and mutually advantageous. Sometimes," he added in a strained voice, "there are children."

Crossing the street, Colter lengthened his stride to catch up with Andre. He studied Andre's drawn features. Colter had always assumed that Andre's dark olive complexion owed itself to a Moorish ancestor. For a moment, he wondered if Andre was trying to tell him something more. He stifled the traitorous thought before it could grow, and asked, "What happens if two men want the same woman?"

"Whoever offers the most will have her."

"Is that what happened here, Andre? Did two of you want the same woman?"

"*Non.* Brice found a widow to console early in the evening and later, I found a game to my liking. My winnings were modest, but at another table, the play was heavy. There was a stir as demand for immediate payment was made. The man, near twice your age, Colter, claimed he had just arrived and had not established credit, but did offer to settle the debt with something more valuable. Within minutes he returned with the most exquisite woman I have seen. She was..." Andre's voice broke. "A dolt could see her fear."

They both stopped to allow a wagon to pass, then crossed another street lined with modest homes. Colter wasn't sure where they were going. He asked nothing, willing to give Andre time to compose himself.

"They were all drunk, not as you and I would be, for I am sure there wasn't a gentleman among them. But I digress. Games were abandoned and an auction was suggested. You have seen this before."

"Several times, when a gambler was down. I also recall a pair who worked small towns, to their profit, I believe, until they were caught. The gambler would be unable to settle his debt, and explain he needed money. Then he would hold an impromptu auction, collect his money, and disappear. The slave always escaped by morning."

"Have you ever bought at an auction?"

Once again, Colter caught the odd note in Andre's voice and chose to ignore it. "What happened last night?"

"They demanded to see what they were getting."

"And you were offended?"

"As you would have been. These were not men, but animals."

"Let me guess," Colter said. "You offered a distraction. A game of chance, perhaps doubling the stakes just to make it enticing enough that none could refuse. And you won."

"When did you come to know me so well?"

"When I first risked my life with you at my back."

Andre stopped in front of a house one shy of the corner. "This is it."

They proceeded up the walk and Colter, ever alert, noticed the slight movement of the lace curtain in an upstairs window. Andre raised the tarnished brass knocker. The door opened almost before he could use it.

As they were ushered into the dimly lit hall, Colter watched the man closing the door behind them. The man ignored Colter, staring instead at Andre.

"You have the money? In gold?"

"Where is she?"

"The money first."

Colter heard the chime of a clock in the next room and turned to the sound. The furniture in the parlor was draped with muslin covers except for a large chair before the fire, which drew his gaze to the mantel. There, resting in lonely splendor, was a miniature replica of a castle. The chime sounded the second hour, and as Colter approached, two heralds sprang from the castle doors. A lilting tune played as they followed tracks that made them appear to march before the castle. Entranced, Colter listened and admired the fine porcelain details. A rose trellis climbed up the wall to a center balcony. As the music played, the dainty figure of a woman came forth, dressed in gold cloth, her arm slowly raised and moving as if she waved to an unseen crowd below.

She retreated, as did the heralds, and the music stopped. Colter didn't realize he had lifted the clock until his attention was taken from it.

"It was a child's delight."

Colter looked at the man by his side. There was a weary stoop to his shoulders and a tremor to the hand that reached for the clock. Colter would not release it.

"How much?"

"It is not for sale."

"It could delight another child. A little girl."

"Yours?"

Colter glanced at the doorway where Andre stood alone in the shadowed light, for the velvet portieres were drawn across the windows. Colter sensed a tension between them, a demand for truth that would again put them on equal footing. Still holding Andre's gaze, he nodded. "Yes. Mine."

Andre spoke rapidly in his native tongue, leaving Colter to stand alone as the man walked away from him, shaking his head in refusal.

If it were possible, Colter believed the man's shoulders bowed even farther as Andre continued, low-voiced, intense, using every bit of flair at his command to gain the clock for him.

"Tell him I'll pay whatever he asks, Andre. Don't bargain. I want the clock."

With an abrupt turn, the man faced Colter. "I wish your child life to enjoy it."

"I can't thank you enough. Wait, I don't know your name."

The man raised a hand in Colter's direction, putting an end to the conversation. He obeyed, but did so out of sensitivity for the man's double loss. Colter set the clock down on the large chair, and used its cast-off muslin cover to wrap the clock carefully. Carrying his gift, Colter reached Andre just as a soft rustle of cloth drew his gaze to the staircase.

The woman was just as Andre claimed—exquisite. She moved with a liquid grace, and her fawnlike eyes met his for a moment before she looked at Andre. Her hair was a mass of ebony curls, her skin the delicate hue of copper. As she neared, Andre raised her hand to his lips.

"As I promised, Naomi, I have come for you."

Her smile was as shy as Elizabeth's had been when he first met her and pierced Colter with a sense of urgency.

"Andre, the matter between us is settled. I leave you to make what arrangements you wish. Time demands that I go."

"I wish you joy, *mon ami.* As I will have."

Colter opened the door and heard a last admonishment from the old man.

"Treasure these gifts. They are priceless."

Chapter Six

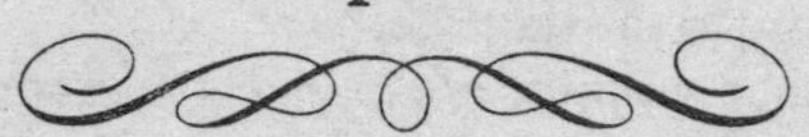

The fire spat and sizzled when sap ran from a green piece of wood, sending a shower of sparks up the chimney. Golden light from the prismed lamp beside the wing chair Colter sat in, reading the newspaper, cast a warm glow over his features. Beyond the lace curtains, the night held the dark and danger that threatened Elizabeth, just as Colter's presence did. Seated before the fire on the settee, Elizabeth stared down at the needlework she'd abandoned.

Upon his return this afternoon, she had voiced protests that he ignored and since then had little to say to him. Colter had succeeded in establishing himself in everyone's good graces.

Rutha held her reserve but couldn't disguise her pleasure as Colter offered to help fill her pantry shelves with staples and delicacies that had long been missing from her kitchen. Mister Josh had unbent long enough to grudgingly admire the four mules that Colter claimed were now his responsibility, but Elizabeth had seen his smile when he unloaded grain for their care.

Emily's defection was accomplished with a book of poetry, a silver-encased vial of rose water and the softest of cashmere shawls in a shade of pink that nearly matched the blush on her cheek.

Elizabeth chided herself for her petty thoughts. She didn't begrudge them the gifts, or their pleasure in having them, but she couldn't ignore the feeling that by making his interest in them widely known, Colter brought danger to them. Alma would never rest until she had Nicole. Elizabeth knew this, and with a sigh, she was forced to accept her place as the one to tell Colter.

She found it difficult to begin, especially with the sound of Nicole's delighted laughter lingering in her mind. How could she harbor even a tiny bit of resentment or anger for a man who had included all of them in presenting his surprise to Nicole?

With her head bent, Elizabeth allowed her smile to widen, recalling Colter's solemn explanation that the timing of his gift had to be perfect. None of them had caught the subtle clue. Eyes aglow with impatience, Nicole had cast aside whatever fear of him lingered to remain close by his side. Supper saw her squirming, bolting her food, constantly interrupting the conversation to ask, "When?"

When had arrived with a ribbon-tied box of bonbons that Rutha set in front of Elizabeth, leaving her no choice but to accept and share them. Nicole obediently closed her eyes at Colter's suggestion and the hour was struck to the lilting tune of the clock Mister Josh set in front of Nicole.

The excited cry, the laughter to see heralds come forth, the enchanting wonder of her daughter's eyes as she gazed at the delicate figure waving brought home to Elizabeth all that they had been denied. Not the material gifts, but the simple sharing that Alma's austere manner had forbidden.

To protect her child, Elizabeth decided to be firm with Colter. She knew her own vulnerability to him, and while she wanted and needed to believe in the security he had created by his presence, she would be a fool to forget his being here was a double-edged sword.

Colter looked up at that moment, watching the firelight cast glimmers of bronze and gold in the lighter strands of her hair. The fragile bend of her bare nape drew his gaze. Desire to love her filled him, a hot surge that rushed through his blood. He wanted to free it, but he had a bittersweet awareness that tempered passion.

Elizabeth was afraid of him.

Elizabeth didn't trust him.

Where had the charming minx, full of laughter, enchanted with life and joyous pleasure, disappeared to? He saw Elizabeth in his daughter. While he had shared his child's joy when the castle clock had been revealed, it had been Elizabeth that he watched in those unguarded moments. Only a blind fool would have missed the shadows in her eyes. He wanted them gone. He refused to believe that his mind had created lies out of his memories of Elizabeth.

He had earned her anger with this day's work. They had sat in silence for nearly an hour since tucking Nicole into bed. Emily had been the last to speak. Her good-night and reminder that Rutha had laid fresh linens in the upstairs front bedroom were joined by a speaking glance that begged Colter's patience.

So he waited. And waited. Elizabeth did not speak. Time was his enemy. He could give her no more.

Setting aside his paper, Colter rose and took the last two logs from the wood box. He placed them on the fire and faced Elizabeth.

"You have an appointment to see Memminger tomorrow."

"Thank you."

"That's it? No questions, just this meek, false acceptance?"

The goad in his voice made Elizabeth look up at him. "What do you want from me, Colter? Do you want me to ask what you told him about me? Do you want me to claim that pride won't allow me to accept your help in gaining me a job that will support us? Live at the mercy of another for every crust of bread, for the joy of seeing your child, and then dare to tell me that I am meek!"

"You're shouting, Elizabeth," he chided.

"Yes. Yes I am."

"And you've quite crushed that bit of cloth in your hand," he pointed out, leaning close to take it from her. He hid his smile at Elizabeth's bemused expression as he set the needlework on the table beside the settee. "But you're not finished yet, are you?" he asked, taking up his position in front of her.

"I don't know what you're implying."

"Not implying, never that, madam," he returned in a stern voice, running one hand through his hair. "You don't trust me and you're afraid of me. I demand to know why. And when you have satisfied my curiosity on that matter, you can tell me why I've angered you over—"

"Enough! I'm not under your military command. You can't badger and demand and..." She bolted from the settee, intending to cross to her room. He caught her arm in a punishing grip and stopped her.

"No more running."

His eyes held a reckless glitter and she raised hostile eyes to meet them.

"I'm not afraid of you, Colter. I fear the harm you can do by calling attention to us. You heard Emily mention the risk. It is to Nicole. Alma will not cease in her search to claim her." Closing her eyes, she bowed her head and felt his grip ease, although he did not release her. "James's father left everything in trust for a grandchild. Without Nicole—"

"But she's not—"

"It doesn't matter. She is claimed as his daughter. Without her, Alma must give over everything to be divided among her husband's brothers. She will never allow that," Elizabeth declared with a violent shudder.

Colter released his hold, only to slip his arms around her, drawing her close to him. With his lips pressed to her temple, he murmured, "And your trust? How do I regain that from you?"

With innate honesty, she answered, "I don't know, Colter."

"Holding you is like holding the summer sun. You are a forever warmth to melt the chill of loneliness."

His emotions poured over her, stealing her breath, quickening her pulse. "Think of what you say. These moments are all stolen."

"And I would steal more."

Husky, caressing, his voice recalled memories of their times together, just as the soothing touch of his hands stroking her back lulled her into believing him.

His scent teased her to taste his kiss and Elizabeth fought to hold on to her sanity.

"Until I know what has happened to James—"

"James isn't here. I am." His lips trailed kisses to her ear. "James doesn't want you. I do." The edge of her earlobe was caught gently by his teeth and she couldn't hold back a shiver of arousal. "And you," he breathed, raising his hand to cup her chin, his gaze holding hers, "you want me, not James."

"I never did. Not the way you believe. I—" His kiss came to taste her mouth, silencing her, bringing desire, not fear.

Colter's mouth. Temptation. Pleasure, hot and wild and passionate. Elizabeth remembered all of these only too well. She opened her mouth as her body softened against his. She was greedy now and wanted him to feel the same need he had unleashed in her.

Colter surrendered the role of aggressor. She took his mouth with a delicate courting that clawed his body with desire. He willingly allowed her to take and give as much as she wanted.

His hand stroked her side, raising her arm to his shoulder, lifting her gently up and into his body. He continued his caress, pressing the heel of his hand to the lush side of her breast, until she clung, breathless and shaking against him.

He gave her mouth a reprieve, ignoring her protest. "Such a greedy little fox," he whispered, finding that he had neglected the sensitive area below her jawline. The teasing kisses brought forth his name in a shuddering cry of demand. "But you enjoy this, don't you?" he asked softly, pulling the net and pins from her hair. "Tell me," he demanded in a passion-rough voice.

"I enjoy—"

"And I want more. Say that, too, little fox."

"And I want—"

"And want," he finished, breathing the words before taking her mouth again.

His kiss stripped her of calm. His fingers threaded into her loosened hair, cupping the back of her head to hold her still. The hand at the small of her back urged her against him. Colter's lips rubbed gently against hers until they parted. His agile tongue claimed her mouth with slow, delicious strokes.

Breathing rapidly, he raised his lips from hers to whisper, "Sweet, sweet little fox, you make my blood run hot." With his mouth open against her throat, he drew the fragile skin against his teeth.

"You'll mark me," she cried out softly.

"Yes." There was a controlled savagery to his voice.

But Elizabeth ignored it. She knew how hot his blood ran, for her own had reached a fevered state. Hungrily she brought his mouth back to hers. Her tongue searched for his and her hands slid into his thick hair, holding him. Pressing against the hard, taut length of his body, all protests faded to whispers in her mind.

Colter had made her glory in the passion they called from each other. He had taught her to share, that the give-and-take between lovers was something rare, always to be treasured. And within her, desire flamed into a passionate glory that demanded consummation.

Colter eased his hold on her head, slid his hand down her back and drew her with him as he stepped toward the wing chair. His mouth teased her with a flirtatious play that begged her to follow him. He sat, positioning Elizabeth between his spread thighs, his hands cupping her hips.

Elizabeth opened her eyes and gazed at the sharp-set features of her lover. A passion flush across his cheeks drew her fingertips, her thumb grazing his mouth. Colter followed her movement, his tongue licking its pad, slowly drawing the tip into the heat of his mouth. She swayed before him, placing one hand on his shoulder for support.

When he released her thumb, she held his gaze and lifted it to her own mouth. "I'll taste of you and me," she murmured, eyes darkening as desire rose to another height.

His own eyes darkened, the lids heavy, watching her gaze lower to the blatant ridge of his arousal. The close-fitting, dove gray pants did nothing to hide his aroused state and with a rueful grin, Colter pulled her down to his lap.

But as he once again moved to claim her lips, she turned her head from him.

Into the silence from the upper reaches of the house came the unmistakable chime of the clock. Elizabeth tensed. Colter had given that clock to Nicole. Her daughter. Was she mad to dally with him as her child slept beneath the same roof?

Warnings and recriminations poured over her like a cold, wet rain. Alma's voice charged from her memory, screaming imprecations. "Trollop! Slattern! Colter's whore! You're not fit to be mother to that child!"

"Love, what's wrong?" he asked in a gentle voice.

Elizabeth didn't answer. She raised a fist to her passion-swelled lips.

Colter sensed her move to bolt and he snaked his arm around her waist, anchoring her in place. For a few moments she struggled silently for release, and he, just as silently, refused to let her go.

"Stop this, Colter. You don't own me. I am not yours. Let me free."

"You're not making any sense, Elizabeth. For the sake of—"

"I won't let you use the passion between us to make me forget who I am," she cried out, striking his shoulder.

"Sweet heaven, Elizabeth," he grated from between clenched teeth, desperate to still the heat of his body and make sense of her sudden withdrawal. "Desist," he finally demanded, "before you hurt yourself."

"Then let me go." Her slender fingers grabbed his wrist, tugging at his viselike hold.

Afraid that he would hurt her, Colter released her. She jumped up and backed away from him, her eyes wide, her chest heaving, no longer with passion, but what he determined was fear. Her hair was a wild tangle that fell to her waist, and he knew that if he dared to move, she would react like a wild creature, prey to predator. His own breathing was unsteady, his body a riot of need. His mind exerted itself to bring order to his thoughts.

Elizabeth watched him as prey would watch its hunter. His eyes seemed to bore into hers, eyes so dark and hard she shivered. Colter's strong features grew tense, his lips compressed, and his jaw went rigid with anger. She could see the ripple of his muscles beneath the linen shirt as he slowly rose from the chair.

Her heart thundered in her chest. She tried to speak, but her throat seemed to close and her mouth was dry as kindling.

She knew her silence caused the look on his face to turn to raw fury. Frozen in place, she could only stand as he came toward her.

In the few seconds she had, Elizabeth urged herself to attack him verbally before he could begin to make his demands. She swallowed repeatedly, skirting the fire, backing toward the safety of her bedroom door.

"No farther, Colter," she warned in an unsteady voice, moistening her lips, frantic to find something to distract him. She could never repeat the names Alma had called her. She could never tell him the guilt she suffered, the shame she had known for loving him.

Colter had her within arm's reach, but he made no move to touch her. He fought for his own control while attempting to find reason for her actions.

Elizabeth's gaze darted about the room, lighting on the half-empty box of candy. "Was it your intent to have me in payment for your lavish gifts?"

"Devil's bitch," he swore in a biting tone that was soft, almost too soft. "If it was, madam, I was sorely cheated. That damn clock cost me two thousand dollars in gold." Colter wasn't looking at her. He couldn't. The course of her attack left him feeling raw.

"Colter! I didn't mean—"

His gaze locked on hers. "Didn't you?"

Elizabeth felt chilled by his cold countenance. He stood, legs spread apart in a challenging stance; she could see their sinewed strength strain against the cloth of his formfitting breeches. The strong beat of the pulse in his throat kept the same wild cadence as her heart.

She closed her eyes for a dizzying moment. What in all of heaven had she done?

"Look at me! No cowardice now, madam," he intoned in a voice that had brought fear to his men. "Find me a brazen whore bold enough to proclaim her wares worthy of that high a price. Find her, damn you!" he commanded, knowing he was losing control.

Startled, Elizabeth looked at him again. She shook to see his hands curled into fists at his sides. "Colter, stop. Please, stop." She raised her hand as if to ward off his blow.

Colter's lips compressed until they were almost white. He hadn't missed her move. "You believe that I would raise my hand to you?"

"No. No, never you." Her hand fell limply to her side, but he wasn't done.

"Well," he asked in a mocking tone, "have you nothing else to say? Do you truly believe," he goaded without mercy, "that my expenses this day were well paid for?"

"Colter, I... no," she finished lamely. Dragging forth her courage, she offered him what she hoped he wanted to hear. "If I let you use me from now until you had to leave, I would not be able to repay your generosity."

Her eyes were glazed with unshed tears, but he was far too incensed to see them and take pity, or to realize that she lied. She had sliced a raw wound in him and his pride demanded satisfaction.

"Come here, Elizabeth," he drawled with soft menace.

Chapter Seven

When she didn't move, he added, "You can't believe that I want to *use* you. It all comes back to your not trusting me, doesn't it?"

His voice still held menace, but there was hurt, too. He blocked her escape to the hallway. She made the mistake of looking behind her toward the bedroom door. He managed to take two steps closer before she turned back and faced him. To his surprise, Elizabeth came forward.

"There's nowhere left to go, is there?" she asked softly.

Anger seeped from his body. Pride caused his brow to lift with disbelief, but slowly, as slowly as her hand rose to touch his cheek, it ceased its demand for satisfaction.

"I've run you a merry chase this night," she said, bowing her head as her hand slid down his chest. "So much power in you, Colter. I envy your strength."

"Elizabeth, I—"

"You want so much from me," she continued in an emotionless voice. "No. Not from me as I am, but from the girl I was." Lifting her head, she studied his face. "Accept what little I can give you and ask for no more. If you do, Colter, you'll end up hating me. What has happened changed me. You want to know all. I can't ever tell you or anyone. But I am not the one who is important, Nicole is. You cannot risk her."

"Then let me help you. Being a broker in Europe for my father and his friends has made me financially secure. I can hire an attorney to fight Alma's claim. I will find out what's happened to James and I can, if you let me, protect you."

She turned away from him. "Colter, if I allow you to do all this, it would take time. What if something happened to me?"

"I don't understand. What could happen?" He tried to hold her and draw her close to him, but she stepped out of his reach.

"If Alma found us, if she took Nicole, I would follow. Alma threatened to kill me. With me dead, James missing and you at war, there's no one to stop her."

"So any query I make, any move—"

"A whisper could bring her here. If you care anything for my child, don't draw attention to us, don't put us at risk."

He saw her shudder as the tension left her, but he made no move near her.

She started toward her room. "Elizabeth, wait."

"Good night, Colter."

It could not have been more final if she said goodbye. The key grating in the lock to her door left him feeling more than physically shut out; he was overwhelmed by the loss of what could never be reclaimed.

* * *

Elizabeth finished her morning ablutions long before the sun rose. Once again wearing the deep plum skirt with its matching pointed bodice, she forced herself to eat a biscuit spread with honey and sipped a second cup of tea, waiting for Colter to wake. Rather than be alone, she had joined Rutha in the kitchen, finding her undemanding presence calming. Separated from the two-story farmhouse by a covered walk, the kitchen was built of brick, with one entire wall taken up by the massive fireplace and baking ovens. The original homestead was over one hundred years old.

"Miz Beth, you gonna eat another biscuit?"

"One was enough, Rutha. Do you want me to take that tray up to Emily?"

Rutha shook her head, setting the china teapot on the linen-draped tray. After she left, Elizabeth gazed around the room that had once served a farm family for eating as well as cooking.

The thick wooden trestle table and benches were still there, although she sat on one of the two chairs that had been added. The wash bench, which she and Rutha took turns using, was against the solid wall, along with tubs once used to salt meat. The wooden meal chest remained but was no longer used for food storage since the pantry had been added. A cheese press gathered dust, for there was no cow, and a spinning wheel that was missing a leg sat abandoned in the corner.

The massive ceiling joists drew her gaze, and Elizabeth tried to picture them as they once might have looked, hung with hams, sides of bacon, onions and the like. It was pleasant to wonder what people had lived here, what laughter and tears they had shared within these walls.

Mister Josh entered the room, distracting her, and she watched him unload an armful of kindling into the wood box.

"Day be fine, Miz Beth. Mules be hitched an' waitin' jus' like the colonel ordered." He helped himself to the dipper hung above the covered barrel of fresh water, drinking thirstily before he replaced the cover and re-hung the dipper. He eyed the basket of biscuits resting on the trestle table. "You et?"

It was hard not to smile when Mister Josh began his role of caretaker. "There's plenty more if you want—"

"Had 'em steamin' out of the oven. Pleased me see my Rutha not havin' to scrape by."

"You like the colonel, don't you, Mister Josh?"

"Well, rides a fine piece of horseflesh, he does. Ain't a mark on him. Tells a body a piece 'bout a man to be seein' how he treats his horse."

Elizabeth couldn't help but laugh. Impulsively she rose and ran to hug him. "You're just what I needed this morning. I admit I'm a little frightened about this appointment with Secretary Memminger. A good dose of your common sense almost has me believing that if the colonel treats his horse well, a person could expect the same from him." Elizabeth stepped back and saw the twinkle in his eye.

"Didn't say so, Miz Beth. Jus' sayin' it's one way to be judgin' the measure of 'im." He looked beyond her, smiling. "Mawnin', Colonel."

Elizabeth turned in time to see Colter nod. He stood in the doorway leading toward the house, one arm raised against the door lintel. She searched his clean-shaven face for a clue to his mood, disappointed when he merely inclined his head in greeting.

"Rutha made biscuits, Colter. And there's tea."

For a moment longer he hesitated, leaving Elizabeth with the strange feeling that he was unsure of his reception. He came to sit at the table, and she took a china cup and saucer from the open shelves. Once she poured the tea and set it before him, she stood behind him, unable to tear her gaze away from the buff-colored frock coat that emphasized the breadth of his shoulders.

"Will you join me?"

Elizabeth looked toward Josh, thinking that Colter offered the invitation to him. But Mister Josh was no longer in the kitchen. Unwilling to further strain the uneasy truce between them, she complied.

He was already breaking open a second biscuit, lavishly spreading honey and eating it before she had taken a sip of tea. His eyes were closed in pleasure and she found herself smiling.

Colter caught the smile and his own was boyish. "Rutha's baking is heaven. The hotel's chef can't hold a candle to her," he said, reaching for a third. "Did she ask you to help her make a list of what other provisions she needs? I promised to bring them back with us."

Edging the rim of her cup with one finger, Elizabeth hesitated in answering him. Trust. Colter wanted her to trust him. But if she was honest, she could endanger Rutha.

"Don't tell me I have begun this day by committing some unpardonable sin?"

The words were harsh, but not his tone. Elizabeth looked up and made her decision. "Rutha doesn't need my help to make up a list of her wants. She is able to read and write."

"She what!"

"Keep your voice down, Colter. You wanted me to trust you. I know it's forbidden for slaves to be taught, but Rutha and Mister Josh are free. From childhood, they were raised to be house servants in Emily's family. When her parents died, she offered to have them come live with her, but gave them their papers. And," she whispered, glaring at him before she leaned across the table and wagged one finger under his nose, "you shall not debate the merits or wisdom of this."

Colter kissed the fingertip that tempted him, leaving behind a small smear of honey. Before he could lure it into his mouth, Elizabeth snatched her hand back and, with an innocent, unconscious move that was nonetheless provocative, licked her finger clean.

Not wishing to provoke himself or Elizabeth, Colter shrugged, finished another biscuit, emptied his cup and, knowing he needed time to carefully word his concerns, used his napkin as if at a formal dinner. When he was done, he leaned back and found her watching him with an arresting expression. He folded his hands across his middle, the deep tan of his skin almost a match for the shade of his waistcoat.

"Elizabeth," he began, "what you have told me is a serious matter. You realize I am—"

"I know who and what you are, Colter!"

"You trusted me. I have no intent of violating that trust, let me reassure you of that. But I worry should anyone else find out. I know from what you've said that you have been isolated from news. But the teaching of slaves to—"

"I told you, they are not slaves," she interrupted.

"To the outside world they are. Teaching them to read and write is illegal. The penalties to Emily would be most severe, and, by association, they would extend to you."

"You believe in slavery?"

He met her gaze with a level look. "I am fighting because I believe in states' rights to govern themselves. Slavery will die of its own, no matter what the outcome of this war. The economic growth of the Northern cities, the near double amount of railroads in the North, along with their greater number of factories, are all working against our way of life. Because of our longer growing seasons, we've been encouraged to be dependent upon the North. Our political, economic and social life has been dominated by the quarter of Southerners who own large numbers of slaves, but that cannot continue much longer."

"You never mentioned your feelings before, Colter."

"And you never asked. Now, as much as I would like to continue, we must leave to keep our appointment with Memminger."

Elizabeth left to get her bonnet. Their brief conversation gave her a better understanding of Colter. She had been right to trust him. Emily would have to be told that he knew, but her step was light as she went outside to join him by the farm wagon.

"I apologize for our mode of transportation, Elizabeth. I didn't think to find a carriage horse. I'll remedy that today."

She accepted his lifting her up to the wooden seat and smoothed her skirts as he sat beside her. "Colter, I would feel better if you didn't buy a horse. The chance of it being stolen—"

"But you'll need the carriage to get to the city."

"No. I'll walk. The less—"

"Attention. Yes, I know."

Guiding the team of mules diverted his attention and Elizabeth was content to remain silent. She wished that Colter were going to come with her, for she would need to lie to the secretary, and his presence could be useful.

As if he had read her thoughts, Colter asked her what she was going to tell Memminger.

"Did you tell him my name?" she countered.

"No. I merely asked him to see one of our gallant Southern ladies, a Virginian by birth, orphaned by the war. I did mention that you were in need of work, that your character is exemplary, your penmanship the finest and—"

"But Colter, you've never seen my writing."

"A minor detail." He glanced at her and offered a roguish grin. "Memminger will take one look at you and know I was right." His gaze coaxed her into a lighter mood, and while her laugh was soft and far too short in duration, it was sweet to hear.

A few moments later he added, "I believe I forgot to mention that he'll have in his possession a letter of recommendation from the secretary of war."

"I don't understand. How could anyone write a letter of recommendation without knowing who I am, or my name?"

"I haven't compromised you, Elizabeth, so lose that frown. It was a personal favor to me, and he stated only that the bearer of the letter was known to him." Urging the team around several deep ruts, Colter continued. "I was surprised to learn that more than a few women have approached the president to intercede for them, and none are shy in mentioning other political connections. I deemed it only fair to give you a similar opportunity."

Placing her hand on his arm, Elizabeth murmured her thanks, trying to still the flutter of her stomach.

Colter drove the wagon through the crowded city streets with patience and skill. Elizabeth glanced up at the building before which he stopped, its white stone brilliant in the sunlight.

"This is now the Note Bureau," Colter explained, setting the pole brake. "Memminger is waiting inside." He climbed down and came around to lift her from the seat. The slight tremble of her body alerted him to her nervousness. "We could avoid this meeting if you would accept my help. There's no need for you to work."

Elizabeth, her hands still braced on his arms, glanced down at the plain gold stickpin nestled in the soft fold of his necktie. Its creamy shade almost matched his linen shirt. There was no doubt that he could easily support her, but it was a choice she couldn't accept. "I didn't realize you intended to come with me."

"I won't be cheated of one moment with you and the matter is not open for discussion. But you haven't answered me."

"Accept my decision, Colter. It is the only one I would be comfortable with."

Her sweet smile of gratitude warmed him, although he wanted more, so much more from her. He contented himself with the knowledge that her acceptance of his company was a step in the right direction. Offering his arm, he escorted her into the former LeFebre Female Academy.

Christopher Memminger, with his sharp, deep-set eyes and manner as stiff as his high starched wing collar and thickly waved hair, proved to be gracious about having his day disrupted. Elizabeth had a feeling that if Colter had not been with her, her time with the secretary would have been short.

As agreed, Colter introduced her by her maiden name of Hammond. He also added that she was from King George County, which caused her to start. How could he have known her letters to Memminger were signed as such? She intended to question Colter later.

Completely at ease, Colter waited until the secretary had finished reading the letter of recommendation. "If you need more," he drawled graciously, "I am sure that Randolph, Seddon or Letcher would be happy to comply. Of course, Miss Hammond is far too modest to prevail upon our first lady, but I know that Varina Davis would personally endorse her application."

"No need, no need," Memminger answered, tossing the letter down amidst the clutter of his desk. "If you would be so kind as to supply me with a sample of your penmanship, Miss Hammond, I am sure we can find a position for you as a note signer. You will be expected to signature or number at least three thousand notes per day. The hours are not strenuous—nine to three o'clock, five days a week. You will be assessed ten cents for each note that is marred or defaced, or should you blot the signature. Salary is sixty-five dollars to start—per month, that is—and we dock three dollars a day for each day that you miss work, unless you supply a physician's excuse. Now, have you any questions?"

Elizabeth, having written her name down one side of the paper he had handed her, looked up and shook her head.

Memminger reached out and she handed him the paper. Without comment, he tossed it aside and rose. "If you would like, I will show you where you will be working."

"Yes, I would. This is very kind of you and I—"

"The secretary is more than happy to do it, Elizabeth," Colter stated, sharing a look with Memminger over her head.

Colter once again offered his arm, and they followed Memminger to the upper floor. Elizabeth stood in the doorway and looked over the workroom, finding it bright and attractive. Women sat at long tables or desks, each busy with her task. Elizabeth had hoped she would be able to meet at least one of the women, but Memminger glanced at his pocket watch and they left.

"When would you like to begin work, Miss Hammond?"

"Oh, tomorrow—"

"Is too soon," Colter finished. "She'll need to make arrangements for transportation, Christopher."

"Nonsense. She can room at the Ballard House. Many of the young ladies reside there. We provide them with an escort to and from work."

"Elizabeth's aunt is elderly and wishes her to remain at home outside the city limit. I'm sure it won't present any problem."

Elizabeth, fuming at his side, was about to stop Colter when the warning look he shot her made her reconsider. As he took their leave, she could barely wait until they were outside.

"Why? Tell me why you had to pretend I wasn't there. I am capable of speaking for myself."

"How well I am coming to know that," he remarked, taking her arm and leading her to the wagon. "Up you go. I still have a few matters to see to. And I spoke for you," he continued, rounding the wagon and climbing up, "simply to avoid having Memminger believe that you had no protector."

"And tossing around those names! I know Letcher is our governor, but the others . . . and telling him Mrs. Davis would personally endorse me! A fraud, that's what you've made me party to."

"Are you finished? Seddon and Randolph are secretaries of war that I count as friends. If it were necessary to obtain the first lady's endorsement, I would have done so. It seems that no matter how I try to please you, you take an opposite stand."

"Colter, I don't mean to appear ungrateful. The truth is that I was frightened he wouldn't give me the job. Obviously, the rumors that political connections help are true. I will simply prove to Mr. Memminger that he has not made a mistake in hiring me."

"Very admirable sentiments, Miss Hammond."

His serious tone was undone by his grin, which widened as Elizabeth tried and failed to look severe. She shared her merry laughter with him, sobering minutes later upon remembering her intent. "Colter, how did you know I mentioned I was from King George County in my letters?"

Busy urging the mules into the flow of traffic on the street, Colter didn't immediately answer. And when he did, he refused to look at her. "Would you believe that I couldn't sleep last night and rode into the city to break into Memminger's office and find your letters?"

"My Lord! Tell me that you didn't?" When her question went unanswered, Elizabeth seriously considered his war activities for the first time. "Is that what you do, Colter? Steal secrets across the Yankee lines?"

"Would that worry you?"

"Yes."

Colter relaxed his grip on the reins. He had feared she wouldn't answer, or if she did, it would not have been the response he was looking for.

"You won't admit it, will you?"

"I can't. But I assure you that I didn't break into Memminger's office. You were born in King George County and moved before your first year."

"You remembered that?"

"I remember everything about you, Elizabeth. Everything. But to continue, since you haven't a facility for lying, it was a simple deduction on my part that you would stretch the truth as best you could."

"I see." Hesitantly Elizabeth glanced at his strong profile. She was both warmed and chilled by his remembering so small a detail. "Are you very good at what you do?"

He thought about a few narrow escapes he had had, his eyes darkening at the memories. But now was not the time to share such things with her, if he ever would. She had her own demons to haunt her nights. He would not add his own to them.

Elizabeth endured the silence, busy with her thoughts. Colter lived with danger, any soldier in the war did, but the time he had been granted before returning to the war was suddenly precious. She had been so wrapped up in her own problems—not that she could cast them aside easily—that she had given little thought to the risk Colter would be facing again in just two days' time. Within reason, without compromising her daughter's safety, Elizabeth vowed to try to give him pleasant memories of their brief time with each other.

A similar vow formed in Colter's mind. Last night, his encounter with Elizabeth had left him with a raw despair, but this morning, new hope was spreading its healing balm. If the Lord, General Lee, the Yankees and his own skills saw fit to grant him life, he would always look back on their time together as a precious gift. And somehow he would find a way to set her demons to rest.

Lost in their own thoughts, neither saw the man who watched them.

Chapter Eight

Later that same afternoon, Elizabeth gathered up fallen hickory nuts in a copse of trees behind the house. From the open kitchen door she heard another burst of shrieks from Nicole, broken by Colter's laugh and Rutha's admonishments.

The awareness that time was both enemy and friend had crumbled her resistance to Colter's presence in their lives. Her decision to trust him with Rutha's and Mister Josh's secret had marked another turning point. It was a test of her own for her to walk away, allowing him the chance to be with their child. *Their child?* The thought made her pause, and she examined her acceptance of calling Nicole theirs. Another squeal of pretend fright came from Nicole, and Elizabeth nodded as she continued her labors. She was theirs.

"Mama! Oh, Mama, come play!"

Elizabeth glanced up to see Nicole dart out of the door. Colter appeared behind her and the girl ran back inside. He waved to her, looking the worse for wear from the mock battle they were having. His hair was mussed, and his shirt and breeches dampened with water.

"Come join us," he called. He gave a start, growled loudly and then he too disappeared.

With a rueful smile Elizabeth glanced down at her half-filled basket and abandoned her chore. At a run she crossed the clearing but stopped just inside the door.

The kitchen was steamy, the air redolent with the spices boiling in a large kettle of water hung from a crane over the fire. As she watched, Rutha warned Nicole to keep away while she stirred the contents of the pot. Water lapped over the kettle's edge, hissing as it hit the glowing coals below, raising another cloud of steam. Sweat sheened Rutha's face, and she wiped it before adding a few pinches of salt.

"Got you!"

Elizabeth didn't know whether to laugh or shout a warning to Colter. Clutched in Nicole's small hand was the largest crab Elizabeth had ever seen, and she was amazed at how skillfully Nicole threatened Colter with its flailing claws.

From Colter's lofty height, not one but two impressively sized crabs held in each of his hands took up her challenge.

"Lordy, Colonel, iffen you don't stop playin' with that chil' we won't ever git supper," Rutha warned with a wink.

Bringing his heels together with a resounding click, arms extended so that the lethal claws offered no danger to Nicole, Colter bowed to her. "You have heard my orders. I must concede the battle to you, my dear, for it is now time." Whistling, Colter assumed a military posture, and Nicole followed suit. They began their march around the trestle table, and then with a shout, both rushed toward Elizabeth.

She grabbed her skirts and ran, falling into their play with screams of terror as they chased her around and around the clearing. Nicole's chubby little legs could not keep up and Elizabeth slowed her pace, but it was Colter, not her daughter, who caught her.

"We have you," he growled with mock ferocity. "Now, my lovely, pay us a forfeit." Her face tilted up towards his and Colter took swift advantage to capture her lush mouth with his own. The touch of her lips was like a match to kindling. The swift rise of passion turned a teasing kiss into savage need.

A heated longing rippled through her. Their tongues touched to ignite a powder keg of new sensations. She sank her teeth into his lower lip, soothing its sting with her tongue.

"Mama, I want one, too."

Elizabeth jerked her head back. Nicole stood beside them, one hand tugging at her skirt, the other still holding the crab.

Colter recovered before she could. "And you shall have whatever you want." Leaning down, he placed gentle kisses on each of his daughter's flushed cheeks, his breathing labored, his gut churning with desire. But there was a sweet peace to be had in gazing at his child that soothed the sharper edges of need.

"Them that helps gits an' them that don't, don't eat," Rutha shouted from the kitchen.

Elizabeth scooped up Nicole and raced Colter back to the kitchen. They arrived laughing and breathless, just as Rutha pulled the burlap sack off a bushel of crabs. Colter rushed to help her by lifting the bushel, and, with Rutha's guidance, the crabs met their demise. Nicole warned him of the two that clung together over the edge, ready to make their escape. Her bright eyes and giggles gave lie to her wail of terror when Colter deftly captured them and added them to the supper pot.

The air held a sharp bite and the clear night sky allowed the brilliancy of the stars to appear like scattered gems across velvet, with wisps of lace to tease and tantalize the eye. Elizabeth gazed back toward the house, reassured by the soft glow of lamps in the upstairs window and back parlor that all within its walls were asleep. Pulling Emily's borrowed wool cape close around her, she walked at Colter's side, sharing with him a quiet contentment so strong, she didn't believe its barrier could be pierced.

"Are you cold?" he asked, placing his hand at the small of her back to guide her along the lane. A quick shake of her head made him doubt she spoke true, but he let the matter pass. "I want to thank you," he said softly, as if he were reluctant to disturb the waiting hush of the night that enfolded them, "for giving me time alone with Nicole today."

"She was as she should be, a little girl, filled with laughter. If anyone should be thanked, it's you, Colter."

Drawing her close to him, his arm around her shoulders, Colter shortened his stride to keep step with her. "I know she is mine, but even if she weren't, I think I would love her. When I leave, I'll take the memory of this time as a treasured gift. I want to believe that the Lord looks down and is pleased to see the lights of a home, lights that serve as a beacon for our love, with our daughter at its heart. And I pray that He protects it."

Elizabeth's step faltered. Loneliness. His somber reflection was filled with loneliness that reminded her the war was waiting to take him away. She wished for more light to see him by than the waning moon could provide.

"When must you leave?" She could ask no more, for his simple words had touched her heart with a rawness she was afraid to confront.

"Tomorrow afternoon." His hand slid from her shoulder, and he continued to walk ahead a bit before stopping near a barrel-trunked oak. Colter leaned back against the tree, his head angled up, aware that she had stopped and stood watching him. How many lonely nights had he stared at the sky and wondered if he would see the morning light? He had never thought to count them. Life was far more precious now. Bringing his gaze back to Elizabeth, he held out his hand.

"Come to me."

The words were similar to those he had uttered with soft menace the night before, yet it wasn't only the absence of threat in his voice that made her go to him, it was her own need she was urged to satisfy.

"I should take you back inside where it's warm," he offered, blowing gently on his fingertips to warm them before he shaped her cheeks and lifted her face upward.

"I can be warm right here." She opened his long, voluminous Garrick coat with its tiered shoulder capes and nestled herself against him. She couldn't tell him there was a deep chill within her that no body warmth could hope to dispel, for it was a dark coldness that shadowed her soul with fear. She pressed her cheek against his heart, drinking in his scent as she rubbed her nose against his shirt. Strength and power. Last night she had told him she envied him for these traits. Now she was becoming aware that she possessed their feminine counterparts that might someday be equal to his.

"There's a danger in this," he warned. The press of her body brought his every nerve ending alive, but he was still able to listen to the prompting of his conscience.

She nodded, unwilling to voice her knowledge of just how dangerous it was. The desire sparked by the kiss they shared this afternoon still simmered inside her, and the hardening tension of Colter's body suggested that his thoughts had taken the same course. She was tired of having to weigh risks, tired of being cautious, tired of being alone. Seeing Colter with Nicole, sharing with them a time of carefree joy, had awakened her to what she could have if she would cease cowering and reach for it. Emily had loved her father without conditions, and mourned his loss as only a woman who had been totally loved in return could. Once she had believed that Colter loved her the same way. Was that belief shattered beyond repair? Elizabeth didn't know. Colter reminded her that life was uncertain. How could she demand promises of tomorrows when she could give none of her own in return?

Tracing the sensuous line of his lips, she felt their shape change as he smiled. Madness. It was a form of madness to encourage the passion between them. She was both afraid and delighted to know her slight touch caused his sharp intake of breath, the quickening beat of his heart.

"Have a care, little fox," he warned with mockery aimed at himself, "teasing games have lost their appeal for me." Yet his actions only encouraged her games, for while he warned her, he had angled his head down to keep her fingertips on his lips.

"To tease you, I would tease myself," she whispered.

"The second time I held you in my arms," Colter murmured, softly again, so as not to break the delicate web being spun, "you touched my mouth like this and wondered aloud why my kisses gave you more pleasure than another's. You beguiled me with your seductive innocence and made me angry as well. It was spring and we stood beneath the dogwood tree. Your gown had the feel of satin, your shawl was a flimsy lace and your skin, love, was as smooth and hot to my lips as the brandy I imbibed far too freely that night."

"You were jealous, Colter. You said it was because I had not saved a waltz for you. And," she primly reminded him, "you had no right to think I would."

"True. But I was jealous of any man that danced with you. I wanted to claim you as mine. It's no longer spring, but I still want to make that claim." He released her and, with a smooth move, slid his hands beneath her cape. She tensed and Colter quickly sought to bring ease. "Blame my greater age for the chill of my hands and let me warm them. My blood doesn't run as hot as yours."

"Colter! You—"

"Spoke a falsehood."

Elizabeth had been lulled by their shared memory. His touch on her back was light, but her body reacted quickly, feeling somewhat heavier, fuller and, of its own volition, rested its weight against him.

Colter smiled, nestling his chin against the top of her head. "Let me see, where was I? The garden . . . I believe there was an intoxicating scent of roses and the moon rode high. You were quite indignant at first that I lured you outside and—"

"You laughed, captured me in your arms—"

"Just so," he finished, hugging her tight and feeling his breath catch and hold before he released it. "Just so," he repeated, his voice husky and dark with emotion. "Yes, love. Lord, yes."

His tone held hunger and desperation. She lifted her head, searching in vain to see the expression in his eyes, finding only shadows. Her mouth was already softening, awaiting his lips with fevered anticipation. *So wrong,* a voice nagged her. *I know. But I've become a thief willing to steal what I can.*

Their mouths fused. The danger came again. But she knew there would always be danger when Colter touched her, kissed her like this, savoring her so thoroughly that he left no doubt of his intense desire.

His tongue anointed the corners of her mouth, and she parted her lips to make him welcome into her moist heat. With his hands splayed wide across her back, he urged her tight to his body, so close that she couldn't tell which one of them tremored. A plea, almost a whimper, escaped her, and she accepted his return invitation to explore the carnal delights his mouth offered, feeling the muscles of his chest bunching beneath her hands. The chill of the night should have cooled their fevered bodies. It was a fleeting thought, for a hot coiling tension had begun to unfurl inside her, and the thrust of Colter's thigh between her own gave a brief surcease.

The world and time faded before the storm of their unleashed passion. She could feel the swell and ache of her breasts, unconsciously twisting her body against his for ease.

"Tell me, love," he whispered, trailing kisses down her neck. "Tell me where you hurt and I'll make it all better."

"You know. You always know."

Colter half turned, taking her weight on one arm, freeing his hand to graze the undercurve of her breast. He could feel her trembling, her legs squeezing his thigh until he groaned with need. Cupping the fullness of one breast, his thumb unerringly found its pebbled tip, and he abraded the cloth across this most sensitive flesh. There was both surrender and enticement to her moan when she moved to cover his hand with her own.

The yielding of her mouth spun another web that pulled him deeper with a lightning savageness that stunned him. He wanted her now. He needed to sheath himself within the silken folds of her body, for making love to Elizabeth had been a renewal of his own life force.

He wanted to claim and repossess what was his by right. And in his soul he had always known that she in turn claimed and possessed him.

She pulled his head down, scattering random kisses over his taut features. Whispering his name over and over, plea and demand melded as he made her want...and want. This is how it had been from the very first—an explosion of desire that clawed inside her, desperate for release, yearning for fulfillment.

But she hadn't known then what waited. Innocent, she had begged for more of the pleasure he offered; his tender tutoring found her a most willing pupil. And in one blazing night of glory, she had discovered that sharing emotions only enhanced the physical joy they gave to each other.

She wanted to share that glory again.

There was an added intoxication of knowing...of anticipating.

"Colter...I want you, I..." She stopped, chafing against the restriction of their clothing as their bodies began to rock together. It was a delicious dance of seduction whose beat held a gentle rage of privation.

His lips fell upon hers with a bruising intensity. She elicited a raw passion in him that overwhelmed thought and clouded his mind. Elizabeth came alive with a thirsting pleasure beneath his hands. Her ragged cry drove him wild as she dug her fingers into the straining muscles of his arms.

Colter suddenly gentled his assault on her mouth. He rimmed her lips with his tongue, grazed her cheek and captured the soft lobe of her ear with a suckling motion.

"Need, love," he whispered, tracing the delicate whorls of her ear, eliciting another, deeper tremble of her body. "I need you so badly it's tearing me up." His lips wandered to her throat and the heat and scent of her aroused skin sent his blood pumping hotly through him. "And I'll please you, little fox," he promised, his voice scorched with passion.

He lowered her to the ground, the thick carpet of leaves crushing beneath the twist of their bodies as he followed her down. His caress of her hip, her rib cage and belly held none of the courting finesse he once used. There was an urgency to his touch that he couldn't still, desperate to release the buttons on her bodice so his lips could taste the silken flesh it concealed.

Elizabeth pushed at his shirt, tearing a button free to slide her hand inside. His chest was hot, the hair soft, and she tossed her head wildly to feel the pounding of his heart. *Need.* She needed water and air, needed her daughter, but Colter...his need became hers. Life. Love. Fire... Her back arched in invitation, the chill air only a momentary distraction, for Colter's lips soon spread heat and moisture across her exposed collarbone. She guided his head down and his mouth teased the swell of her breast.

So long. It had been years since she had come alive for him, every nerve singing with passion. And James had stolen the years with his lies. So long... She knew he shared the wildness that raged inside her.

"Be gentle, Colter...please, love," she cried out, losing her voice as his mouth closed over her and he began suckling. Her fingers clutched his head, holding him, her body racked with tremors that stoked a flame into fire. Again and again she cried out for tenderness, even as pleasure so intense surged forth to dissipate fear.

But Colter heard her cry at last and eased his mouth from the berry-hard tip covered by the wet, sheer lawn of her camisole. "Sweet blessed heaven, Elizabeth," he whispered, dazed and raw. Hurting from the ravenous hunger that seared like wildfire in his blood, he tensed with an agony he couldn't hide and shifted his weight from her.

"Colter?"

He shook his head, unable to look at her. "I've never lost control like this, never! I almost took you here like a camp whore. . . ." His hoarse, stunned voice trailed away. He rolled to his side, one arm flung out, clawing the earth, the other covering his eyes.

"Get back to the house." He fought to drag air into his lungs, welcoming the sharp chill of it, hoping it would quickly cool his body. When he sensed that she remained as he left her, his rage against himself snapped. "Get the hell away from me!" he lashed out with a savageness that could leave her no choice but to obey. "Move, Elizabeth. Damn you, go, or the love I claim is a lie." The touch of her hand made him jerk away. "What devils you?"

She found her voice at last. "You knew? You knew what names Alma called me?" She staggered to her feet, uncaring that her bodice gaped open. Pressing her hands to her mouth, she stifled the scream inside. Elizabeth did not cry, but slowly backed away from his prone body, shamed.

The mention of Alma's name and what followed slammed into his gut like a fist. "I didn't know!" He came to his feet. "How can I know what you won't tell me?"

To her ears, his tone condemned her. "She was right." With her stomach churning, she turned, ignoring his plea to listen to him. *Alma was right.* She hadn't cared where they were, her need demanded that Colter ease the torment of her body. Again and again, Colter called her name, but she was running. Running not from Colter, but from herself.

With impotent fury Colter watched her disappear. His body still fought a battle with his mind. Emotions ran riot with need.

But there was no choice. From the moment he had found Elizabeth again, there never had been. At a run, he went after her.

Chapter Nine

Elizabeth lay where she had tripped and fallen. She heard Colter whispering her name, shivered and huddled her body so he couldn't find her. But minutes later, he lifted her up into his arms, and without a word, carried her into the house.

With his foot he dragged a bench closer to the kitchen fire, then he set her down gently. She sat while he added kindling and small logs to the banked coals. She lost track of time as he left and returned, offering her a glass of brandy.

"Drink it down, Elizabeth, and then we'll talk." Colter tossed off his own drink, refilled his glass from the bottle he brought with him and sat beside her.

Sipping gingerly at the liquor, Elizabeth watched the flames greedily lick at the wood. With the glass clasped between his hands, Colter drew her gaze as he leaned forward, resting his elbows on his spread knees. The growing light flickered shadows over his face, and she welcomed the burning swallow of brandy she took to help still the clamor of her body.

She still wanted him.

He saw the tremble of her hand and set his glass down to remove his coat. She was shaking by the time he draped it over her shoulders. For a moment he stood behind her, wanting to touch, to bring cessation to the seething emotions he sensed in her. He didn't trust himself to be gentle. Picking up his glass, he sat staring at the fire.

Impatient to begin, he looked at her glass and realized that Elizabeth, given any more time, would build a solid wall he couldn't hope to break down. He was a soldier, he reminded himself, good at his job. He knew how to find a weakness in an enemy's fortification.

"I apologize," he stated abruptly, "for what I said. I was angry with myself for losing control, not you."

"Forgiveness? Acquittal? Whatever it is that you want, Colter, you have it. But, please, if you have any mercy, leave the matter be."

In a very controlled, soft voice he asked, "Have you already twisted what I said? Do you believe that I called you 'whore'?" His fingers clenched the glass until his knuckles whitened. "Have you, Elizabeth?" he repeated without looking at her. He didn't dare glance her way. His control was shredding. "You asked me for mercy, madam. If you have any of your own, you will answer me." Every breath he drew was released slowly. He was trying. He was!

"Damn you! I did *not* call you a whore!" Shattered glass punctuated his caustic cry. The flames leaped out at them, fueled by the splash of brandy.

Devastated by his explosion, Elizabeth dropped her own glass.

"Why the hell don't you run now?"

"I can't, Colter," she whispered, knowing it was the truth. "I told you last night, there is nowhere left to go."

The utter defeat of her voice defused his rage. He was stunned by how quickly she had unwound him. Colter looked at her and saw in her eyes pain and acceptance.

"What have I done to you?" he asked, almost of himself. His hand shook as he reached out to touch her cheek. Soft. So soft. But her skin was cold. "I thought to bring you my protection against whatever might harm you. Instead, I find that you most need protection from me."

His voice was tormented. His eyes reflected the agony in his soul. Elizabeth wanted to close her eyes, seal her heart and deny him the comfort he needed from her. But her hand rose, not to push his away, but to cover it, pressing its warmth to her cheek.

"I would not have you leave without peace between us. I have no right to the protection you offer, but I will accept it for Nicole." She saw the storm gathering in his eyes before she felt the tension in his hand. "You must listen and accept what I say. I will not try to stop you from seeing her whenever you can, nor will I deny Emily and the others what you can do to ease their lot. But I am to blame for what happened out there tonight—me, Colter, not you. I have forgotten that I am James's wife—"

"No! I will not—"

"Colter." Just this once she let the love she felt shine in her eyes. "Until I know what has happened to him, I am his wife. Until the war is over, you're not free. If there even is a freedom to be had."

"Your terms of compromise are harsh, Elizabeth. Perhaps I should have sought a position with the secretary of war for you."

"But you will accept them?" she pleaded, knowing that if he did not...no, it was cruel to think of not seeing him again. With gentle persuasion she urged his hand to her lips and kissed his palm.

"I will find out what happened to James," he proclaimed in a strident voice.

"I pray you do."

Her sigh fluttered her breath across his palm and no more was said. But Colter had never been one to accept defeat meekly. He didn't intend to begin now.

Like a child, Elizabeth wanted to hold back time, greedy over every moment that slipped away until it was time for Colter to leave. Her thought from the night before that she was a thief willing to steal what she could was grounded in fact. She had stolen Colter's shirt, guiltily hiding it beneath her pillow. It turned out to be a needless act. Acting on faith that she would keep her word and allow him to return, Colter left behind whatever belongings he had brought with him.

Mister Josh led Colter's horse to the front door, where they all waited. "Take care of this here horse, Colonel," Josh said by way of parting, and handed over the reins.

Rutha gave him a tied napkin bundle. "'Pears I's givin' back your own, Colonel. Jus' ham an' biscuits to keep you until I get to feed you again."

"You keep that fire going and make a little extra come supper, Rutha. I'll be back," he promised, tucking the bundle into his saddlebag.

"My prayers go with you, Colter," Emily said when he turned to walk back. She blushed as prettily as a maid when he kissed her cheek and whispered something to her. Then he kneeled down and opened his arms to Nicole.

"A soldier can't go off to fight unless his princess gives him a token." Expecting her hug, Colter received more. Kisses. As many as she could place wherever she could reach. He used untold strength to control his own hug of her small body. Colter blessed and cursed the war that had brought him his daughter only to tear him away from her again. "Nicole," he whispered, "you take good care of everyone for me. Especially yourself."

She solemnly nodded. "An' you promise—"

"I'll remember my promise." Reluctantly he released her and forced himself to stand. He saw Elizabeth look askance and hurried to explain, unaware that he absently rubbed his daughter's head and held her by his side.

"Each night at five o'clock I've promised to look at my pocket watch and remember that Nicole will be listening to the chimes in her castle while she prays for me."

"As I will. As we all will pray for your safety." With a pleading look, Elizabeth found support from Emily and Rutha. Between them they managed to get Nicole to return to the house. Now Elizabeth and Colter stood alone and she didn't know what to say. Admonishments for him to take care, keep warm and stay out of harm's way all seemed foolish to whisper, yet those were the words that welled up. As did tears.

Bareheaded, Colter closed the distance between them. He lifted her chin and with his lips drank each tear.

"You are the only truth I have ever known. I love you, Elizabeth, and maybe..." His voice faltered, and he had to swallow before he could finish. "Maybe that is all I need to know." His lips caressed her mouth with a tender but fleeting touch.

She closed her eyes, knowing by the creak of leather that he had mounted. When she was sure he had gone, she whispered, "Come home to me, Colter. I love you."

Elizabeth thought she had heard the last of Colter for some time to come, but as they sat down for supper that night, a private arrived with a message from him. Rutha fed the young man and sent him on his way before Elizabeth read Colter's missive.

Her name was scrawled in bold masculine script across the top of the parchment. With one finger she traced the letters, feeling the power of Colter's hand, joyful that whatever its content, he had been thinking of her. But as she began to read, she chided herself for even harboring the thought that he had sent a declaration of his feelings.

I beg you, Elizabeth, to make the acquaintance of Mrs. Hugh Morgan, arrived this day in Richmond. Her husband, you will recall, is known to you and is a man I respect and count as my friend. As of this writing, her residence is uncertain. A position is being secured for her at the Treasury, likely in the note department. She is alone in our city, Elizabeth, so whatever comfort you offer to improve her lot will place me in your debt.

Colter Wade Saxton
Colonel Confederate Army

Pressing the note to her breast, she wondered what Colter would be thinking of to ask her to befriend a stranger. But no matter its content, she would treasure this first written missive from him.

Emily grew concerned at her continued silence and asked if the news could be shared. Elizabeth read her the note and then explained her own fears.

"I do not mean to make light of them, Elizabeth, but, my dear, Colter would not put you or Nicole at risk. Remember," she stated, and then went on in a softer voice, "I may be a foolish old woman—"

"No. Never foolish, Emily."

"Well, I believe this is his way of asking for your trust. The time he spent here has already determined your course." Holding out her hand in both a gesture of comfort and to stop Elizabeth from speaking, Emily gently squeezed the younger woman's fingers. "The way is a difficult one, with hard choices. You know you have my support. And what possible harm could come from doing as he asked and making this woman's acquaintance? You need say no more than you wish if you find she is not to your liking."

"You're right." Freeing her hand, Elizabeth folded her letter and smoothed it on her lap. "But Emily, I did meet Hugh Morgan and he knows I'm married. If this—"

"Do you believe Colter would leave you exposed to a lie?"

"I don't know. But if his wife asks, if anyone overheard her reveal who I am . . . I know you've told me that Alma couldn't find us here, but there is a feeling I can't explain that warns me to caution."

"Then you must heed it," Emily returned in her practical manner, knowing if she gave way to the fear and pain that Elizabeth expressed, the young woman would falter. "Wait until you attend work in the morning. She may not be there, and if she is, you will simply deal with the matter. If you continue this fretting, you'll find yourself fearful and as useless to yourself and your child as a man attempting to saw sawdust. Now, I am going to retire. I suggest you do the same."

Elizabeth nodded, indicating her agreement, but inside, the warning to be cautious flared brighter.

"The colonel say I take you," Mister Josh insisted when Elizabeth refused his intent to drive her into the city.

"The colonel isn't here, I am. And I will walk."

"Now, Miz Elizabeth, the colonel warned me. He says, 'Mister Josh, you take her an' handle her like the mules. Ain't much to tellin' them 'part 'ceptin' their ears.' "

Elizabeth glared at him, her hand still on the crochet-covered button that secured her lace collar. "You and the colonel are more like mules than I'll ever be." But her protest signaled the end of her argument, and she climbed up onto the wooden seat.

It was a crisp, clear morning, the sun strengthening as they rode along at a brisk pace. Elizabeth was nervous about starting her job and all of Secretary Memminger's warnings and expectations drove other thoughts from her mind.

They approached the city and, to distract herself, Elizabeth began to admire the gracious homes set close to the street. More than a few were elegant houses of brick, built in a style touted as Greek revival. Two stories high, they had their own stables, quarters and kitchens in the yards behind, and were ornamented by well-tended gardens. She could almost imagine the scent of roses from the vines that clung to house walls. In spring, the jessamine, azaleas and japonicas, shrub and vine would all provide a glory of color and fragrance to intoxicate the senses and make one doubt there was a war going on.

But as Mister Josh directed the team closer to the location of the Note Bureau, Elizabeth saw wounded men, and women and children with dazed faces that brought back the reality of war.

Elizabeth straightened her bonnet when Mister Josh brought the wagon to a stop in front of the building. One of two soldiers on guard duty sprang forward to help her down. She thought about telling Josh that she would walk home but dismissed the idea, unwilling to argue with him again.

"Three o'clock, Josh."

"I'll be waitin'."

Feminine voices of every pitch sang a chaotic opera inside the hall and Elizabeth, bemused, stared at their comings and goings. A portly matron of considerable years, a widow by her dress, finally noticed her and asked her business. When Elizabeth explained, she was told to follow. They ascended the stairs, the widow introducing herself as Mrs. Marstand. She proceeded to inform Elizabeth that the company of the women was pleasant, the work itself was not strenuous and the atmosphere many thought more suitable to a tea party than an office.

Within minutes of being shown her place at a table beneath a window that offered a view of the city, Elizabeth made the acquaintance of the two women who would train her.

Mrs. Thomas Galwey, slender and pale, projected a tragic air that was reenforced by the streak of pure white in her dark brown hair. She wore spectacles and her voice, the soft, melodious drawl of southern Virginia, reminded Elizabeth of home. Mrs. Candace Sawyer, with a lively pair of blue eyes and dimples she showed to advantage each time she smiled—which Elizabeth would come to learn was often—had a flighty nature that revealed itself in her speech. She would ask a question and before Elizabeth could form an answer, proceed to another subject.

The work, just as Mrs. Marstand claimed, was not difficult. Presented with pen, inkwell and a stack of unsigned treasury notes, Elizabeth had to number them. Several women walked the large room, their sole job to remove finished piles of notes and replace them as needed. Numbered stacks were carried to the front where they were signed and dated. Elizabeth had a tally sheet that listed the beginning number she was to start with, and it was her responsibility to note at day's end the number that would begin her next morning's work.

Writing consecutive numbers was not hard, but it was boring. She found herself listening to the gossip of the women around her. Most discussed with varying degrees of agitation the rising cost of flour. Last week it had been sixteen dollars a barrel, this week it was forty. Shoes and boots, she learned, when they could be had, were almost fifty dollars a pair. Salt, so indispensable, brought a loud chorus of groans that the price had fluctuated madly. One day it was seventy-five cents a pound, and the next day the city council had offered each person a pound at five cents. There were complaints that shirts cost twelve dollars and that the Negroes were better dressed than whites.

On and on . . .

Mrs. Galwey, when asked, began a discourse about the speculators, quartermasters and the commissaries, pointing out in her quiet way their underhanded dealings.

All agreed there was little they could do, but by that time, it was announced the workday was done. Wishing Mrs. Galwey, who had unbent enough to suggest Elizabeth might use her name, Tilda, good-night, Elizabeth took her mantle and bonnet from the hook assigned to her and left the building alone. Mister Josh was waiting as were other wagons and carriages, although most of the women were escorted to several hotels nearby where they roomed.

Reassured by Mister Josh that Nicole had been no more troublesome than any other child, Elizabeth let her thoughts drift to Colter. As Emily had pointed out last night, it was senseless for her to worry over what she couldn't control, but she did hope that wherever he was, he would be safe.

Conversation at supper was enlivened by her relating her first day of work. The only somber note was Nicole's listlessness. Elizabeth took care to spend the time before bed playing with her, but Nicole kept asking when Colter would return.

Sensing there was something wrong, Elizabeth sat on her daughter's bed, stroking her hair. "Did something happen today, precious?"

"I picked nuts with Rua an' Mister Josh found me a tree."

"A tree?"

"For the swing."

"You don't sound too happy about it, Nicole. I thought that was what you wanted." For a few moments, Elizabeth thought she was asleep and leaned over to place a last kiss on her forehead. But Nicole was still awake. Racking her mind, Elizabeth finally asked, "Did you do anything to make Mister Josh or Rutha yell at you?"

"Oh, no, Mama. I didn't. I didn't."

Her small hand nestled into Elizabeth's, leaving her mother at a loss to find out what was wrong. Nicole wasn't frightened, she didn't cling, not like those first nights... but what had disturbed her?

"Honey, you know you can tell Mama if you were bad. Telling the truth is more important than worrying about being punished. You know that. Please, sweet, tell me or I'll worry."

"I saw a man."

"Oh, dear Lord!"

"I wasn't bad."

"No. No, of course not, Nicole." Urging herself to be calm, Elizabeth brushed the hair back from her child's temple. "Did you tell Mister Josh?" Nicole shook her head. "Why not? He wouldn't let anyone hurt you. Do Rutha or Miss Emily know about this?" She realized that it was a foolish question; they would have told her. Trying to keep panic locked inside so she would not frighten Nicole, Elizabeth cuddled her close. "Did the man talk to you?"

"No. He watched."

"Mister Josh didn't see him?"

Again Nicole shook her head, clinging tightly to her mother's hand. "He'd say I was 'tending again."

"Tending? Pretending that you saw someone? Yes," she answered herself before Nicole could, "of course he would think that. Well, my darling, you are not to worry. Mama will explain this to Mister Josh and Rutha. And I promise you they will keep watch to see if the man comes back. You know they love you and wouldn't let anyone hurt you while Mama isn't here."

It was a long while before she could bring herself to leave her daughter. She spoke to Rutha and Josh alone, unwilling to alarm Emily, once again stressing to them her own nagging fear. They both promised to keep a closer watch on Nicole, and Josh said he would make sure no deserter was camping close by.

Elizabeth had to be satisfied with their assurances, but as she lay in bed that night, clutching Colter's shirt to her cheek, she knew she would have to find a way to better protect her child. Colter might not return for months, and while she knew she would tell him about this, he couldn't be depended upon to ensure their safety.

Thanksgiving was two weeks away and Mrs. Marstand mentioned they would be paid before the week's end. Thanks to Colter's generosity in filling their larder, she wouldn't immediately need to buy foodstuffs. But she decided what her money could buy.

A gun. Josh had a ball-and-powder hunting rifle, but Elizabeth wanted a handgun. She had never used a weapon, but she could learn. Alma was not going to take her daughter. And no matter who believed her, she was sure that the woman had somehow found them.

The wind picked up, its wail almost mournful, and her sleep was restless, haunted by the past.

Outside, the man watching the house settled a thick wool blanket around his shoulders and leaned against a tree trunk, hoping there wouldn't be snow before morning. He waited, keeping his vigil as he had been ordered.

And another unseen presence watched him.

Chapter Ten

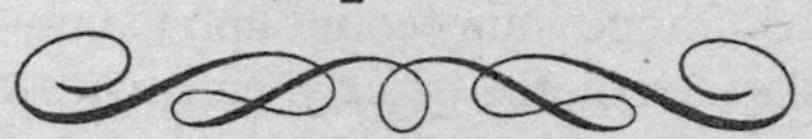

There were no more sightings of the mysterious man in the next few days. Elizabeth, still nagged by instinct to be cautious, harried Josh and Rutha to be cautious, as well.

Work had settled into a boring routine. Since she did not encourage questions about herself, she found her note numbering edged over the three-thousand mark within the first week of working as a "treasury girl," a name the women coined for themselves.

The following Monday she made the acquaintance of Mrs. Hugh Morgan. Jenna, the woman was quick to suggest as she was shown the seat next to hers.

Elizabeth noticed the other women's shocked reaction to Jenna before she realized that the violet-eyed young woman with thick, upswept auburn hair, spoke with a harsh intonation that declared her a Yankee.

Whispered protests were followed by chairs scraping as, one after another, women rose and went en masse to register complaints.

Elizabeth felt torn. She had Colter's request to consider, along with the fact that she had met the woman's husband and found him to be the kindest of

Colter's young men. Surely, she argued with herself, it would be unfair to judge Jenna Morgan by an accident of birth.

Mrs. Marstand approached them. "Elizabeth, I fear it will take some time explaining and time for the others to reconcile themselves to having Mrs. Morgan work with us. I hope I may count upon you—"

"Yes," she interrupted quickly, embarrassed for the other woman to hear herself discussed in such a manner. With a consoling pat on her shoulder, Mrs. Marstand left them.

"I warned Hugh he should find me a position where I could work alone. I write a fine hand and often helped my father with business. Hugh was the one who insisted that I would enjoy being with other women. Just like a man to believe such nonsense."

"I'm sure it will be fine once they get to know you, Mrs.—"

"Jenna, please. And may I call you Elizabeth?"

Elizabeth decided by the close of the day that Jenna Morgan wielded an arrogant manner to hide a sensitive nature. Compassion overruled caution when Jenna, near to tears, revealed that she had ruined several notes and would be penalized her first day, perhaps costing her the position. Discarding her own work, Elizabeth managed to rework the numbers with careful strokes, blotting her own sequence in the process. The thought that Jenna may have taken work from a Southern woman in need disappeared the moment Jenna confessed that she had lost her child. Elizabeth saw the young woman's hunger for friendship and her loneliness for her husband when Jenna related the details of her illness before and after the birth of her child. The debts were so staggering her family and Hugh could not hope to pay them alone, and so she had to work.

Shocked by the woman's emotional outpouring, Elizabeth prayed that Jenna would not expect her to return such intimate confidences. On the contrary, Jenna's mood seemed to lighten, and Elizabeth fell in with her wish to discuss the war and what was happening in Richmond. She was disappointed that Jenna could shed no light on where Colter and Hugh had gone, thinking herself clever in her roundabout questioning.

As she told Emily that night, one of her fears had been groundless. "Jenna mentioned that she knew I could not fully understand all she had been through since I was not married."

"There, Elizabeth, just as I hoped. And it will be good for you to have a young woman your own age to help pass the time."

"We'll see." But Elizabeth knew she would encourage the friendship, since Jenna innocently gossiped about Colter and she was hungry to learn what she could.

By the end of Elizabeth's second week of work and Jenna's first, Elizabeth was settled in her decision to befriend Jenna. She became angry that the other women continued to shun Jenna and aligned herself with Jenna, even if she understood the motives that prompted such action.

It appeared that Jenna rewarded her loyalty with added tales of several social occasions that she, Hugh and Colter had attended, often singing Colter's praises. She also informed Elizabeth that Colter never fixed his attentions on any one woman, though it was not for their lack of trying.

Jenna's frequent mistakes with her notes continued, causing an incident that Elizabeth could not put out of her mind.

"I assure you, Mrs. Marstand," Jenna protested, voice quavering in light of the woman's accusatory tone, "I was given short count."

"But that is impossible. It has never, do you hear, *never* happened before."

"Surely, Mrs. Marstand," Elizabeth interrupted, "you are aware of the circumstances that exist? Won't you allow for the possibility of it happening?"

"Well...well, yes," the woman stuttered, quite taken aback at the thought. She then quickly rallied. "Mrs. Morgan, we are all aware that your sympathies may be divided, but those of a treasury girl cannot be. We must make every effort to protect our treasury from having counterfeited notes fall into enemy hands. It is no secret that the gold reserves are dwindling and have been since long before our declaration of fighting for states' rights. But this condition exists for Yankees as well. If I accept your word that you were short counted, I must accept the implication that another woman here is guilty of a gross violation of trust. However, I will have the matter looked into and see that it is not repeated."

"Yes, ma'am," Jenna conceded meekly as the woman went off in a huff.

Elizabeth could have sworn that she saw a brief flash of triumph in Jenna's eyes before a sweep of her light-tipped lashes hid them from view. The incident raised suspicions in Elizabeth's mind. The more she thought about it, the more she felt it didn't make sense. What could Jenna think to accomplish by taking a few notes? There had been twenty uncorrectable mistakes to date. Twenty? Elizabeth frowned. When had she begun to keep a mental tally of the ruined notes? She certainly had lost count of the many she had shown Jenna how to fix. Why keep account of the supposedly ruined ones?

Supposedly? Well, it was true. She had not seen the notes.

With a slight shake of her head, Elizabeth refused to believe it. Jenna was simply afraid to be penalized two dollars. Likely, she was upset by being treated as if her place of birth had somehow stigmatized her beyond redemption. There was also the threat of losing her position.

Resolving to keep watch for her own peace of mind, Elizabeth decided she would tell Emily about this and hope that the older woman would confirm her conclusions.

The stress had built to a headache by the time Josh came to get her. Halfway home, an icy rain began to fall. Shaking from the chill, Elizabeth forgot Jenna and her desire to talk to Emily.

If she hadn't, the shock of finding Colter waiting would have driven it from her mind.

Their initial greeting was a silent exchange of glances. Colter rushed to help Josh stable the mules while Rutha fussed over Elizabeth. She couldn't make a single protest. The chill had seeped into her bones and her lips felt numb.

Hot coffee liberally dosed with brandy warmed her, but it was Colter's embrace that turned the winter night into summer after he sent Rutha to tend to her husband.

His kiss stole her breath and replaced it with his own. "You taste like heaven," he whispered against her lips, his tongue gliding against hers to relearn the hot, silken textures of her mouth.

Spirals of intense pleasure flooded her with yearning, making her ache with desire. "I missed you...missed you so," she murmured, peppering kisses across his chin before his lips found hers once more and offered a taste of sweet promise.

Elizabeth stood with her back to the fire in the small parlor, her bare toes first curling into the carpet, then stretching to lift her closer to him. Colter's arm caught around her hips, raising her up and into his body so tightly a feather couldn't have fit between them.

Again and again, their lips met and parted, half words and fragmented phrases interspersed between ever-deepening kisses until they were both breathless.

"When did you come?"

"An hour ago, no more."

"How long can you stay?" she managed.

Her wide eyes pleaded as eloquently as her soft, shaken voice. Colter smoothed the loose tendrils of hair from her face. He wanted to lie but couldn't. "A few hours. I'm stealing them as is."

Fear made her jerk her head back, her hands framing his beard-stubbled cheeks, holding him still, forcing him to meet her gaze. "Will you court trouble by doing so?"

"No. Lord, no," he ground out with intensity. "The trouble comes from not being able to hold you, not seeing you. Please, love, don't think. Don't do anything more than give me your mouth." His lips brushed hers, willing her to lose reason, wanting to drag her into the thunder and fire that churned within him.

With surprising strength she held him at bay. "Colter, think. You can't risk—"

"I can. I will. I need you, Elizabeth. I need your warmth and your love, not war. I've had enough of war."

She fought off a shiver of apprehension. Helpless to argue, she gave him what he claimed he wanted. Her warmth. Her unspoken love. Her mouth.

And he took all he could, savoring these moments to stave off the growing darkness within his soul.

Her heart ached. The wildness that had overtaken them led to a danger point she could not cross. She sensed that Colter was aware of this, too. His kisses became soft touches, as if unwilling to part from her tender offerings. Slowly, so slowly, she listened to his breathing become deeper, steadier, and it helped her to still the pounding of her heart, the coil of tension unfurling inside her.

He cradled her head to his chest, one hand working the pins free until her hair tumbled down in a thick mass. Elizabeth tilted her head to one side to see his face. She was arrested by the sensual line of his mouth and his eyes, indolently watching her. A roguish grin flirted with his lips, but without a word, he granted her the tranquillity of being held without further demand.

Her fingers teased the ragged edge of his sideburn, lingering, without thought to arousing him, to trace the shape of his ear. He drew her fingertips down to place a gentle kiss upon them, then settled her hand on his chest.

"You'd tempt a devil to breach heaven's gate, love, with your touch. I'm not a saint, Elizabeth, I've never claimed to be, but knowing that you wait here makes this a corner of heaven for me."

Her lashes lifted, revealing eyes bright with the start of tears that she attempted to blink away. Meeting Colter's gaze, she encountered a hungry look that flushed her cheeks with color. For a few moments more, she held on to the sweet delirium his words offered; they did have something special to cherish even if they could not claim it. Colter embodied both anguish and ecstasy. Anguish for being the man she loved but did not marry, and ecstasy for making her flower again with the ardent passion he openly displayed.

Safety lay in distance. But both her will and her flesh were weak. She did not want to leave the heat and security that being held by him offered.

Colter contemplated her beautiful upturned face, knowing full well the battle raging within her, tempted despite his unspoken vow of patience to persuade her that denial was not the better part of valor. The thought of seducing Elizabeth rose to tantalize him.

As if she sensed the turn of his thoughts, Elizabeth found her will strengthened and she managed to break away. "Have you eaten?" she asked, taking several steps toward the door. It was just now dawning on her that no one, not even Nicole, had come to disturb them.

"My efforts to charm you are poor indeed if you're thinking about food."

"Oh, no. You mustn't believe that." She made an effort to keep her tone as light and teasing as his. "I'm thoroughly charmed. If you dare to charm me any further, Colonel, I shall expire at your feet."

"The idea," he remarked with a decided drawl, "has possibilities." He offered a considering look that swept her from tangled curls to bare toes.

The silly banter stopped abruptly. Colter's eyes burned as they held hers in thrall. Languorous memory seemed to glaze her eyes and he was stabbed by an agony of need. The curve of her lush lips, the heightened color of her skin, the hint of a smile, the sudden shudder of a released breath all claimed, I yield.

"Colter, I beg you, don't," she implored, frantic to break the web of sexual tension stretching between them.

He turned away. "If you'll put on dry slippers, we'll join the others."

Elizabeth hurried, for his sake and her own. But as they were about to leave the parlor, Colter stopped.

"I've meant to ask, why do you sleep down here, apart from everyone?"

"It's private."

"Were you planning some entertainment that would disturb their sleep?"

The keenly honed edge in his voice forced her to look at him. "I sometimes have nightmares and wake Nicole."

"Nightmares?" he repeated softly, almost too softly. He caught her hand with his, raising it to his lips. "Someday, Elizabeth, you must decide to tell me about them." Using the thumb of his free hand, he brushed lightly at the skin beneath her eyes. "And when that someday comes, little fox, the only shadows that will bruise these eyes will come from spending a night being so loved that rest is denied to you."

His tenderness was balm to her conscience. She nodded, unwilling to explain that dreams of him had replaced the nightmares, allowing her peace, until Nicole had seen the man lurking nearby. She remembered her promise that she would tell Colter about him, but not now.

The hours flew quickly. Nicole, behaving like a frisky puppy, claimed Colter's lap, insisting he play the wooden whistle he had given her. Taking up the hand-carved instrument embellished with flowers, he explained that many of the soldiers whittled to pass the long hours. Nicole refused her bedtime with his support, her tiny arms locked around his neck, her head nestled on his broad shoulder. There she finally slept.

Elizabeth was touched by a flicker of envy. It shamed her to admit that she wanted to steal their child's position for herself. She smiled at him, silently offering thanks for his generous sharing with Nicole. All too soon, Rutha was lifting the child to carry her up to bed, and Colter rose. It was time for him to leave.

"One last thing before I leave you, Elizabeth. Josh told me what happened with Nicole. I confess, I am at fault for not telling you that he's my man. I couldn't rest easy without knowing there was someone here that could protect you both."

She couldn't be angry. He meant well, but the fright she had suffered had left its mark. Emily quietly retired after bidding him a safe journey, Josh left to fetch Colter's horse, and they were once again alone. She smoothed the tiered cape of his greatcoat, needing to touch him until the last bitter minute.

"Josh," Colter continued briskly, "has already made a place in the hayloft for my man to keep him out of the elements, but within good watching distance. Allow me this, Elizabeth, for it offers peace of mind."

"As you wish," she returned, knowing she would promise him anything he asked for right now.

"And you, little fox," he murmured, caressing her hair with a swift bold stroke, "keep yourself and our child safe and warm." He pulled on his gauntlets and took his hat from her, bending to kiss her with a fierce intensity. With her whisper for him to keep safe and warm, as well, Colter left.

He rode out in the icy rain, refusing to dwell on parting, keeping the few hours of peace as a talisman against the coming days.

Hugh Morgan also rode out from Richmond, heading toward their planned rendezvous, but with a despair that caused him no end of anguish.

Jenna was not safely ensconced in their hotel room. No one remembered seeing her since the morning, when she had been escorted to work. The precious hours that Colter had stolen for all of them were wasted in a futile search.

By the time he reached their point of meeting outside the city, Brice, Andre and Colter were there. Hugh longed to hear Colter tell him that Jenna had been with Elizabeth. When he made no mention, Hugh felt his last hope was crushed. He said nothing as they rode north, for he knew what insidious fear could do to a man about to engage the enemy.

But it crept its way inside him, leaving him most vulnerable.

Chapter Eleven

It seemed to Elizabeth, during the week following Colter's brief visit, that the world she knew was rushing toward destruction.

The threat of the Yankees firing upon Fredericksburg had trains bound for Richmond crowded with women and children trying to leave before the fighting began. Last spring, the enemy had almost come to the gates of Richmond. General Lee had managed to drive them out and in turn marched into Maryland. No matter how loyal she believed herself, she wondered why, with the Yankees led by Burnside deep on Virginia soil, General Lee seemed reluctant to fight him now. The prayers of the women she worked with had failed to bring enough snow to call a respite until spring. Everyone lived with a sense of danger.

Refugees poured into Richmond and Elizabeth wondered if their own fear had chased them from their homes rather than the enemy. It was an uncharitable thought, one that made her contrite, but she knew herself not to be alone. Many women were expressing their fear that smallpox would sweep the city. Elizabeth was torn. Tilda Galwey claimed that several doctors wanted to vaccinate healthy children, save the scabs and use them to immunize adults. How could she protect Nicole and herself without exposing them to a greater risk?

The dilemma plagued her throughout the days at work, where the hours were spent exchanging gossip and rumors that made tempers wax hot.

General Lee believed the Yankees would cut off the railroad, leaving Richmond dependent upon getting food and goods that came up from the Danvillc area if another rail could be laid.

Daily, women spoke in hushed whispers of friends that were buying steamers to run the blockade. If this news wasn't enough to shock the delicate sensibilities of Southern womanhood, the rumor that President Davis intended to trade the South's cotton to the Yankees for salt gave them the vapors.

Claiming that her knowledge came from reading every available newspaper, Jenna added that the North was more than willing to trade clothing, meat, shoes and blankets, all desperately needed items by the South, in return for their cotton. The North needed the cotton to keep their mills open. Any item was open for trade but guns and ammunition.

"And," she added with a sly look around the room, "I believe a way could be found around that restriction." When Elizabeth refused to respond to that provocative remark, Jenna continued, "Davis is—"

"*President* Davis," Elizabeth corrected, unaware of how often she had to remind Jenna.

"Yes, President Davis, well, he hopes to get fifteen to twenty sacks of salt for a bale of cotton and will be fortunate to get ten. The men who handle the business will likely get the difference."

"How could you know that from a newspaper?"

"Oh, you forget, Elizabeth, I room at a hotel filled with the military."

"Those men who would profit are nothing but speculators getting rich off the war."

"As they have throughout history, Elizabeth. My, you are in a cantankerous mood of late."

"I find it upsetting to think of vultures profiting without thought to the women and children who go hungry."

"But thankfully you're not numbered among them," Jenna snapped, bending once more to her work.

Guilt that she and her child had more than enough to eat stilled Elizabeth's tongue. Of late, she was uncomfortable with Jenna. The feeling, now that she thought about it, could be traced back to the day after Colter's visit.

She had come to work, hugging the joy of her secret to herself, wishing she could share it. When Jenna casually mentioned that she had had a delightful time after accepting a supper invitation from another soldier's wife who worked for the Quartermaster Department, and so missed seeing her husband, Elizabeth was shocked.

She certainly didn't expect handwringing or tears, as she had already judged Jenna's makeup to lack strong emotional extremes, but lack of any reaction, not even disappointment, left Elizabeth unsettled. It was not her place or right to ponder the personal relationship between Jenna and Hugh. No matter how many times she warned herself, however, the fact that something was wrong nagged her.

But over the past days Jenna's mistakes had lessened to the point that Mrs. Marstand mentioned they were being considered to replace two note signers who were returning to their homes, which both cheered and reassured Elizabeth somewhat.

Her days were also brighter because she knew her daughter was protected when she couldn't be with her. Colter's man—Dobie, she learned, although she couldn't ascertain if that was a first or last name—was taciturn to the point of rudeness. But she couldn't fault the man's alertness.

She was proud, too, that the lessening worry seemed to allow her to become proficient at note numbering. Her tally at day's end was close to thirty-five hundred. She coped with a recurring hand cramp by using an ointment Mrs. Marstand made and sold for extra funds. Rutha had to know what was in it before she would allow Elizabeth to use it, and the widow had been kind enough to tell her. The boiled bark of white oak and apple had to be reduced to a thick substance and simmered with goose grease or oil, then rubbed well into the stiffened joint. Elizabeth prevailed upon Emily to try some and found it offered the older woman a bit of relief.

Tomorrow she would receive her first pay, and having discarded the thought of buying a gun, Elizabeth planned a few special treats for their Thanksgiving meal. And she had so much to be thankful for this year, she reflected, her mood lasting long into the night.

More than she knew, for Colter came again, this time in the hours before dawn.

Colter stole into the house, Dobie the only one aware that he was here. But unlike a thief, he left behind a trail of his presence from his boots and weapons in the kitchen, hat and gauntlets in the dining room, down to his coat draped over the wing chair in the back parlor where he took a moment to light a candle. Two long pulls of brandy from the decanter chased the chill from his body. He stirred the banked coals, added kindling and, once it caught, placed a log on the fire.

The bedroom door was open and he walked in, setting the candle in its tin flower-shaped holder on the dresser. Its wavering light allowed him to fill his sight and senses with a sleeping Elizabeth.

She was lying on her back, one arm flung above her head. Her hair, shimmering where light chased the night shadows, fell across a lace-trimmed pillow like a spill of warm spices, framing her delicate features. From her lashes came intriguing shadows on her sleep-flushed cheeks, and the bruised crescents of a few weeks ago were gone. Lush and slightly parted, her lips drew his gaze for long moments.

The quilt and linen sheet were partially cast aside, revealing the light, even rise and fall of her breasts. Her neck appeared fragile, surrounded by a loose, rounded neck.... Colter stopped.

A slow move creased his lips into a decidedly masculine smile that was both sensuous and satisfied.

Elizabeth was sleeping in his missing shirt.

Memories assailed him as he stood there, her gay laughter, the incredible softness of her skin, the sweetly heated taste of her on his mouth. Tension made his muscles knot.

Colter unbuttoned his tunic. He could have her passion, but this night, to chase the specter of death, he needed her laughter. Dropping his tunic to the floor, he retraced his steps to the parlor and lifted his haversack. He debated removing one or two of the items within and leaving it, but with a shrug, carried the leather bag back to the bedroom.

His gifts were stolen from a Yankee whose barn he had been forced to hide in. Looking at Elizabeth, Colter lifted one of his gifts from the bag, absently rubbing it against his trouser leg before he bit into the ripe flesh. Juice, tart and sweet, filled his mouth as he leaned over her sleeping form. With a brush of his lips he left a residue on her mouth and watched as, still asleep, she licked it with a languid tongue that tempted him to capture it. Her head turned to the side, lips pursed as if to receive more. Colter couldn't refuse this silent entreaty. He lowered his mouth once again.

The touch was tender, far too brief, but he found a well of infinite patience as he watched and waited for her to follow the elusive taste, murmuring a soft unconscious protest.

Without a sound Colter settled on his knees beside the bed, nibbling on the ripe apple held in his left hand while the other lightly stroked the tousled curls from her forehead. She frowned, turning from his touch, but his mouth coaxed her back to face him.

Elizabeth was dreaming. She had to be. But never had a dream seemed so real. She tasted the tart flavor of apple on her lips, not once but repeatedly. The added potency of brandy along with the sweetness of the fruit brought her hand from her side to touch her mouth.

Very gently, Colter blew on her fingertips.

Elizabeth's lashes fluttered. "Apples," she murmured, drawing her brows together. She stirred, restless, once again inhaling the scent. Her nose twitched. A hint of a smile lifted the corners of her mouth. It was apples. Apples and brandy and...her eyes opened. "Colter?"

A feather brush of his lips closed her eyes. She was dreaming. And she didn't want to wake. Snuggling her cheek against the soft pillow, she saw again bronze light and shadows playing over Colter's face. His bare shoulders...yes, they were bare, and her fingers curled with a longing to touch him.

"Such a shy little fox," he whispered, stroking her cheek, offering random kisses to her sleep-flushed features.

Shivers of awareness coursed through her. But she fought them, unwilling to wake, unwilling to face being alone. The soft, fleeting caresses continued, and she knew her body's restless stir came from the warmth that began to build inside her.

She fought against the pull that wanted to drag her into wakefulness. The dream was too good, so real, and she needed to hold on to it longer.

"No," she moaned, when once more she was pulled toward waking, flinging her arm across the bed as if to ward off an unseen presence.

"Say yes, love," he whispered, fitting his mouth over hers in one smooth motion. Colter reached for her hands, lacing his fingers with hers, knowing she was no longer asleep by the sudden tension that bowed her body. And just as quickly, with a deep shudder, she was pliant for him, her kiss welcoming.

When he lifted his head and looked down, her eyes silently begged for more. The soft linen of his shirt draped the lush swell of her breasts, the sensitive tips hardening to points even as he watched. With a deliberate move, Colter brushed his arm across one peak and felt the deep quiver of her body in response.

"So hungry?" he asked, repeating the move, her small sound and catch of breath all the answer he needed.

"Colter?" She gazed up into his eyes, eyes that were the dark green of a hidden forest glen splintered with shafts of sunlight that burned with desire.

His mouth lavished the sweet taste of fruit on her lips for long moments before he lifted his head. "What do you want, love, my hands or my mouth?"

Still dazed by sleep, Elizabeth couldn't answer him. She shifted toward him, brushing her breasts against his chest. Colter moved in counterpoint, softly abrading the cloth across her skin. And still he did not touch her. Her hands reached for his arms, sliding upward slowly, a sigh escaping her to feel the latent power of his muscles and the heat of his skin.

"I came," he whispered, brushing her cheek with his lips, "to steal your laughter tonight. But like any good thief I'll take whatever I can." His mouth drifted with tiny kisses to her ear, and his teeth, with gentle restraint, worried the velvet heat of her lobe. He felt her cry and tremor deep, deep inside him.

Elizabeth unconsciously arched her neck to give his lips access. She closed her eyes and used her hands to test the smooth slope of his broad shoulders, flexing her fingers against his heat and power when he groaned in response. The tiny love bites he took, then soothed with his tongue, sent a spiral of fever rushing over her, and she kicked free of the confining covers.

Colter stroked the length of her body, easing up to cover her breast. Her back bowed reflexively, her breathing suddenly ragged and his a perfect mate. With a gentle finesse that belied his passion-taut features, he smoothed the cloth over his prize, breathing so close to its peak, he could almost feel it draw tight.

"Both, Colter," she whispered, urging him closer with her hands locked behind his neck.

"Love?" he queried, his voice harsh with need.

"I want your hands and your mouth." Her eyes were half-closed, watching him, knowing how bold her answer was and beyond caring, as long as he eased the ache he had skillfully kindled.

He pleased her. The huskiness of her moan incited him like an intimate caress. He nibbled gently, offering silken kisses that grew deeper, hotter, until she rubbed her fingers through his hair, holding his head hard against her breast.

She arched helplessly when he responded with an urgent suckling that brought a cry of pleasure. Tension coiled inside her, and she wanted him to know the hunger that violently stormed her body. She shifted her head, restless, her hands sliding down to the dark curling hair on his chest, small sounds of need forcing him to lift his head.

"Tell me, love. I'll give you—"

"You. I want to touch you, Colter." Words and gesture invited him onto the bed.

Colter didn't immediately take it. "Look at you, love," he murmured, one finger brushing the wet cloth over the erect nipple. "So much fire."

Elizabeth was shaking. But she returned his caress, finding the tiny hard point of his nipple and rubbing it between her fingers. Wavering candlelight gilded his flesh, and she threaded her fingers into the soft hair on his chest, his hoarse groan another sensation that shivered through her.

"I want you, little fox. But if you're going to refuse me, say so now." His eyes targeted hers, and he wondered at his own sanity for giving her a choice.

"Colter, I—"

"Only one word, love, that's all you have to say."

"Why? Why are—"

"Wrong word."

She searched his face and met his gaze with a feeling of being cornered that she knew he could see by the cynical smile on his lips.

"Tell me why you're doing this."

Desperation underscored each word. Colter heard and understood, even as he cursed himself. "I want you with a hunger that eats at me. But I won't take. I won't be accused of seducing you. I told you I came to steal your laughter, but I can't touch you without passion flaring up between us." She closed her eyes, and anger found its home. "Look at me, Elizabeth. I won't let you deny it any longer." And when she refused to respond, he taunted her. "If you won't look at me, then look at yourself. See if your body can lie to you. Mine can't."

With an abrupt move he grabbed her arm and pulled her close. Taking her wrist in one hand, he used the other to uncurl her tense fingers, his leashed strength overcoming her attempt to fist her hand.

"No more lies," he whispered, lifting her hand to brush the back of it across her breast. "You're aroused and aching, aren't you? Aren't you?" he repeated, driven to have an answer.

"Yes. Damn you, yes."

"So am I." There was a seductive darkness in his voice that should have warned her.

But she was exactly what he had proved her to be, aroused and aching. To find her hand suddenly splayed across the rigid length of his male flesh, singed by the heat, brought a violent tremble that coursed endlessly through her body.

He released her hand, unable to stand her touch, knowing he had forced it, and realizing too, that his own exhaustion had sapped whatever reason he had.

"I won't touch you again, Elizabeth, until you come to me."

She looked at him as he stood, and wanted to lash out at him for making her want him and then forcing her to knowingly admit it. He rubbed the back of his neck and she knew that tension had taken hold. She saw for the first time the exhausted lines of his face and bit her lip to keep silent.

He turned away and she knew she couldn't let him go.

"Colter, wait. I can't tell you what you want to hear. But don't leave this anger between us. I can't help what I feel, no more than you can." She slid from the bed and took up her wrapper. Slipping it on, she tied the belt, walking around the bed to where he stood.

He nudged the haversack with his foot and several bright red apples spilled out. "I wanted to surprise you and Nicole with these. For Thanksgiving," he added, swaying where he stood.

The candle flame sputtered and wax spilled down. Elizabeth wanted to touch him but was afraid. She was still trembling from the desire that shimmered inside and knew by the shuddering breath he released that he was still aroused.

Gray light filtered through the lace curtains, warning of daybreak. "Colter, why not rest here. I'll leave. It's almost time to—"

"No. Stay with me." Bleak eyes met hers. "I've made a mistake by cornering you, little fox. Blame the damn war. It claims a man's soul."

"Tell me. Talk to me Colter."

There was a plea in her gaze and voice that he didn't want to ignore. But tell her...he couldn't. Taking a man's life to protect your own belonged in that dark, secret recess of the mind and soul that no man would expose.

Elizabeth was beset by an intense need to know what brought such blackness to his eyes, as if a light had been snuffed out. She wanted to know him. When they first met, there hadn't been time to share hopes and fears. The incredible passion that flared between them consumed every moment they could be together.

Elizabeth offered him her hand, and when he laced his fingers with hers, she led him to the bed.

Colter glanced at the window, shook his head as if to shake off the exhaustion that raked over him and judged the time. "An hour, no more. I must be in Richmond before eight."

She didn't bother to ask why, he wouldn't answer. She nodded, quickly fluffing the pillows and smoothing the linen-covered tick. "Come rest. I won't let anyone disturb you. And if you want to talk, I'll be here with you."

"Sometimes, it's too late for talk." But he accepted her offer and stretched out on the bed.

Colter's eyes closed and she hesitated before slipping into bed at his side, holding her breath a moment before she felt him relax. Taking hold of his hand, she prayed he would share his thoughts with her.

"You bring me peace from turmoil, love," he said in a hoarse whisper that she strained to hear. "And I, I bring you a sometimes haunted man."

"Then tell me what haunts you and we'll chase the ghosts together," she returned, rubbing her thumb over the back of his hand, thankful the tension there was easing.

"Such a sly little fox," he murmured in a tired voice. "You'll have my secrets and give up none of your own." He felt her turn to face him and managed to drag his arm up so she could nestle her head against his shoulder. Absently he began stroking her arm.

"Before I returned home, it was easy to talk of the war. My cousins retold stories of their fathers who fought under Wellington. But talk does not come close to the reality of the destruction war can bring." His hand stilled, and he found himself struggling to keep his mind clear. He had to remember not to reveal too much.

"Colter?" she whispered, thinking him asleep.

"I came home to serve, but I wanted to still the voices of the high-minded idealists who spoke of death before surrender. They have never faced a superior force in battle. And it sickened me to know men who bought others to substitute for them." He squeezed her arm, unaware, lost in some world that beckoned him to ease his burden. He had to make her understand what drove him.

"No one knows how many have already deserted. The conscription law makes it easy for rich men to avoid the fight and for poor men to die. Deserters are shot and no one seems to care. God." The word grated from between his clenched teeth. "How do we kill our own for leaving a war that gains them nothing? How can a man live with his conscience for turning in another who hides in the woods by day and farms his field by night to feed his family?"

Elizabeth was unsure if Colter talked of himself. The doubt left her almost immediately. Colter would never turn such a man in. Lifting her head, she smoothed the hair from his brow, listening to his uneven breathing.

"Sleep, love," she murmured, longing to comfort him as she would Nicole, wishing she could bring him peace.

"The Yankees are going to trample every inch of our soil and there's damn little we can do to stop them."

She stilled her hand. His voice was faint but hot with anguish.

"I want, I need to believe that even a disaster is not without hope, but Lee and most of us know that we are playing out an ill-fated scenario. And until it's over, we'll watch men die...."

His voice faded and through a blur of tears, she saw that sleep finally claimed him. Inside her, a fire burned to fiercely protect this man she loved.

The last of his words lingered in her mind... *we'll watch men die....* "But not you, my love, not you," she mouthed silently. She felt grieved that he had not touched the true blackness that ate at him, and perhaps he never would. Just as she knew she would keep from him secrets of the past that could not be undone.

Resting her cheek on his chest, she felt the heat of his skin. She stroked the sleek dark mat of hair that covered his naked torso, thinking the pelt almost silky. Her fingers touched a puckered ridge of flesh on his rib cage and once again his words crept forth.

We'll watch men die. With a start, Elizabeth guiltily questioned if that had been James's fate. If only she knew... if only...

To the beat of Colter's heart she slept. When Nicole came to wake her, he was gone.

And apples were strewn over the bed.

Chapter Twelve

Thanksgiving passed quietly and the prayers continued that winter would come, making movement of the armies impossible. The first day of December saw ice covering the water pitcher in Elizabeth's room, a bitter wind bearing testimony that hopes could be realized.

A few days later, news came that Fredericksburg was under fire and the night was once more warm. Fear became a daily companion. The Yankees had crossed the river. Rumors flew, battles were won and lost, and there was victory to cheer, defeat to moan.

Colter didn't come again. But there were mornings when evidence of his stopping, or having sent someone, awaited her. A wooden top with string for Nicole, a leather-bound volume of Tennyson's poems for Emily, whose reading of "Nothing Will Die" infused them all with hope.

Elizabeth cherished the memory of Rutha's smile when she would find a packet of cinnamon bark or a length of soft calico. Another time there was real coffee to share, and even Josh was remembered with a finely made knife. For herself, there appeared one morning a brown velvet-and-satin hair bow and much needed gloves of black Marseilles kid, trimmed with an embroidered spray of yellow and brown silk flowers.

Yes, she cherished his thoughtfulness toward all of them, but she longed to see him, for the fear for his safety rose as the weather turned to a springlike warmth. On Monday morning at work, Elizabeth learned that the fighting had taken the lives of General Cobb and countless others. General Hood was severely wounded, but the Yankees had been repulsed.

As she worked, a litany played over and over in her mind. The waiting and waiting without news of Colter was going to drive her mad. She thought of visiting the secretary of war—after all, Colter had claimed friendship with the man—but if her suspicions about Colter were true, no one would tell her anything.

The wounded began to arrive and women were asked to volunteer their time at the hospitals. Elizabeth wanted to give her time, but Emily cautioned against it.

"What if you are recognized? Would you undo all we've taken pains to ensure?"

Conceding that she was right, Elizabeth made her excuses and was left with a vague feeling that she had lost the respect of her fellow workers.

News came from General Lee that Burnside had withdrawn to the hills beyond the Rappahannock. Winter brought them a time of peaceful security.

Elizabeth now waited with restless anticipation for Colter to return. Her feelings toward Jenna began to border on mistrust. Twice now, Hugh's wife had revealed information that Elizabeth knew she could not have gathered from reading a newspaper or hearing talk from their own military. Yet some instinct cautioned her not to reveal what she believed.

Everyone talked about the congressional elections held in October and November, which had increased the Democratic delegation from forty-four to seventy-five, but the Republican majority was saved, to the surprise of many, by the New England and western Mississippi regions. A few days after the battle of Fredericksburg, Jenna mentioned that Senator Sumner, during a caucus of the Republican members of Congress, had appointed a committee of seven radicals to call on Lincoln to demand that Secretary of State William Seward, a close friend of McClellan's, be removed.

By itself, Elizabeth was not alarmed that Jenna knew. It was that Jenna continued to discuss the jealousy between Seward and Salmon Chase, the Union secretary of the Treasury. To hear Jenna speak knowingly of Chase's ambitions to run for president and have her add that Senator Browning, an intimate friend of President Lincoln, had offered a solution to his having a radical cabinet, Elizabeth could scarce hold her tongue.

"Is it through your family that you are well acquainted with these men, Jenna?" Elizabeth watched Jenna's reaction closely. Her smile was cool, just as her gaze was.

"No, I merely repeat rumors."

"The security of the Yankee government must be loose indeed to allow such gossip to flourish. I have always believed there must be a seed of truth in all rumors."

Directing a wry look at Elizabeth, Jenna murmured, "Perhaps you are right."

That was the first incident. The second was a blatant lie of a personal nature. Elizabeth knew of Lincoln's using presidential authority to call for enlistments not yet sanctioned by Congress, in his declaring of the blockade, and the suspension of the writ of habeas corpus in Maryland. During a brief respite from work, Mrs. Galwey, as she often did, was reading aloud. She recounted an outrage that sprang from this suspension of rights. A judge who had charged a grand jury to inquire into illegal acts of government officials was set upon by soldiers while his court was in session. He had been beaten, dragged from his bench and imprisoned. This provoked an outcry from all who listened.

"God save us if the Yankees take Richmond," one matron exclaimed.

"This power-hungry warmonger Lincoln will show us no mercy," yet another declared.

"Fools," Jenna whispered. "So he arrests and imprisons those with Southern sympathies."

"Jenna! You can't support his actions." Elizabeth was furious.

"You misunderstand. This is war. Each side will do whatever must be done. It is foolish to decry what we cannot help."

Elizabeth dropped her blotter just as Jenna bent to reach for her reticule. Their hands entangled and the contents of Jenna's purse spilled. Before she could kneel to pick them up, Elizabeth saw the bold scrawl on a missive dated the previous Sunday. *My darling Jenna, meet me*...

So hungry for news of Colter, Elizabeth spoke without thinking. "You've had word from Hugh?"

"No," Jenna snapped, shoving the paper into her bag. "Not for weeks."

Frowning, Elizabeth gazed after Jenna's retreating back. There was no doubt that the note was from a man. Elizabeth's mind was dulled by lack of sleep, but she refused to doubt what she saw. What possible reason could Jenna have for lying? Were the other women right and Elizabeth's own judgment at fault? Should Jenna's loyalty be questioned? The thought made her uncomfortable. She did not want to accuse her falsely. Not out of a sense to protect Jenna, but to protect Colter, who used his influence to obtain this position for Jenna.

Living out of the city left her without means to watch Jenna and there was no one she could trust with her suspicions. Yet it troubled her to leave the matter unresolved.

Her mood remained pensive on the ride home. Josh mentioned that Nicole had been restless all day, comparing her to a pea jumping around in a hot skillet. Elizabeth blamed the unseasonable weather changes for Nicole's recent slight cold, but now that her daughter was feeling better she knew that for everyone's peace, she had to spend some time out of doors with her.

As had become the custom, Dobie helped Josh take the mules from their traces when they arrived home. Elizabeth's greeting elicited a curt nod from Dobie before he went into the barn and climbed the loft where she knew he would sleep until supper. He had refused all her overtures to draw him out, but she couldn't help wondering about a man who slept during the day and kept guard all night.

"Don't be frettin' over him, Miz Elizabeth," Josh advised, seeing that she still gazed at the shadowed barn opening where Dobie had disappeared.

"I can't help it, Mister Josh, I'm curious about him. I wonder where the colonel found him."

"He ain't sayin' an' I ain't askin'."

"I am sure that is the wisest course."

"Prove to the colonel you ain't like them mules."

"That's where you are wrong, Josh. I am just as stubborn." But she was laughing as she walked toward the house.

Nicole pounced on her the moment she walked inside. "Mama! Mama, can we play?"

"Chil'," Rutha scolded, "let your mama catch her breath. Ants has got you fidgetin' an' frettin' all day."

"Has not! Has not," Nicole repeatedly denied.

Elizabeth let her imagination fill in what had gone on all day. Rutha appeared on the verge of losing her patience.

"Nicole, let me change and we'll go outside."

"I don't wanna wait."

She glared at her daughter. Nicole's mouth was a sullen pout, her eyes almost defiant. Elizabeth drew on her own store of patience and guilt that she wasn't able to be home with Nicole, making her temper her response.

"I'll hurry, precious, and we'll have almost two hours before dark. We can stay out the whole time."

"Oh, Mama, you're the bestest."

Elizabeth braced herself as Nicole came flying at her, hugging her tight. For a moment she met Rutha's gaze, letting her eyes blaze with the fury she felt, and found that Rutha felt the same. Alma's threat was denying Nicole other children to play with, forcing her to remain hidden away from any diversion.

Releasing her daughter before Nicole could sense her tension, Elizabeth hurried to change.

For a little while they played tag in the yard, Josh teasing them as he split wood. The day was still warm and Emily joined them outside, seated in a chair near the kitchen door. Rutha was humming and Elizabeth felt her mood lift with each new burst of laughter from Nicole.

When she pleaded for a walk in the woods, Elizabeth hesitated, although she was unsure why. Glancing back to see Josh close by, drawing water from the well, Elizabeth dismissed her unease as foolish. She called out to him that they were going for a short walk.

Holding hands with Nicole, Elizabeth raced down the knoll that took them out of sight of the house. She smiled to see her daughter's bright eyes, flushed cheeks and sturdy little body twirling around and around.

"Catch me, Mama. Catch me," Nicole teased as soon as her mother released her hand.

"Oh, love, give Mama a moment to catch her breath and then I'll chase you around and around." Elizabeth sat hugging her knees, unaware of the growing twilight. Nicole was suddenly still, looking up at the sky, and Elizabeth followed her gaze.

Two pure white birds with large wingspans were overhead. Elizabeth repeated her daughter's murmur that they were beautiful, for the birds seemed to be putting on an exhibition that showed off their grace in flight. A soft whistling noise came from them. Elizabeth was unsure if it was caused by the movement of their wings or was a sound swans usually made.

"Oh, no, Mama," Nicole cried, already running to keep the birds in sight.

"Wait, Nicole!" Elizabeth scrambled to stand, her heel caught in her skirt hem. With a feeling of annoyance she ripped it free and turned to see Nicole disappearing into the woods. She called her daughter back, for the tall pines would make it impossible for the child to see any more of the graceful swans.

Walking steadily toward the forest, Elizabeth caught the aromatic scent of the waxy bayberry fruit and made herself a promise to pick some for their candle making.

"Nicole," she called, glancing about. Low-spread oaks mingled with the pines, and some had vines twisted in their branches. The floor was covered with russet brown pine needles, carpeting each step that Elizabeth took. She was suddenly aware of how quiet it was.

"Precious, answer Mama. This isn't a game anymore." Elizabeth stopped where she stood, hoping to catch sight of Nicole's pale blue frock or hear her giggle, a sign that she had hidden and was ready to be found.

The forest was silent. Fear pervaded every bone in her body.

"Nicole," she called again, loudly this time, demand clear in her tone. She strained again to listen and, when the silence remained unbroken, took a few steps forward. She staggered, her legs trembling and a fear unlike any she had experienced taking hold. "Nicole,'' she screamed over and over, tearing aside low-growing bushes in her rush.

''She's fallen and can't answer me,'' Elizabeth said to herself as panic shivered through her body. Her heart seemed to stop whenever she did, and then beat out a frantic rhythm. Her breathing became erratic.

''Baby, baby, where are you? It's all right. Come out now, Mama won't be angry. Just answer me. Tell me where you are. Tell me,'' she wailed in terror.

Up at the house, Josh was poised with the ax raised above his shoulder. He frowned and listened, hearing Elizabeth's voice. About to finish the downward swing, he realized that she was screaming. His arms trembled for a moment before he flung down the ax and yelled for Dobie.

Musket in one hand, pistol in the other, Dobie charged out of the barn. His doze had been light, yet he shook his head as if to clear the sleep from his mind. Bits of straw clung to his shirt and the thick waves of his blond hair. His narrowed eyes targeted Josh's.

''Where?''

''Forest over the knoll,'' Josh answered, bending to pick up his ax. He followed the ground-eating lope of the bigger man. It didn't surprise him that Dobie asked no more questions. He knew that Josh wouldn't have called him unless something was wrong. Guilt grayed Josh's skin. He shouldn't have let them go off by themselves.

From below, they both could hear the terrified wails that Elizabeth made. Dobie gestured for Josh to hold up at the forest edge. He scanned the already darkening sky, heard again the feminine screams that the forest seemed to gather and then fling out in all directions.

A less experienced man would not have been able to pinpoint its source.

Elizabeth felt her knees buckle and grabbed hold of a sapling for support. She dragged air into her lungs. Tears blinded her. She wiped them with her torn sleeve. Her throat was raw, and there was no moisture left to soothe it so she could scream again.

Pushing away from the support, she realized the twisting and turning path she followed had left her without sense of direction. The night hovered as if it were a huge quilt waiting to smother her.

"Nicole," she called weakly, sweeping her gaze over the dark shifting shadows that held an unseen menace.

Time and again, her steps faltered, but she wrenched strength from an inner core, knowing only that her child needed her. In a small clearing, Elizabeth stopped and stood with head bowed, praying.

A tiny sound made her spin wildly. Was it a muffled cry she heard? She didn't know, couldn't tell. Tears poured down her face. Where was her baby? The nightmares of the past came alive again. She could feel the ache of empty arms, the physical pain that rendered her helpless and the emotional desolation.

"No! No, it can't happen again," she cried out. A surge of rage filled her, imbuing her with a furious determination not to be a victim. Nicole was never going to be lost to her again.

For she knew with a clarity that cut through the panic and madness of her plight that Alma had found them. Alma, whose own madness had nearly driven Elizabeth insane.

Twigs snapped behind her, but Elizabeth was running forward where she was sure she had heard a muffled cry.

Roots tripped her and she fell in a jarring sprawl. Don't let her defeat you, she whispered to herself, ignoring the sting of scrapes and her belabored breath to stand.

And there, through a grove of trees, she caught a glimpse of light cloth in the purpling shadows of twilight.

She had no weapon but herself. It would have to serve. Elizabeth hurled herself after the barely discernible shape of a man carrying Nicole, her only thought to free her child.

The force of a man's arm clamping around her waist, sweeping her off her feet, stunned her. A cry ripped its way up from deep inside her, only to be choked off.

Chapter Thirteen

For a moment, Elizabeth hung limp, then her fury exploded. She clawed the arms that held her prisoner. Violence seethed inside her. She kicked back, satisfied to hear a grunt of pain. But a second attempt missed its mark.

"Be still, still!"

She heard the words from far off. Dizzying black spots danced in front of her eyes. She couldn't breathe. The pressure of the arm around her waist eased. Her feet felt the solid earth beneath them. And again, she heard the command in the gruff male voice for her to be still.

"You'll obey."

It wasn't a question. She found herself struggling to nod. She had to get free. She had to save Nicole.

"Stay."

Elizabeth wasn't sure what alerted her that she was not going to be harmed. She managed to push aside the tangle of her hair and turned to see her captor.

Dobie. She mouthed the name, no sound coming forth from her throat. He shook his head, warning her to be silent, and she obeyed him. Emotions unraveled rapidly until she found simple gratitude that he was here.

Released, she swayed a moment where he left her while he picked up his weapons. Before he was lost from sight, she followed him.

Dobie never looked back, never said a word, but Elizabeth knew he didn't want her with him. She tried to make her footsteps as quiet as Dobie's.

As her head cleared, Elizabeth heard the sounds of Nicole's captor as he ran from them. She prayed that he would not fall and hurt her child, for it was dark within the forest. How Dobie managed to find his way she didn't know but was most thankful that he had.

At a slight sound, Elizabeth glanced to her left, biting her lip not to cry out. She would swear that someone was running parallel to them. But before them came the continued noise of someone thrashing as if they had lost their way. Dobie suddenly stopped, as she did well behind him.

"Mam—!"

Nicole's cry was strangled. It was cut off so fast, Elizabeth doubted at first whether she heard it at all. She didn't even know she was running toward the sound until Dobie gripped her arm.

"He's cornered and knows it. Let me do my job."

Fear held her still, held her silent, but would not hold her back.

"Josh is circling," Dobie whispered against her ear so the sound would not carry beyond a few feet.

Elizabeth knew she should allow them to rescue her daughter. But some instinct, some dark emotion drove her, and when Dobie moved off toward the right and was swallowed noiselessly by a thick brush of low-hanging branches, she crept forward.

Dobie had his pistol and musket, and she had to assume that Josh was armed. But what of Nicole's captor? Would he have a weapon? And if he did, would he use it on her child to gain his freedom? Or would he try to kill either of the men attempting to rescue her daughter?

Her fears were realized when a cry and shot rang out simultaneously.

"Let the child go," Dobie ordered.

A growl of rage. A child's cry. Elizabeth's heart froze in her chest. She didn't even realize she had come upon them until the vague shape of a man loomed in front of her. She never knew if she actually saw her child or it was only her mind's eye that pictured Nicole's terrified face, but the sight spurred her to act.

With a snarl of blind rage, she lashed out with her fists, beating the man's back, kicking him where she could, trying to tear his arm from Nicole's body. Cornered he may have been, but a spinning turn of his body sent his hammered fist into her side and Elizabeth dropped to her knees with a scream.

Sounds blurred. Dobie's demand for the release of the child. Josh's liquid threatening drawl. Nicole's cries. Elizabeth heard them, tried to sort them out, pain lancing her as she struggled to rise and fight the lure of the black well of unconsciousness waiting to claim her.

"You want her? Here!"

Dobie had to drop his weapons to catch the little body hurled at him. The dark cloak of night was impenetrable; he called out for Josh to wait.

It was all the time the man needed. He dragged Elizabeth to her feet, yanking her arm, pulling her backward with him.

She didn't care. Nicole was safe and that was all that mattered. She couldn't fight, she had no strength left. Her body was bruised and battered, so much so that she felt little of the pain. Time lost meaning. She heard the sounds of pursuit and wanted to warn them back.

Suddenly she was free. With a moan, she curled into herself.

Dobie struggled with her abductor, barely escaping swipes from a wicked, gleaming knife.

"I'm going to kill you for daring to touch them," Elizabeth heard Dobie promise.

There was a grunt, a harsh laugh, and threats in return.

She couldn't tell who cried out a moment later, but one man fell to his knee, the other stood poised for a moment and then lunged.

Dobie's arm bled freely, but when his assailant charged him, he raised powerful hands to grab the man's arm from underneath, bringing his knee up at the same time. Bone ground against bone with a sickening thud. A knife fell from the man's hand to the ground. The kidnapper's arm hung useless.

"Elizabeth," Dobie ordered, "get away from here."

She looked up and barely made out Dobie towering over the other man, but his voice, that colorless voice, frightened her.

"What will you do to him?" she managed to say, feeling the rawness of her throat.

"Just go."

"Where's Nicole?"

"With Josh. Safe."

She knew Dobie meant to kill him. For now, she appeased her need to see that Nicole was unharmed. Revenge for what they had undergone surfaced. Hate and fury made her rejoice for a wild second that Dobie would make the man pay the ultimate price for what he had dared. But with each breath, each agonizing move she made to force herself to stand, saner thoughts began to prevail.

"Don't stain yourself with his blood, Dobie," she whispered, limping to his side. There she turned to look at the shadowed figure of the man Alma had hired. She couldn't see his face, but then, Elizabeth didn't want to have a face to add to her nightmares. She saw only that he clutched his broken arm to his chest.

"Tell Mrs. Waring that she'll never have my child. Tell her that I will kill her if she dares to try and take her again."

He didn't answer her. Elizabeth had not expected him to. Dobie urged her to move, and when she stood firm, he pushed her aside. Elizabeth grabbed his arm without thought.

The man fled.

Dobie shoved her away and went after him.

Elizabeth tried not to think of what would happen when Dobie caught him. She had no doubt that Dobie would try to kill him. She began to walk, her steps slow, using the filtering light of the rising moon to guide her.

When she heard steps behind her, she didn't flinch.

"Dobie, I don't think I can walk much farther."

He didn't answer, but when he offered his arm for her support, she could feel the fury radiating from him.

"He escaped, didn't he? It doesn't matter. I'm almost grateful that he did. Alma wouldn't have paid him in advance. He'll go back to her and she'll know to never try this again."

"You're calm," he said, an observation that was both statement and question.

"No," Elizabeth answered softly, knowing very well how little control she had over her teeming emotions. She longed for Colter, needed his comfort and strength. The thought of him prompted her to add, "If you're worried about the colonel, I'm sure he will not fault you. Nicole is safe." Wanting to make sure, she hurried her steps.

"Don't interfere between me and the colonel," he warned.

They climbed the knoll up to the house, the yard lit with torchlights.

Colter didn't see them as he first rode in. The lights alarmed him and his hunter reared at Colter's sudden tug on the reins.

"Josh! Josh, what the devil is going on?" Colter demanded, bringing his horse under control. "Dobie! Damn! Where's everyone?"

"Colonel?" Rutha yelled from the upstairs window. "Somethin'—"

"Colter!" Elizabeth called, using the last remains of her strength to run toward him.

He swung his horse around and with a touch of his knees raced to meet her. Leaning down, he caught her up with one arm. With the other, he fought to slow the hunter's pace. Dobie's presence barely registered. Elizabeth clinging to him, shaking, crying his name over and over was his only concern. His soothing voice calmed his horse, even as the words he spoke calmed Elizabeth. At a walk he returned to the yard and lowered her to stand before he quickly dismounted.

Elizabeth couldn't stop crying. Shielded in Colter's arms, she released the terror of the past hours, her words incoherent.

Colter rocked her, cradling her close, watching as Dobie approached them, his gaze locking on the weapons Dobie carried. Their exchange over Elizabeth's head was silent.

With a spare, barely discernible shake of his head, Dobie summed up the only words Colter cared about. His daughter and woman were unharmed and the man escaped.

"Colonel," Dobie said, meeting Colter's gaze with a level, direct one, "I'd be obliged to be relieved."

"Not now, man. Can't you see—"

"I failed to carry out your orders. And now's as good a time as any."

With her sobs quieting, Elizabeth heard the last. "That's not true, Colter. Dobie did all he could. If he had not come..." Her voice trailed off and once again she was overcome by uncontrollable trembling. "I... don't want anyone else here."

"Ma'am, you're not thinking too clear—"

"That's enough, Dobie," Colter cut in. "Elizabeth may be shaken, but she knows her own mind."

Dobie walked away, but Colter called him and he turned.

"Thank you. They're more precious than my own life and I already owe you that, Dobie."

He nodded, standing a little taller, but Colter was already sweeping Elizabeth up into his arms and carrying her into the house.

With her head cradled on his shoulder, Elizabeth felt emotions wash over and around her until she couldn't think. But as Colter moved to enter the hall, she asked him to take her to Nicole.

"In a little while, love. You'll frighten her if she sees you now." Colter's calm voice belied the rage seething inside him. Elizabeth surprised him by agreeing. His glance took in her torn clothes, the scratches and scrapes that bruised her flesh, the pine needles and bits of bark entangled in her hair and the puff of her lower lip where she had bitten it, a drop of blood still welled there. He brushed it away with his own lips, wishing he could as easily heal her from the trauma she experienced.

He knew that the full impact of what she had been through hadn't yet broken, and he was not looking forward to the storm. Colter wasn't sure he had the strength to hear her rightful recriminations for his promise of safety and failure to deliver it.

Emily, leaning heavily on her walking stick, came down the stairs and paused at the foot of them. Elizabeth's eyes were closed and she addressed her question to Colter.

"Is she injured?"

"Not that I can tell," he answered, noticing the tremble in Emily's voice and hands that betrayed her state. "I will tend to Elizabeth. And Nicole?"

"Rutha is bathing her. She wants her mother." But she too noticed the damage done. "I'll get some hot water and clean clothes. Together we'll—"

"No. I'll take care of her."

His self-accusation was apparent in the look he gave her and in his voice. "You cannot blame yourself or anyone that this happened, Colter. I'm afraid that we grew lax in our vigilance. It is obvious we all underestimated Alma's determination. I never thought she would find Elizabeth here with me."

"Emily," Colter softly warned, "you tell me not to blame myself, yet that is what I hear you doing. Blaming yourself."

"No. I didn't mean to do so. I was thinking of the cold Nicole had, and how with the weather's turn to springlike warmth she infected us with a child's natural need to be outside and free. I feel guilty, as I know Rutha and Josh do, that Nicole's giving us no peace, made us toss out caution to quiet her."

"Emily," Elizabeth said after hearing all she could, "I don't want anyone blaming themselves. Alma's plan failed and that is all that matters. Now, where is Josh? He wasn't hurt, was he?"

"Other than a bruised ego reminding him he isn't as spry as he likes to believe, he's fine." Emily patted Elizabeth's hand in both thanks and reassurance. "I'll get that hot water so you can hurry and see Nicole."

"She wasn't—"

"Nicole isn't..."

Emily looked from one to the other as they both spoke at the same time. She forced herself to meet Elizabeth's pleading gaze, even as her words sought to calm Colter. "All I can see are minor scratches. What I can't see, I can't tell you about, dears. Only time will reveal the answer."

Colter bit back an angry retort, afraid that Elizabeth would panic. But she merely nodded and once again rested her head on his shoulder. He brushed past Emily and carried Elizabeth into the bedroom where he set her on the bed.

Colter forced himself to remove her clothes with a gentleness he hoped would soothe her. Elizabeth's docility didn't fool him. He sensed she was reliving every moment of terror.

Wrapping her in the quilt, he retrieved the decanter of brandy and a glass from the parlor and poured a small bit for her to sip. She pulled away when the liquor stung her lip, and Colter didn't try to force her to drink more. He didn't have any himself. The little that was left wouldn't remove his feelings of guilt. He paced until Emily, followed by Josh, came with hot water and clean cloths. When they tried to talk to Elizabeth, he cut them off and ushered them out of the room.

Elizabeth sat unseeing, offering no resistance as Colter tenderly bathed her face and then lowered the quilt to expose her shoulders. He had turned to rinse the cloth and wring it out when he caught sight of his face in the mirror, quickly forcing his expression of pain and fury to disappear. Her skin was marred by an already darkening bruise, and before he washed it, his lips offered the healing balm of his kiss.

Over and over, he repeated his actions, masking his reaction to every slight scratch, each scrape, offering no words, just his silent, gentle kisses until he knelt before her, drying her feet. The quilt had shifted so that one leg was bare, and he rested his bowed head against it, praying to find the right words to say. His fingertips skimmed the outline of purpling flesh on her rib cage, and his throat closed, just as his mind refused to find words.

Elizabeth roused herself and with one hand brushed his hair. The tender ministrations, his silent declarations of love, flooded her heart. She knew in the ensuing moments that, even if he never asked her to break vows she had made before God and man, she would break them. And rejoice while doing so. Colter's love was a gift that she could no longer deny. He was her strength. For she sensed, as she focused her gaze fully on him, that Colter was flaying himself over what had happened. By making himself this vulnerable, and allowing her to see him so, he made her strong.

The moments were few before he accepted that no words would come and helped her into her night rail and wrapper. Neither spoke, but there was a shared serenity in their looks, a sense of their willingness to wait. Their child needed them now. Later there would be time for talk and for love.

Colter once again lifted her into his arms and, when she protested, said, "I need to hold you. Don't deny me this."

And silently she whispered to herself, *I can deny you nothing, love, nothing.*

Three lamps lit Nicole's room. Rutha rose from her place by the bed as they entered. Neither of them noticed when she left them; Colter placed Elizabeth on one side of Nicole and himself on the other.

Colter's heart filled to overflowing when Elizabeth joined her hand with his across their child's body and raised his to her lips. Her light kiss and look seemed both to beg support and offer him courage before she turned to Nicole.

"We both came to make sure that you feel safe, precious."

"Did you slay him?" Nicole asked Colter, her eyes wide, her small mouth quivering before she pressed her lips together. Her little hand crept out from beneath the quilt to touch Colter's arm.

Squeezing Elizabeth's hand to still the betraying tremble of his own, Colter shifted so that Nicole nestled closer to his body. He had to swallow several times before he could trust himself to speak without venting the coil of emotions that rocked him. She was his princess and he her promised knight, who had vowed to slay all her dragons. He longed to tell her, yes, he had slain the creature that would be the subject of his daughter's night terrors.

"I arrived too late to chase him down, Nicole," he finally answered. "But I wanted to hurt him for hurting you and your mother."

"He's awful bad. An' Mister Josh an' Dobie gots scared. Mama hit him. An' then I think Dobie gots mad."

"Yes, he was bad and you're right to believe that Dobie was mad. Mama was brave. But they all love you, princess. Just like Rutha and Miss Emily. But you remember that no one loves you more than Mama and me. And when you love someone, you want them to be safe where no one can harm them," he whispered just as his voice broke. Colter brushed a kiss across her temple, breathing in the sweet scent that belonged to her, feeling a loosening of the band that held his heart. He fought a burning sensation in his eyes when Nicole's lips touched his cheek.

"I don't have a papa to love. So can I love you?"

Colter's eyes closed to hide the rush of tears that he rapidly blinked away. "All you want," he managed to say past the lump in his throat.

"You mustn't be so sad, Mister Colonel. I'm the bad one. I runned after the pretty swans an' didn't come to Mama when she called. I didn't know the bad man was there. He wouldn't let me scream. But I kicked him, real hard. Dobie told me to."

"When did Dobie tell you that, love?" Elizabeth asked, forcing the words out. She wished to bury these past hours but knew Nicole had to talk about it if she was ever to forget it.

"We 'tended. Dobie says it's the goodest game."

"Tended?" Colter asked, dragging his gaze from Nicole's face to look at Elizabeth.

"Nicole loves to play pretend," she explained, feeling a sense of healing as they talked. "I have much to thank Dobie for."

"We *both* do," Colter said, once more turning his attention to his daughter.

"You're a very brave princess and Mama is proud of you," Elizabeth whispered, but her eyes met Colter's, filled with anger that their child had to suffer any fear.

Nicole wiggled about, freeing her other hand and bringing theirs to cover hers. "Rua gave me tea, Mama," she said with a yawn. Her eyelids fluttered once, twice and then closed.

"Sleep, precious. Sleep with the sweetest of dreams."

To muffle the sob she couldn't contain, Elizabeth bit her puffed lip and heard Colter repeat her words.

Colter's throat closed again. Among the warring emotions he felt, pride for his child's courage overcame his own feelings of inadequacy and failure. He spent a long time gazing at her sleeping face before he looked at Elizabeth with a new tenderness in his eyes.

"With all my heart I thank you for giving me the gift of this beautiful child. No soldier in the field could match her spirit and courage."

In that moment, when she saw the adoration for her and their child, Elizabeth stripped away the last trace of betrayal from the past.

"No, Colter, I am the one who was given the gift of having Nicole as a living reminder of your love for me."

They stayed and watched until Colter knew that Nicole's sleep was peaceful. Only then did he once more insist on carrying Elizabeth downstairs to the parlor.

At her demand, he set her on her feet. A small fire was already burning in the fireplace, adding its warmth to the balmy night. Colter opened his tunic buttons, suddenly realizing it was the first time in three days he had done so.

"Colter, Rutha fixed you a tray," she said, calling his attention to the linen-draped tray on the sideboard.

"Are you sure you wouldn't be more comfortable in bed, Elizabeth?"

"Oh, I will be," she answered, hiding a small secret smile as she fixed a plate of cold ham, biscuits and slices of hard winter pears for him. "Would you like a glass of cider?"

Bemused, he didn't answer her.

"Colter?" She turned to find his expression puzzled. "What's wrong?"

"I might ask you the same," he returned, coming to her side.

"You haven't eaten, have you?" He shook his head. "I thought as much. And it's likely you haven't had a rest or a chance to bathe. I wouldn't be surprised to find fresh hot water in the bedroom along with clean linens for you."

"At this point, I wouldn't be surprised, either."

"Good. Then you won't waste time arguing." She turned back to the plate she was arranging, her breaths shallow until he moved away. "You needn't worry so, Colter. I simply want the pleasure of taking care of you for a little while. A return of—"

"Don't," he intoned in a mock-stern voice, "say favor, little fox. I'd never believe it."

"Then I won't." She glanced up and offered him a too bright smile. Colter stepped closer to the bedroom doorway. Water was steaming from the china basin, his razor and strop were neatly laid on linen and his clothes draped over the straight chair. "When did you manage to have this arranged?"

"I didn't. We all care a great deal about you. And each one tries to show you how much in his own way." Elizabeth couldn't meet his penetrating gaze.

"That's all this is?" he asked, his voice soft.

"Yes."

Rubbing his unshaven jaw, Colter grinned. "Can't deny I stink like a bluebelly and—"

"No," she cut in, looking directly at him, "you don't *stink*. I'm not wrinkling up my nose, am I? I love being near you, for you are all that a man—"

"Hold that thought, Elizabeth," he whispered, ducking into the bedroom. Desire blazed in his eyes.

Chapter Fourteen

Colter took his time. But when he finished shaving, he began to think of the news he had brought for her. How was he going to tell her what he had learned so far about James?

Stripped of his uniform, he washed absently, still trying to marshal his emotions into order. Barefoot, he padded over to the bed, tossing aside his shirt and putting on his close-fitting breeches. He carefully brushed the bits of bark that had fallen from her hair and scooped them up with the pine needles that clung to the quilt.

For a moment, he relived terrifying minutes when he first saw her and held her close, fear exploding through him. Fisting his hand around these reminders, he walked back and let them fall into the basin, watching as they floated. Harmless debris, that is all they were, all he must let them be.

And to ensure that, he removed Elizabeth's hairbrush from her dresser, taking it with him into the parlor.

Elizabeth sat on the carpet before the fire, gilded in its light. Colter paused, studying her profile, his mind making a new memory to replace his earlier one of her. There was something serene in the delicate bones of her features as she contemplated the flames, and he had no wish to make his presence known.

But she turned then, a shy smile tilting her lips. "Come, sit beside me," she offered, gesturing to one side. "I have your food here." But she averted her gaze from the sight of his bare chest. "I know you must be hungry."

Elizabeth felt her ears burn as she heard what she said. The room had seemed restful before he entered it; now it was charged with a current of awareness that made her tense.

Seeking to put her at ease, Colter joined her on the floor, using the settee as a backrest and stretching out his long legs before him. He watched her come to her knees with a graceful move, placing the plate on his lap before she sat on his left, partially turned to the fire.

"What did you eat, Elizabeth?"

She turned quickly, almost losing her balance. "I didn't eat."

"I thought as much. Well, you can't expect me to finish this alone. You'll have to help me." Colter offered her a charming smile, meant to entice not to alarm. "Come, lean back here, and we'll share."

Elizabeth gazed up at him, finding within the gold flecks of his dark green eyes a reflection of the flames. She gained no insight to his thoughts or his intent. His smile was fixed, and she couldn't help but respond to it, just as she responded to the promise in his voice to share food. Her conscience had reemerged and she was unsure of what she would do if he asked more of her. Settling at his side, she noticed the hairbrush.

"Why did you bring that out with you?"

"Because there wasn't time before to untangle your hair."

"Oh, I see."

"I doubt it, love, but you will allow me my pleasure, too."

She accepted a bit of ham from his hand, then shared a slice of winter pear.

"If you want to talk to me, Elizabeth, I'm here for you." *Now,* his mind supplied with a bitter lash of guilt.

"Do you make that same offer to your soldiers under fire? To listen, I mean. I don't know," she continued in a rush, "if I want to talk about it, Colter. I feel guilty, at fault, and wonder how I'll cope now that I'm sure Alma has found us."

"One thing you won't do, love, is cope with this alone." An idea began to form, but he wasn't ready to discuss it with her. Nor was she ready to hear it. But he could lay the groundwork. "You're isolated here and I worry about all of you. Dobie is good, but I can't assign another man—"

"How did you manage to have him here?"

"That, Elizabeth," he chided with a light tap on her nose, "I cannot tell you. I am not denying the Confederate forces of his valuable services." He glanced away, chewing slowly, knowing that truth lay beneath his lie. Dobie was valuable, and the Confederacy would only waste his talents while he served out his sentence for repeated insubordination, but having Elizabeth know this wouldn't serve to reassure her. He took her silence on the matter as acceptance.

"To continue what I was saying, I worry. If you had close neighbors, or lived in the city, the attempt to take Nicole may not have been made. It is something to think about." He felt her shiver and, while he regretted having caused it, knew playing on her fear would eventually help him ensure her and Nicole's safety.

He tried tempting her to eat more, but she refused and Colter set the plate aside. He thought again of his news. While it was inconclusive, it still offered him hope that he would have an answer soon about James's fate. If Elizabeth felt out of control, what he had to tell her might give her back a small measure of security.

"Love, you remember I promised to find out what I could about James?"

"Don't, Colter. Not now." Elizabeth shuddered. Just his mention of James's name when she was warring with her conscience jarred her.

Colter sighed, letting the matter drop. Perhaps the timing was wrong. And it wasn't as if he could say with certainty that James was dead or alive. He brushed a fleeting kiss over her hair and slammed the door on his own conscience.

Elizabeth closed her eyes and leaned back against his shoulder, letting his warmth seep into her own chilled body. But the sights that waited for her behind closed lids were those of looming shadows and massive trees that shut her away from Nicole. Rigid, she jerked forward, panting as she stared unseeing at the fire, willing the flames to burn terror to ash.

With a gentle touch, Colter urged her back against his chest. Her soft wool wrapper brushed against his flesh. He murmured meaningless sounds and as the minutes passed, felt her body soften as her breathing grew even. He rubbed his chin against her hair, feeling the prick of the pine needles and wanting them gone. Using one hand, he eased into the tangle and with long soothing strokes, kneaded the tension from her neck and scalp. Rewarded with her small sounds of pleasure, he continued.

Elizabeth shifted closer to him and her hand brushed the blunt ridge of flesh rising from his breeches. She knew Colter wanted her and couldn't prevent his desire from showing. But once again, her heart opened to his love, touched by his not pushing her to make a decision when she was still unsure. Her eyes drifted closed and the nightmare was held at bay as she was lulled by his soothing, gentle massage.

Colter watched the delicate shadows created by the twin light-tipped lashes on her cheeks. He kissed her hair, so lightly that she didn't stir, and then he picked up the brush.

"Don't stop," she whispered, an intoxicating languor pervading her body.

"I won't, little fox. I just want to give you more pleasure." He brushed her hair slowly, stopping to work through knotted tangles, whispering velvet apologies when he inadvertently hurt her. He was uncaring of time, for being near her offered his mind and body the peace they craved. And as her pleasurable murmurs grew and her hair became more softly curled and silky to his touch, he was given a sensual caress against his skin in payment.

Setting aside the brush, he used his hands, his eyelids heavy as he watched the curled strands cling to his fingers like a lover's teasing strokes. Her lavish appreciative murmurs of his name, whispered over and over as her body relaxed and grew heavy against his, added an exquisite coil of tension that fevered his blood.

The flame heated the spice color of her hair so she appeared seductive, but the curled length fell against her creamy colored, almost virginally cut wrapper, making him think of her innocence.

Elizabeth twisted in his arms, turning to face him. For a moment she stared up at the dark, masculine features that loomed above her. His lips were full, slightly parted, adding to the sensual flare of his nostrils. With her eyes holding his, she reached up to thread her fingers through his hair, longing to return each lavish sensation that embraced her. His eyes were already kindled with an insistent passion that bathed her senses with rapture. Colter's lips brushed against hers with a delicacy both tender and enticing, and a ripple of desire misted through her. With a sweet gossamer touch, she returned his kiss, feeling her unwanted conscience raise its warnings.

She refused to consider her actions, refused to think of the future. The terror of the day, the desperation of believing their daughter lost, the twists of the past, all proved how uncertain their lives were. No matter how she longed to bury the knowledge, Colter was a soldier at war. He was the only man she had ever loved, would ever love. Acknowledging that simple, unadulterated fact forced her conscience into hiding.

And she flowered under the tender stroke of his hand, which chased knots of tension from her back and replaced them with slender, heated satin threads of passion that spun her into a web of ecstasy.

Colter's eyes were dark with an uncompromising hunger, but he was solicitous of her bruises as he eased himself down to lie full length against the carpet and urged her to rest on him. The pads of his fingers graced her hips briefly before he raised his hands to hold her head and bring her mouth to his.

"I want to take and take from you, love, all your sweetness, all your passion, all that is mine," he declared in a hard, masculine voice. "But if you will once more deny me and yourself, say it now."

With her hands splayed out against his chest, Elizabeth tossed back her head to remove the curtain of her hair so she could see him.

"I cannot deny you, Colter. To deny my love is to deny life and hope, and I will not do that again." Her body trembled, but her voice was firm with conviction. With her mouth in offering, she leaned down to kiss him.

He took the kiss, using his lips and tongue to evoke memories of the night she had surrendered all that she was to him. He was reminded anew of how soft her mouth was, how sweet she tasted to his tongue, how her own desire grew hungry and her lips parted to get more of him until her body melted against his like warm honey. There was a lush taking and giving to their kisses, as if time had stopped to allow passion to spread through them. And Colter praised his generous lover as his kisses relearned each delicate feature, each velvet shadow that heated to the play of his mouth.

Elizabeth dragged her lips down the corded length of his neck, unwilling to lift her mouth from his skin. Her tongue dipped into the hollow of his collarbone, placing teasing swirls that ended with her own moan of pleasure as Colter returned the caress. She was barely conscious of the slide of cloth over her shoulders, for

Colter's mouth followed, the heat and pliant touch of his tongue soothing and enticing her flesh.

She rubbed her palms over the hard nubs of his nipples, feeling an answering ache in her own, wanting his hands to assuage the swollen peaks.

Her restless move alerted Colter. "What's wrong, love?" he queried in a passion-taut voice, deftly untying her wrapper and lifting her away so that it fell open. She rose above him, cheeks flushed, lips glistening with moisture, intriguing shadows from the lush fullness of her breasts teasing him through the thin lawn night rail.

He wanted it gone. He wanted nothing but his lips, his skin, to touch her. "Tell me what you want, little fox. Don't be shy with me. I'll give you all I can." He turned his cheek and brushed it against the taut peak of her breast. Her breath shuddered out and her body tremored against him.

"I want you, Colter. I want you now."

"I know," he whispered in return, seeing her desire in the dark, dreamy eyes that locked with his, feeling how ready she was by the taste of her mouth, by the sliding caress of her body as he lifted and fitted her over his.

His hands curved over her hips and she arched instinctively into his hands. He pressed her into the cradle of his thighs, proving that he wanted her just as strongly.

Elizabeth lowered her head until her cheek rested on his chest. She rubbed back and forth, loving the feel of his skin, the soft abrading hair that curled on his chest and entangled itself in her own long curls. She murmured her pleasure to him, loving the strength of his broad shoulders and the heat of his skin, and she smiled against his chest to hear the ragged edge of his breathing as his body tightened beneath hers.

She swept her hair aside and trailed her hand down to his narrow hip, pleased she could make him tremble from the light touch she feathered down his thigh.

"When I first saw you, Colter, I was afraid of your power. But you were always so gentle with me."

"Is that what you crave from me, Elizabeth? Do you need me to be gentle?" he asked, but doubted he could give her gentleness when need clawed his body.

She kissed him just as her fingertips brushed his erect flesh, eliciting a groan of dark need that came from deep, deep inside him.

Lifting her lips a bare fraction from his, she whispered, "No, I don't want you to be gentle. I want the power of your love and I need the wildness that you once showed me."

He reacted with a violent shudder as the words exploded through him, almost snapping his control, the last sane corner of his mind reminding him that she was bruised.

But she pressed against the throbbing flesh as if she knew he fought a battle with himself and intended, by scattering sweetly heated strokes of her tongue across his chest, to overcome his will.

"Colter," she groaned softly, "I need you to love me." With delicate restraint, she raked her teeth over his nipple, soothing it with her tongue. "I need to love you," she whispered, her look and voice offering both promise and challenge.

As he eased her arms from the wrapper, the lift and twists of her body as he sought to pull it free fanned a fire, already smouldering, to consume him. He tossed the unwanted cloth aside, stroking the bared length of her thigh until she called his name with impatient sighs. The edge of the night rail was caught between the press of their bodies, hindering him from baring her flesh to lips that hungered to taste her. He caught the length of her hair with one hand, angling her head to the side, his mouth taking hers with a possessive kiss that was primitive in its demand. His arm cushioned her back as he lowered her to the carpet, sweeping the thin lawn cloth up over her hips until the folds rested beneath the lush curves of her breasts.

His tongue laid claim to the secrets of her mouth and now he sought sweeter flesh to worship. Yet, for all his compelling need, he was careful to take time to remove the night rail without hurting her. To his eyes, her body, bathed in the fire's glow, was exquisite perfection.

"A glorious angel who offers me heaven," he murmured, lowering his head to graze his mouth over one nipple.

"A fallen angel, if any, my love," she returned before closing her eyes and letting bliss bathe her senses. When his mouth closed over her breast, suckling on the swollen peak, she cried out softly to feel the tightening in her womb. She pulled his head closer and opened herself to the full force of his passion.

Elizabeth unleashed the wildness that he had held back with every restless move of her body, twisting with slow caresses of her legs against his, and increased his ardor with the tremulous cries from her lips.

Colter pulled back, his breathing ragged, using almost jerky moves to strip his breeches off. His hand shook as he caressed the graceful curve of her calf up to her raised knee. His lips were moist as he kissed her thigh, drinking the tremor from her skin and feeling it deep inside himself. The crease of her leg held a velvet shadow that lured his mouth, and his cheek brushed the soft nest of curls that hid sweeter, hotter shadows.

Elizabeth felt the build of silken tremors that coursed over her body without end. She touched his back, wanting to pull him over her, needing to know again the swift rise to glory that loving Colter would bring, but even her fevered plea would not deter him from the lavish exploration his mouth tendered to her heated flesh.

His tongue dipped with the delicacy of a butterfly's wing to her navel. She moaned his name. His mouth learned the curve of her stomach and she felt her insides draw tight. In a lover's coaxing voice, she asked for and received the first touch of his fingers on the soft feminine core that she willingly yielded. She heard with satisfaction the changed tempo of his breathing, and her own rendered shallow drafts of air that brought their mingled aroused scent to her. But when he stroked more deeply inside her, her breath was suspended; she struggled to draw air as knots inside her seemed to coil and coil, tight, and then tighter still.

Colter spoke to her with words that roused and sparked conflagration, with kisses and touches that drove her to exquisite peaks over and over until she lay spent and trembling, cradled in his arms.

Using savage control over his body, Colter brushed aside the damp tendrils of her hair, his lips sealing hers with tenderness that deepened with the potency of his need.

Her flesh gleamed with a passion mist that fed his senses as he positioned himself over her. "Look at me, love," he urged softly, "watch me make you mine, again."

Her eyes opened even as she shifted her legs to welcome him. "Now," she whispered, drawing his mouth to hers. Elizabeth felt him hold back. His muscles etched rigid in the firelight and the sharp features of his face were bronzed and shadowed. Tension caused his body to tremble. "Come to me, love. Make me whole again. Make me yours."

And in welcome she lifted her hips, taking his mouth in a kiss that reveled in the wanton rapture she felt as their bodies merged into one.

But even as the power of his need called to him, Colter stilled, giving her time to adjust to the hard intrusion of his body. Tiny ripples of her pleasure coursed around his throbbing flesh as she melted against him. His control shredded as she used her body to signal how ready she was for him.

Emotions rioted with passion and Elizabeth let herself be swept away by both. Colter set a powerful rhythm for their lovemaking and she responded with every fiber of her being. Suddenly there were no thoughts as her own hunger reached out for fulfillment.

Colter yielded to her feminine entreaty, slipping his hands beneath her hips and fusing her body to his. He had claimed he wanted to take all that she was, all that she could give, and he reenforced that claim with the hard, driving thrusts of his body that took all she offered to him and dared to demand more.

Her body tightened. Elizabeth knew Colter experienced the same savage need. His mouth joined with hers and the pleasure that coursed through her became almost unbearable. Cries erupted from her throat and he answered.

She wanted . . . and wanted . . . and Colter was there, bringing to her an explosive ecstasy that ripped through her a moment before he joined her with racking shudders as he poured himself into her.

Elizabeth drifted in a sweetly sated world. Colter's half-coherent whispers, lavishing praise, inciting hunger, grew more tender with each kiss he bestowed. She nestled at his side, smiling to feel the possessive move of his leg over hers to anchor her to his body.

Colter braced himself up on one arm, looking down at his lover. Her eyes were closed, and he paid homage to them with gentle kisses. Her hair was spread on the carpet, its spiced warm colors gleaming under the dying light of the fire. His smile was frankly sensual. There was a hint of the erotic in her finely etched profile that drew his gaze. The lush fullness of her lips beckoned and tempted him to taste.

And her whispered "Yes" made him obey.

Elizabeth offered her mouth, and his taking of her lower lip into the heat of his, suckling so tenderly while his tongue stroked with seductive skill, sparked fire inside. She ran her fingers through his hair and trembled to feel his sweat-sheened skin cover hers with a sliding caress of their naked bodies. Desire was not sated, she realized. Passion's turmoil churned between them once again.

As Colter reluctantly eased his mouth from hers and lifted his head, he was captivated anew by the satin texture of her skin and the seductive glow in her eyes when she opened them to gaze at him. He stroked her slender waist, watching her respond with a natural candor he had never known from another woman. He wanted to drown in her. The full, lush swell of her breast fitted perfectly to his hand, and he gently tugged the sensitive tip until her skin flushed and she shook with the same need that tremored his body.

Colter gathered her body against his. "Love, I want you again."

"Yes," she whispered, needing him as badly.

He rose and carried her into her bedroom where he set her down on the bed. "You know there's no going back for either of us, Elizabeth," he warned, covering her body with his.

Desire blazed in his eyes, and she gazed at them while her hands framed his face. "I don't want to go back, Colter. There's no life, no love waiting for me there." She kissed him with all the pent-up emotions that were inside her. "Only with you," she murmured against his lips, "can both love and life be mine."

"Show me," he urged with a lover's silken coaxing, melding his flesh with hers. "Show me."

Chapter Fifteen

Morning. Elizabeth wished it never had arrived. The sunlight filtered through the lace curtains, playing a blurred pattern on Colter's back. The hard stamp that usually marked his masculine features was gone, replaced by a softening peace that made him appear younger than his twenty-eight years.

Tears misted her eyes. She loved him so. And when his own cry, telling her how much he loved her, had broken from his lips, she felt her soul was healed from doubts that had wounded her.

No going back. Colter's words. Her promise to both herself and him. The joy of being loved and returning that love filled her. And while her body was still so as not to wake him, her thoughts seemed to reach out and curl their warmth around Colter's mind, for he opened his eyes.

He eased from the tangle of covers, kissing Elizabeth again and again, smiling to hear her sleepy good-morning as she reached for him. Emotions and feelings he couldn't sort, couldn't name, churned through him. He knew they were powerful, explosive, like the desire that was eased but never fully sated as they loved each other through the night. She gave him pleasure that was sweetly piercing and hotter each time.

"I've never heard a little fox purr, love," he whispered, taking her hand and placing a kiss against her palm. "And I never knew that making love with you could bring me not only a peaceful heaven, but a joyous celebration of life."

"Oh, Colter, I love you so."

He nuzzled her lips, but she pulled him close, teasing the corners of his lips with her tongue. The kiss deepened and before it was done, passion's demand claimed them.

He smoothed the silken flesh of her thigh, cupped her hip and, with a light brush of his fingertips, skimmed the bruise on her rib cage before he took in the soft weight of her breast. "Can morning make you taste sweeter, love?" he murmured thoughtfully, his voice husky.

"You've never loved me in the morning, Colter." And there was invitation in the dark glow of her eyes that told him of the blood already beginning to beat heavily through her body.

"But I will," he promised, teasing her nipple into a taut peak of desire. "Like velvet, but hard," he whispered, leisurely rubbing the tight crown with his thumb. "But how could you taste sweeter than when you make me a part of you and cry my name?"

He took her mouth with a lover's ease, sliding his tongue between her teeth, drinking in the small catches of her breath, her soft moan.

Elizabeth held him, feeling the increased beats of their hearts, loving him so much she ached.

When he parted their lips, Colter lifted his head. "I love you, Elizabeth." Delicately he finessed the taut peak he had teased, raking his teeth over the bud until she trembled for him. He paid equal homage to its twin and gazed at the woman who set him on fire with a look and with the precious gift of her love. His hand brushed across her breasts, and he smiled as she arched her back. "Soft to hard, sweet to velvet. But there's one place you remain so incredibly soft, love," he whispered with exquisite restraint. His fingertips grazed her tremoring skin down to her thighs.

He sought and found her most sensitive flesh, groaning as he felt her change for him, but his tender touch revealed a satin heat that was swollen. "Love, you'd tell me if I hurt you?"

Elizabeth smiled. "You can't hurt me, Colter." Her lashes fluttered and she moved her hips against his caressing hand. "How can pleasure hurt? You touched me so..." Her voice trailed off; tension raked her and she drew him close. "Just knowing what awaits when you become part of me..." Once again she lost her voice, melting with a soft, shimmering shiver. She slid her hands down his body and caressed his hard length. Her smile promised the same pleasure as her eyes when she looked at him.

"Come be a part of me, Colter," she murmured. "Come to me, love." Her knee flexed and moved with restless need.

And Colter stored in his memory her sensuality, her joy and her beauty.

Elizabeth nipped his shoulder and gently tugged his aroused flesh. She could feel the blood throb and pool, and was challenged to break his control. Gracefully she shifted her body, kissing his hard nipples. "Soft to hard, sweet to velvet," she whispered, repeating his own words. And she smiled, rubbing her cheek against the curled hair, feeling the wild beat of his heart, the heat of his skin and the shudder that he couldn't control.

"Unlike me, Colter," she teased in a sultry voice, glorying in his acceptance of her power to arouse him, "you're never incredibly soft." The wild heat of passion drove her to let him know the loving intimacy of her mouth.

Colter was seized by desire that flamed so hot he could hardly draw breath. Need forced a groan from his throat. He reached for her, feeling the silky caress of her hair across his sensitive flesh, but even as he urged her back up his body, she gracefully eluded his hands, intent on giving him pleasure. Hunger smoldered in his blood. His hands clenched at his sides, for she had taken herself out of reach of his touch.

And he found himself calling for her, torn by the seething violence of his need.

The hoarse, trembling urgency of his voice brought her flowing up over his body, and he lifted her over him. A wildness cascaded through her to see his dark eyes almost black, his cheeks flushed and lips taut, his body hard and tight. She shivered, overcome with fevered need as he slid deeply into her softness with a smooth thrust of his hips.

For the first time she watched as her lover came apart with a pleasure so intense that it increased the rapture spreading through her body. She abandoned herself to him, just as he had to her, shattered by the feeling of being reborn, dying and finding life once more before she collapsed across his broad chest.

Smoothing the tangle of her hair back, Colter framed her face with his hands. "If I died today," he said, his voice tight and husky, "and I was offered heaven, there could be no greater joy waiting there, than that of loving you."

Elizabeth paled. His words made tears blur her eyes until his features wavered before her. Her mind recoiled from his mention of death, but as she slowly blinked to clear her vision, she knew from the seriousness of his dark gaze that living with the fear of death was as much a part of Colter as all that she loved about him.

"I've frightened you, love."

"Yes," she answered without hesitation, kissing his lips. And against them she whispered, "But my love, you are so much a man to tell me of your fear."

"I love you, I love you," he repeated, rolling over to his side and taking her with him. Cradling her in his arms, Colter knew he would tell of his fears. "It is not my own fear of dying that plagues me, but the lies I am forced to tell when men who are sick of war look to me to restore their sense of honor and valor. I must turn away from the plea of a boy who's never been away from home and longs for his family, wishing I could get him a furlough. Tedium and terror are the soldiers' constant companions in the camps, and I don't know how to combat them."

Elizabeth made a choked sound. She lifted his hand and smoothed it against her cheek, then pressed a kiss into his hard palm. She understood about fears, but she didn't have Colter's courage to share hers with him. "Tell me," she whispered, knowing there was more.

He cupped her chin and tilted her face up toward his. "I risk lives, other men's lives, and can't always live with myself when they die." He could see that she ached for him, but he was grateful there was no pity in her eyes.

"Colter, caring doesn't make you weak, it makes you strong." But she cried for him, appalled that he endured these experiences. As the moments passed, she knew, too, that his offering this trust forged another bond between them.

His lips brushed the tears from her cheeks. "That's why I need your love. I need to know that you are waiting and safe for me to retreat to for a few stolen hours of peace."

Colter tucked her head beneath his chin, holding her for long minutes, letting her cry for both of them. He found that sharing what he had never told to another eased the burden he carried alone. Her generous love, her compassion, would be talismans when the black nightmares came in the middle of the night to wake him with a clammy, cold fear. Time with Elizabeth made sweet, warm memories to hold fear at bay.

She quieted, but he wouldn't let her go until the sounds of others stirring in the house reached him. It wasn't long before he heard Rutha gently scolding Nicole that she couldn't wake her mama. Torn between needing to spend a few more stolen minutes with Elizabeth and wanting to be with his daughter, Colter finally forced himself from her side.

Elizabeth's lashes were spiked with wetness and her eyes were still sleepy.

"Stay, love, and rest. I'll see to Nicole," he said, slipping from the bed and out into the parlor to retrieve his clothes.

She wanted to call out and stop him, biting back the words. Nicole and Colter needed each other for a little while.

With a sigh she turned back to rest her head on the pillow that still held the imprint of his head. She smiled softly to inhale a faint, lingering masculine scent. The war, Alma, James's unknown fate, all faded. Even work was forgotten. She slept to the lullaby of Nicole's sweet, innocent laughter joined with Colter's.

It was almost midday when kisses tempted Elizabeth from her sleep. Her smile was dreamy until she opened her eyes and gave a start. Her cheeks were pressed between two pairs of lips. One pair was soft and sticky with jam, and the other pair was surrounded by beard stubble. She teased them by closing her eyes and sighing, nestling her head deeper into the pillow. She heard Nicole whisper to Colter, "Our lady won't wake up." Colter's answer to the problem was a tussle-and-tickle match, with Elizabeth in the middle until she cried off with a burst of laughter.

She realized he had returned and managed to slip on her wrapper while she slept. When she turned to him, his look was cherishing. "Thank you," she whispered, offering him a warm smile.

"Madam, the pleasure, I assure you, was all mine." His grin was frankly sensual, the light in his eyes wicked. She turned her attention to Nicole. "Coward," he murmured close to her ear, and laughed.

Her hair bow undone, flour smudges on her cheeks and down her cornflower blue frock, Nicole began bouncing on the bed, demolishing any semblance to neatness that Rutha had attempted. "We played, Mama. We played the bestest games. Now you come, too!" she demanded, tugging on her hand.

Colter's face loomed over Elizabeth's. "Oh, yes, *Mama,* do come and play the very bestest of games with us," he teased with a mock leer, made comic by the streak of flour across the dark of his eyebrow. Suddenly he scooped Elizabeth up into his arms and came to his knees. "What should I do with our captive now that we have her secure, princess?"

"Colter!"

"Shall we gag her to prevent her giving our secret away?" he asked Nicole, trying to contain a squirming Elizabeth. "Think quickly, or she'll get free."

"What secret?"

"We're hiding," Nicole explained, looking at her mother with frowning concentration. "We can't be mean," she told Colter.

"No meanness," he repeated, taking a firmer grip on his captive.

"I know. Feed her lots of jam an' make her sticky," she cried, clapping her small hands while wearing a smile of unholy glee.

"The jam pot it is, my lady." And to Elizabeth, he threatened, "Prepare yourself, madam, you are about to meet your fate."

Elizabeth tried hard not to laugh. She thought she managed to look sufficiently frightened.

Colter thought otherwise. "Here now, let's have a proper reaction at hearing the terrible fate that awaits you."

The very stern tone of his voice prompted her to release a wail of horror.

"We've got her! We've got her," Nicole yelled, jumping off the bed and running from the room.

Elizabeth linked her arms around Colter's shoulders. "I seem to be thanking you for so much, but this one is from my heart for giving her laughter to replace yesterday."

Colter allowed the serious turn, for the moment. "She hasn't forgotten. We talked this morning. But children will allow healing where adults cannot." He backed off the bed, holding her securely in his arms. "And now, to please my princess, I must bring you to her." But his whispers had nothing to do with childish games. The bare length of her thigh peeking from the ill-draped wrapper, the hint of shadowed cleavage, the passion swell lingering on her mouth, all caught his noted attention as he carried her out into the parlor.

The jam pot was waiting. Nicole held it clenched in her chubby hands.

Colter placed Elizabeth on the settee, smiling to see the flushed tint of her cheeks before he stepped back. He began a poor imitation of a drumroll. Nicole came forward as the notes died away and Colter backed around the settee.

Elizabeth's gaze darted between the two of them. "Surely you don't intend to allow her—"

"Princess," he said, standing behind Elizabeth, "the captive is all yours."

Nicole tried hard to look serious. Her lips pursed. The jam pot shook in her hands. A smothered giggle escaped her. Then another.

"You go first," she said to Colter.

Elizabeth screamed.

Colter whipped a plate of misshapen, charred biscuits up to her nose. Nicole thrust the jam pot into her mother's hands.

"Eat!" they both ordered at the same time.

Biscuits, jam pot and plate went flying as Nicole launched herself at Elizabeth. Colter made an attempt to save the jam pot and only succeeded in having his hand covered. When he tried to retrieve it, the jam smeared across Elizabeth's wrapper and Nicole's shoulder. Laughter erupted, biscuits crumbled, but when they were done, Elizabeth did manage to taste their efforts at baking. She heard that Rutha had threatened them with a broom to leave the kitchen, Miss Emily had chased them from the parlor when they attempted to offer her a taste of their baking effort, and even Josh had ordered them from the barn because the smell of their burned biscuits was making his mules rambunctious.

Silly smiles and bouts of giggles marked the early afternoon hours, until Nicole, happily exhausted, took a nap.

Colter sat on the wooden front porch railing as Elizabeth came out to join him. He slipped an arm around her waist and held her at his side.

"Happy?" he murmured, brushing a kiss across her hair.

"Very," she returned with a deep sigh of contentment. Elizabeth had no wish to ever let reality intrude, but his pensive look prompted her to speak. "I feel guilty that I shirked my duties by not attending work today. But even more so for not asking how long you can stay."

"I've been out here thinking while you settled Nicole for her nap," he answered, deliberately avoiding a direct response to her. "You must see after what's happened that you cannot remain here."

"But Colter—"

"Wait. Hear me out, love. I want to take you to Richmond. I know the risks, but feel remaining here where you are isolated from all help is the greater one."

"Colter, Emily will never leave her home and I can't leave her alone."

"I understand and even applaud your feelings of loyalty and caring for Emily, but I beg you to give my suggestion careful consideration."

Elizabeth angled her head to see his face. "Are you making a suggestion or giving me an order, Colter?" For a fraction of a second, she swore his jaw clenched, and when he didn't immediately answer, she repeated her query.

"If I demand it, you'll tell me that I have no right to order you. If I say it is a suggestion that holds a great deal of merit, you will agree to consider it, but never go. You present me with the devil's dilemma."

He tightened his grip around her waist and gazed down into her eyes, which were churning with storm warnings. "I have better protection to offer you and Nicole in Richmond. And," he added with an attempt at a smile, "I will likely be able to spend more time with you."

"As an added inducement, Colonel. The idea is charming." Elizabeth was hurt by her belief that he was reducing her to a role of convenient bed warmer.

"Don't play the grand dame with me, Elizabeth." With a sudden gleam in his dark eyes, he said, "Please don't twist what I meant."

"You implied—"

"I love you. Don't ever reduce what I feel for you to anything but respect and love."

"Colter, please," she whispered, cupping his cheek with one hand. "I'm sorry."

"I wish I could give you...never mind. I don't have time. I leave for Richmond within the hour," he stated impatiently. "You must decide. If you agree to go, I'll have arrangements to make. If you refuse..." He stopped himself from outwardly threatening her but knew she sensed that was what he wanted to do. This time when she pulled away from him, he let her go.

She assumed a protective pose, arms folded across her chest, head bowed and spine rigid. A flush of anger rose in Colter. *Did she feel she needed protection from him?*

Elizabeth remained turned away from him, knowing she could not voice her thoughts to Colter. He would likely be shocked at their turn. She did not question the merit of his suggestion, having decided to be generous and believe that was what he had presented. She found herself reluctant to give up her own independence. Making a move to Richmond, being under his protection, seemed a decisive step toward total dependence upon Colter. A step he would more than welcome. His motives, beyond this, were unquestionable. He would do anything to protect them, but she wondered if he had realized the exposure to gossip that this move could bring. And as unwanted as the thought was, she had to consider the fact that she might have a husband somewhere. The mere thought of James coming back into her life made her shiver. Her reluctance to discuss this with Colter stemmed from his bald announcement of his leaving within the hour. Now was not the time.

Colter had had enough. He stepped up behind her and cupped her shoulders. "Whatever it is that troubles you, Elizabeth, share it with me."

"You ask for too quick a decision."

"I have a war at my back, in case you've forgotten."

The sharp edge of his voice made her turn around to face him. "If I do, blame yourself, Colonel. You make it far too easy to forget everything."

"Why are we fighting?" he asked, drawing her close.

His soft tone disarmed her. Tension seeped from her body. "I honestly don't know. I don't want to send you away angry, but you must understand I need more time."

"Elizabeth, there's only one answer. Time is the one thing I can't grant you."

Confusion clouded her eyes and she gazed out over the barren field. "If I leave Emily, Rutha and Josh will stay with her. But I want to keep my work. I would need a place to stay, and to find someone trustworthy to care for Nicole."

"I have both," he stated.

"Both?" she asked, unconsciously condemning him with a look. When he nodded, she threw caution to the wind. "Did you plan all this before ever mentioning it to me?"

"Walk soft with your anger, love. I haven't been held accountable for my actions—"

"How well I can attest to that."

"Since I was in brace-supported trousers," he finished on a stringent note. When he saw by the stubborn set of her chin that she would not relent, Colter heaved a sigh and gave in. "Listen to me. Yes, I admit I wanted this move before the kidnapping attempt. But the reasons concern Andre, not just my own desire."

"Andre? Why? Has he a mistress and child hidden away somewhere, too?"

"Snap that tongue at me one more time, madam, and I'll show you . . . no. No," he repeated, unclenching his fingers so they were no longer gripping her. "This stops now. My friend, Andre, has fallen in love with a lovely woman, Naomi. She, like you, dearest, is rather too independent for her own good. Having you room together will serve the dual purpose of giving her a chance to work by caring for Nicole, and keeping you both under Dobie's watchful eye."

Colter refrained from mentioning Dobie could also keep watch over Hugh's wife, Jenna. He didn't wish to add an additional burden to Elizabeth just now.

"You still hesitate, Elizabeth? What more can I say? Naomi is young, but of a serious nature. She is in possession of a suite of rooms in a private home. The area is quiet and the houses modest, but—"

"Oh, hush, Colter. You sound as if you are procuring—"

"Proposing," he interjected.

"Proposing what, exactly?"

"Have I told you," he whispered, hugging her close and placing a kiss on the tip of her nose, "that I adore you when you assume that prim manner?"

"And have I told you, that your charming wiles work too well on me, Colonel?"

"You'll say yes?"

"To what?"

"To everything, love, to everything."

Chapter Sixteen

Elizabeth said yes. No matter what excuses she offered to herself and Emily, she knew she could not allow Colter to return to his war duties worrying about her and Nicole.

Making that simple admission allowed her to bring order to the whirlwind that followed their announcement.

"Shouldn't you warn this young woman—"

"Naomi," Colter supplied, carrying out Nicole's trunk to be loaded onto the wagon.

"Yes, this Naomi. Shouldn't she be told we're coming?"

"Already taken care of, love. Dobie left..." He caught himself before letting her know just when it was the Dobie left for Richmond.

"Colter."

He refused to hear the warning in her voice. "You said yes, love. It is too late to change your mind."

That was an understatement, and Elizabeth knew it. He had promptly told Nicole as soon as she showed her sleepy little face. Her excitement had kept them all at a fever pitch of activity.

Emily, she reflected as she packed the last of her own few clothes, had proved to be understanding, even going so far as to say that Colter was right in his choice.

Elizabeth swore silently that she knew exactly how the city of Richmond had felt when the Yankees were camped less than nine miles from their gates—besieged on all sides by the enemy.

But she was smiling as she joined them outside. There were hugs and kisses to give and receive, along with the promise to return for Christmas. Elizabeth avoided looking at Colter when Emily mentioned the upcoming holiday, for she knew without asking that he wouldn't be with them.

Finally Josh complained that they had to leave or he would be returning in the dark. Elizabeth was crushed between Josh and Colter on the wooden seat, with Nicole settled on Colter's lap.

She was grateful that Colter kept their child amused on the ride to the city, for she was suddenly beset by doubts about the move.

Comforting herself with Emily's parting words that she could come back if these arrangements proved unsuitable, Elizabeth shook off her dour mood. Colter gave Josh the directions and she was pleasantly surprised when he turned onto Franklin Street and guided the team down a narrow alley. Steps led up to a garden gate, and above the high retaining wall she glimpsed the brick two-story house.

"Nicole will have a yard to play in," Colter remarked, lowering his daughter to Josh's waiting arms. He jumped down and, with his hands on Elizabeth's waist, swung her off the wagon. "And you'll be able to watch her, since the lower floor contains your rooms."

Nervous, Elizabeth nodded, busy fussing with Nicole's bonnet and then with her own. Josh had already opened the gate, and Elizabeth looked up into the yard where two great sycamores and a magnolia tree offered shade.

Colter took hold of her hand and with his other lifted Nicole into his arms. He smiled and squeezed Elizabeth's hand. "You won't regret this, I promise."

Josh followed them with one small trunk as Colter led them through the well-tended garden to the back door. At his knock, Dobie opened it and stood aside to let them enter.

High ceilings for coolness, bare plaster walls trimmed with mahogany moldings, and a wide central staircase were all Elizabeth saw before Colter drew her attention to the young woman approaching them.

"Elizabeth, this is Naomi."

"An' me," Nicole piped up, staring with childish curiosity at Naomi.

"And you, princess," Colter said, unaware of the pride in his voice or the look he bestowed on his child. "This is Miss Nicole..." A hectic flush tinted his cheek and he turned away.

Elizabeth hurried to his side, realizing what he had been about to say. She was unsure of how to greet the graceful, lovely woman who watched them all with a serene expression. Was she free or a slave? Nicole, growing impatient, took the choice from her.

"Will you play with me? Can you make best honey cakes like Rua? I wanna get down," she demanded of Colter.

Naomi offered her hand to the child Colter set down. "Yes, I will play with you. But I do not know these honey cakes. Perhaps you will like my *crème brûlée,*" she suggested in a rich, liquid voice.

"What's that?"

"A sweet crème like a custard. It is my favorite treat."

"I wanna see my room."

"Nicole, we ask, not demand," Elizabeth scolded.

"Sorry, Mama. May I?"

"With your permission, madam?" Naomi asked.

Elizabeth noted there was nothing servile in either Naomi's gaze or manner. She nodded, strangely unsettled by the quadroon's poise.

"While Naomi shows Nicole her room, we can use the drawing room, Elizabeth."

He ushered her inside before she could express her vague misgivings. The room was narrow, but the careful placement of the dark mahogany furniture gave a feeling of spaciousness. A plain wooden mantel over the fireplace was graced with a gilt clock flanked by two gilt candle holders. The mirror above, also framed in gilt, reflected Elizabeth's image. Her travel dress was plain and dusty. She couldn't help but compare it to the richer cloth of Naomi's gown, although that dress had been simply adorned at the neckline, sleeve and hem with matching bands of ribbon in a muted shade of blue that complemented her bronze skin.

"You don't like her," Colter said, coming to stand behind her.

"What a foolish thing to say. I don't know her."

"But you've judged her and found some flaw that has made you uncomfortable. Because she is a woman of color?"

Elizabeth took a few steps away but kept her back toward him. "She's lovely."

"Andre believes so. Now, stop fencing with me and tell me what's wrong. I wish I could stay but I must—"

"I'm sorry, Colter. You've told me so little about her." With a slight shrug, Elizabeth turned. "I'm being foolish, and you must leave." She started toward him, but Colter was already closing the distance between them.

With a soft cry, Elizabeth held him tight.

For a moment, Colter wanted to make rash promises. He kept silent and savored the feel of her in his arms before he kissed her. When desire demanded a deepening of kiss and touch, Colter broke away.

"I'll try and come back tonight, but I can't promise that I will. And Naomi will tell you what you need to know."

"I love you. Go, and may the Lord keep you safe."

There was more Colter longed to say, but Josh was at the doorway. "Got all the belongings unloaded, Miss Elizabeth. Reckon I'll be gettin' back. Colonel, suh, will you be needin' a ride?"

"No, Josh, but before you go back I want you to..."

Elizabeth didn't hear the rest. Colter had walked out into the hallway with Josh, and she heard Nicole call him. There were no tears this time. She refused to think of his leaving at all.

Colter did not come back. Disappointed, Elizabeth did, however, try her best to become acquainted with Naomi. Nicole was completely won over, but then she was a child easily pleased by anyone who offered her attention. Elizabeth could not fault Naomi by manner or word, for she was warm and generous, as well as patient with her daughter.

Once Nicole was settled in bed, her pride and joy castle clock set in the center of the bureau, Elizabeth offered to make tea for the two of them. Naomi gently insisted that she would make a tray for them and bring it into the parlor.

The windows were hung with full lace curtains that swept the floor with their hems. A Brussels carpet in a floral pattern of blues, grays and green set the restful mood of the room. The corner cupboard was bare, but the wood gleamed from recent polishing. Elizabeth was pleased with the pianoforte set against one wall, for she loved to play and had often wished she could teach Nicole. The two settees that flanked the fireplace were upholstered in green silk brocade, and the smaller occasional chairs of carved ebony were worked in a needlepoint tapestry. A few marble-topped tables completed the room.

She didn't realize she was smiling until Naomi entered and remarked, "You find the room pleasing."

"Yes, it is charming." She watched Naomi, once more struck by the grace of every move she made.

The china service was Derby, blue bordered with gilt, and Naomi handled the delicate pieces as if she had done so all her life. Elizabeth admitted she was curious, yet good manners forbade her asking direct questions. Once more, Naomi seemed to know the direction of her thoughts.

"My father is white and was once wealthy. All my life I have been surrounded by elegance and the best that his gold could buy. Including my mother. She was his mistress and she died when I was not ready to become a woman." With a sad smile, Naomi set her cup down.

"Please, don't talk about this if it—"

"But you wish to know, do you not?" she queried in her rich voice.

There was no censure in the gaze she directed at Elizabeth. With a charming shrug of her shoulders, she said, "It is of no import to me, but to you this matters a great deal. My father lost his fortune. We traveled north to Virginia and he decided to resettle here. But when his gambling losses proved too much, he decided to use me to settle them. Andre was there and chose not to allow that to happen. He found me these rooms, provides my clothes, my food—"

"Naomi, stop, please. I have no right to pry." For a moment Elizabeth debated with herself. Honesty won.

"In a way, I believe you and I are—"

"Both very loved by two very kind gentlemen," Naomi finished for her and then freed a soft, almost natural musical laugh.

They spoke far into the night, from practical matters such as arranging schedules around Elizabeth's work hours, to sharing their concerns for the outcome of the war. By the time Elizabeth suggested they retire, she found herself almost happy that Colter had brought her here, even if she missed Emily, Rutha and Josh.

Their days fell into a pattern that provided them both with needed friendship, along with complete agreement as to the sharing of household chores. Dobie remained unobtrusive, refusing to take his meals with them, but Elizabeth learned to appreciate his escort as the Christmas season approached and Richmond grew more and more crowded.

There was a rumor that Secretary Memminger wanted to move part of his department out of Richmond. Gossip ran hot, for the idea provoked a storm of controversy. Officials argued that having the notes printed and signed in the same place reduced the chance of forgery and theft. Elizabeth was torn. She could not lose her job, but the thought of moving so far and being unable to see Colter was agony.

Both she and Naomi managed to earn a little extra money by sewing for the clothing bureau. Mrs. Galwey made the arrangements. They earned one dollar for each shirt, and four dollars for a coat that required days to complete. Food prices were soaring, so there was no choice. And when the decision came to retain the Treasury in Richmond, many heaved sighs of relief.

Emily sent Josh with an invitation to come out and stay for Christmas. Elizabeth argued with Naomi to come with them, but she refused.

"If my Andre comes, I wish to be here for him."

"But we can leave him a note," Elizabeth suggested. "Colter will likely stop there first if he is able to get home."

"Then you must take your lovely little girl and be there waiting for him."

Perhaps it was the spirit of the season that prompted Elizabeth to then extend an invitation to Jenna. But unlike Naomi, she did not mention the possibility of Hugh coming to her. She refused to leave the city so she would not miss the parties she had received invitations to.

Naomi and Nicole had decorated their parlor with boughs of pines that Dobie had taken them out to gather. Ribbon streamers lent a festive air with their bright red color. A small tree sat in one corner, trimmed with yarn bows from scraps found in an old workbasket in the pantry. Naomi, clever with a needle, had made lace flowers, and Dobie surprised them with a wooden star shining with gilt. Candles were missing from the holders, but they were expensive now and Elizabeth had to forgo buying them. As it was she paid dearly for a pair of lace-trimmed hankies to give Naomi. They had agreed that Dobie needed a new shirt, and they both had a hand in making one for him. These gifts were exchanged the afternoon of Christmas Eve when Elizabeth returned home from work.

Nicole was in a fever of excitement to leave, and there was a great deal of giggling with Naomi that ceased whenever Elizabeth approached them. By the time Josh came for them, Nicole had a covered basket that she refused to part with, and Elizabeth had wished a peaceful holiday to Naomi. Dobie was already mounted on his horse, waiting.

The air was chill and Elizabeth tucked a blanket over Nicole's legs to keep her warm. With her daughter cuddled at her side, she asked Josh about Emily and Rutha, learning they were well, but upset to hear that stragglers from both armies had been sighted close to the farmhouse.

"Took to hidin' the foodstuffs, Miss Elizabeth. Ain't tellin' when they'll come 'round to stealin'. Preacher man came by an' stayed for supper. Said folks been losin' horses, mules, pigs an' whatever else could be carried off."

"Maybe Miss Emily should reconsider coming to live with us in Richmond. It would be a little crowded, but we could manage. You all would be safer there."

"You can try talkin' to her, but I doubt she'll go."

Nicole had fallen asleep by the time they reached the farm. It was almost dusk, but Rutha came from the kitchen, laughing and crying to see them. The aroma of roasting meat drifted out into the night air as baskets were lifted and carried inside.

Once told that Miss Emily was in the front parlor, Nicole ran off to see her. Elizabeth unpacked her small contributions to their holiday meals.

"A *whole* loaf of sugar," Rutha said, smiling as she took the napkin-wrapped loaf from Elizabeth. She licked her lips and rolled her eyes, making Elizabeth laugh.

"And there's rice, white potatoes and a slab of bacon." Elizabeth looked up from the basket and reached for the one Josh was carrying inside. "Now Rutha, I don't want you to be insulted, but there are two pies in here, a gift from the young woman who cares for Nicole."

Rutha looked at them, muttering to herself as she stored them on a shelf in the pantry. Elizabeth motioned for Josh to take her brown burlap-wrapped packages. "For the tree," she whispered. At the bottom of the basket was a doll for Nicole, but she would put that out after Nicole was asleep. Hanging her cloak and bonnet on hooks near the door, she smoothed her hair and went to greet Emily.

After supper, when the gifts were beneath the tree, Elizabeth sat on the carpet by Emily's chair. Earlier, to please Nicole, they had lit the ten candles Rutha managed to make for the tree holders. Light reflected off shining tin star shapes, and red velvet bows cut from an old gown of Emily's added bright color.

"Nicole should be pleased with her new boots."

"I hope so, Emily. I paid dearly for them, but she's growing so fast, I worry what will happen this time next year. The shortages of food and clothing are no longer occasional, they are constant. I don't know how long the additional sewing Naomi and I do will last. And I've told you about the rumor to move part of the Treasury away from Richmond." With her cheek resting on Emily's knee, she sighed.

"You're thinking about Colter, aren't you?"

"The nights are long, and yes, when I am not keeping myself busy with work, I think far too much about him. This is a night of peace, but for many there is none."

"When you were a little girl, your father would take you outside on Christmas Eve, before you went to bed, and show you the brightest star."

A warmth stole through Elizabeth at Emily's mention of a forgotten childhood memory. She reached up to clasp her hand gently with her own.

"Thank you for that gift. It doesn't surprise me that he shared that with you."

"But there is a question in your voice," Emily noted softly, raising her other hand to stroke Elizabeth's head. "It wasn't easy for me to cope with missing him. No woman will miss her love the same way. But you're strong, Elizabeth. You'll manage to live through this, and when the war is over I hope that there will be a way for you and Colter to be together. He loves you so."

When she left Emily to seek her bed, Elizabeth fell asleep to the refrain, when the war is over....

All too soon, dawn broke the night sky and Nicole was whispering for her to hurry and wake. Rutha had a tray of honey cakes and cups filled with hot cider waiting as Emily joined them around the tree.

They held hands to pray, Nicole curbing her impatience when Dobie gave her a stern look. Rutha, with her rich voice, led them to sing hymns until the words of peace gave each person a measure of it.

Since Nicole's boots and porcelain doll, dressed in gay pink brocade, were unwrapped, they were the first gifts claimed, and shown off with excited cries. Emily, seated near the fireplace, cried, too, but her tears were a blend of joy and sadness when she opened the music box to the lilting tune of a waltz that she often hummed. Nicole danced and, to everyone's surprise, Dobie partnered her, restoring a happier mood. Elizabeth gave Josh a new wool jacket and Rutha a leather-bound Bible that she often wished for. When Dobie received new wool socks, he mentioned they had already given him a new shirt, but Nicole explained that she had helped her mother count the stitches to knit these for him.

Josh had made Nicole a wooden stool with her name carved above a little bird, and from Emily, who supplied the velvet, and Rutha, who sewed, Nicole had a lovely red Christmas dress with a matching bow.

Nicole had everyone sit while she gave Elizabeth her present. Opening the basket where the gift had been hidden, Elizabeth removed her little girl's first sampler. The word *mother* was stitched in uneven letters in blue thread, and on either side were fair renditions of a heart in red.

"Naomi helped me," Nicole said, standing before her mother. She anxiously watched her trace over the letters, but a smile broke when Elizabeth hugged her tight and assured her that it was beautiful, the bestest of all presents she ever had.

When it had been properly exclaimed over by all to Nicole's satisfaction, Emily announced that she had gifts for everyone from Colter. Rutha brought her the small boxes, where Emily found, to her surprise, a cameo pin for herself that Colter had asked Dobie to purchase for him. Nicole had a locket on thin red velvet ribbon to match her new dress, and Rutha and Josh had their first gold coins to treasure. For Elizabeth, there were creamy pearl-drop earrings and a note.

> *Think of me whispering I love you each time you wear these. And while I adore your delicate ears, they are not where I wish to put my ring. But someday...*
>
> Colter

Yes, my love, someday, when the war is over, she silently promised, refusing to dispel their gaiety or to allow the shadows of the past to intrude on this day.

Supper was a feast of roast turkey and Rutha's special ham, baked in a crust. Biscuits, sweet potatoes swimming in syrup, stuffing, rice spiced with a blend of herbs and for dessert, Naomi's pies along with raisin custard.

All too soon, it was time to pack and make the trip back to Richmond. Elizabeth finally gave up hope that

Colter would come. But as she gathered her gifts from her room, she gazed at the bed where he had loved her and once again sent out her thoughts, wishing him peace wherever he was.

Candles burned in the windows of the homes they rode past. Sometimes voices were raised in song, or the merry tunes being played on pianos and fiddles reached them. But as they neared what Elizabeth now thought of as home, the house was dark.

Thinking that Naomi had retired early, she wasn't alarmed. But once Dobie had carried their gifts and baskets inside, Elizabeth was struck by a sense of emptiness. Naomi's room was empty, the bed unslept in and, on her own, she found a note.

Word has come that my Andre has been wounded. I have gone to care for him.

"Dobie, Dobie," she called, running through the hall. "Naomi is gone." She showed him the note, realizing too late that Dobie couldn't read. Ignoring his embarrassment, she told him its brief contents. "She cannot travel alone. If only we knew when she learned of this. You've got to find her."

"I can't be leaving you or—"

"Dobie!" Livid, Elizabeth's voice sliced across his. "Naomi is lovely, young and Negro. She will be at the mercy of any white man that accosts her." Rubbing her head, she tried to think. "First we must find out how she would try to travel. Why didn't she come with us? We could have helped her."

"Ain't no sense in gettin' yourself all fretted. If you promise to stay put, I'll see what I can find out."

"The hotel, Dobie. Go to the hotel. There will be officers there. Maybe they know what happened. And hurry. I..." Elizabeth couldn't put her fear into words, and Dobie, thankfully, didn't wait.

Chapter Seventeen

An exhausted Dobie returned midmorning. He shook his head at Elizabeth's questions. "Nothing," he said in a flat voice. "No one saw her, and I couldn't find out where she had gotten the news."

Elizabeth offered him a cup of coffee and some of the leftovers that Rutha had packed for them. Dobie ate, and Elizabeth paced.

"Dobie, I need to go to work. It's not only that I worry about keeping my job, but perhaps there I could find out some news. Would you watch Nicole?"

"I reckon I can."

An idea began to form, but she wasn't ready to share it with him. "I may be late returning this afternoon. I have someone to see who may be able to help us find out what happened to Naomi."

At work, after she made her late excuse and was docked the time, Elizabeth learned that the smallpox was worse. To her disappointment, Jenna was not there, nor did she appear.

She smiled with those women who had been reunited with family members and commiserated with those who had not.

When Mrs. Marstand came to collect her finished stack of signed notes the first time, Elizabeth paid no attention to her recounting them again before she moved away. But the second time it happened, she questioned her about what was wrong.

"Over a hundred notes were discovered missing on Christmas Eve. With everyone in a rush to get to their families, only a few of us stayed to make a final count."

"But surely you don't believe—"

"I have my instructions, Elizabeth, and no one is above suspicion. The stolen notes could be used to create forgeries, weakening our Treasury. The theft could also be by someone who was in desperate need and wanted to make the holiday an occasion of joy. I do not know."

But Elizabeth noticed that the woman glared more than once at Jenna's empty chair. It firmed her decision to visit the hotel where Jenna had a room. After all, the woman could be ill. But she knew that was a flimsy excuse.

The streets were crowded, and on corners anger rode in men's and women's voices as they damned Lincoln's coming proclamation to free the slaves. News spread quickly that a parade would be held in celebration for the Negroes in Yankee-held Norfolk. And as she hurried along, she heard the pride rise in voices that shouted what President Davis's answer would be: hang any Yankee officer captured as high as John Brown, and in the next battle, an order for no prisoners to be taken.

There were arguments about whether England and France would take the South's side, rumors that the

North was ready to sue for peace. But others discounted this gossip, stating that the Northern armies were still in Virginia, near Suffolk, where they marched toward Petersburg but turned back when a spy who declared they could take the city was not believed. The Yankees were still camped opposite Fredericksburg, and even as some mentioned a great victory in Tennessee that General Bragg had won, others countered that, as usual, it would lead to nothing.

And Elizabeth wondered where Colter was.

By the time she reached the hotel, Elizabeth was aching, for the bitter cold of winter was making itself felt. The lobby was warm and filled with a milling group of men and women. She had to wait her turn to question the harried desk clerk.

"Mrs. Hugh Morgan, could you tell me if she is in her room?" Elizabeth clasped her reticule tight as he turned to survey the rows of neatly numbered boxes behind him.

"Sorry, ma'am, her key is here."

"May I wait in—"

"You're welcome," he rudely cut her off, turning to the next gentleman in line. "May I help you, sir?"

About to demand his attention, Elizabeth changed her mind. She found a place in the far corner where she could watch the comings and goings of people through the lobby doors and listened to snatches of conversations that reflected much of the talk she had heard on the way here. When the light outside began to fade, she knew she could not wait any longer. As it was, she would need to hurry to be home before dark.

She approached the clerk again, asking for a pen and paper, intending to leave a note for Jenna. After several false starts, she crumpled the paper and left.

By the time she arrived home she was dispirited, but Dobie offered a bit of hope when he announced that he would go down to the rail station again.

Nicole added prayers for Naomi to her bedtime ritual, and Elizabeth managed to tell her a story before she went to sleep.

For herself, she paced and sat and paced again, all the while thinking of what Mrs. Marstand had told her. She knew that Jenna was the thief, but Elizabeth hated to make the accusation. Once again, she thought of Colter and his friendship for Hugh. But there was no way to rationalize the harm Jenna could do if she was forging treasury notes.

Elizabeth had thought often of turning back time; now, she only wished she had told Colter of her suspicions regarding Jenna.

By the time a discouraged Dobie returned, it was long past midnight. He sought his bed, as she did hers, each hoping that tomorrow would bring word about Naomi.

Jenna's place remained empty, and when Elizabeth noted that yet another woman's chair was unfilled as the day wore on, she was told the woman's son was injured in a fight that had broken out between soldiers and those they called "bombproofs." The son was one of many young men who filled Richmond, kept out of the war by influence or purchase of a detail. They had earned the contempt of many. With reports of winter snows blanketing the hills of Virginia, tempers were hot. Their soldiers were ill clad to bear the cold.

As she worked, enduring the repeat of yesterday's recounting of notes by Mrs. Marstand, Elizabeth's thoughts strayed from concern over Naomi to worry about Colter. She touched her earrings, renewing her faith that he would be safe and warm somewhere and assured that she thought constantly of him.

Before she left work, Elizabeth asked Mrs. Marstand if she had word from Jenna.

"No. I believe she mentioned visiting a friend's family for the holiday, but I cannot recall if she mentioned where."

Far from reassured, Elizabeth once again visited the hotel. When informed that Jenna's key was still in her box, she demanded that the clerk accompany her to Jenna's room, expressing her fear that she might be ill and no one aware of it.

With less than gracious manner, he led the way.

Elizabeth tapped her foot impatiently while he knocked repeatedly, but when he moved from the door without attempting to open it, she grabbed the key from his hand.

"Ma'am, I cannot allow—"

"If Mrs. Morgan is ill and in bed, your presence will be most improper. Mine will not."

The room was small and the light dim. Elizabeth barely glanced at the unmade bed. She opened the wardrobe and was surprised to see that Jenna's clothes filled it. A quick check of the bureau drawers showed them to contain all that was proper. It was obvious that Elizabeth had been wrong in her belief that Jenna had left the city and did not intend to return.

The clerk's impatience allowed her no more time, and reluctantly Elizabeth returned the key and watched him lock the door.

That night followed a repeat of the last, with Dobie returning after midnight again without a clue to where Naomi had gone.

New Year's Day they rode out together to visit with Emily, where Elizabeth explained all that had happened and confessed her suspicions about Jenna.

"I can understand your desire to protect Colter and Hugh, Elizabeth," Emily said when she was done, "but in this case, you might consider your own association with her. I know you are guiltless, but would this Mrs. Marstand believe that?"

"Why wouldn't she? I've never given anyone cause to think I..." Elizabeth stopped herself and remembered the first week of Jenna's working with her. How many times had she covered up the mistakes Jenna made? Didn't she know of Jenna's disposing of ruined notes? If they ever were ruined.

"Yes, my dear, I believe your thoughts are following mine."

"Emily, what am I going to do? Without Jenna I cannot prove my innocence."

"Perhaps adopting a wait-and-see position would be best for now. When Jenna returns, and by indication of her belongings in the hotel room she must, you should consider a direct confrontation. My dear, no one need know the outcome but yourself. And by then you may feel ready to make a decision."

As far as a temporary solution went, Elizabeth knew she had no alternative.

The days of early January dragged for her. The winter was bitter with rain and cold, and Nicole, housebound, had nearly driven Dobie to the end of his patience. Elizabeth missed the warm companionship of Naomi, needed Colter and faced each day as if it were the one that would snap her own temper.

General Lee came to the city, and once again the Yankees, under General Burnside, began to stir in their camps across the river.

Elizabeth did not bother to listen to the rumors that there was a falling out between the Confederate generals Longstreet and Jackson. She feared the news that followed a few days later of the Yankees trying to move down river. There were more than sighs of relief when it was learned that the wagons and guns the Yankees attempted to move had mired in the mud.

And still no word came from Colter.

Nor did Jenna return.

The house remained empty of Naomi's warm presence. As if her nerves were not strung tight enough, Elizabeth faced yet another blow. Dobie had been ordered to return to active duty.

"It's my own fault. All this questioning about Naomi brought the wrong kind of attention to me. I've been ordered to help the construction of more defensive positions outside the city."

Elizabeth merely nodded and listened to his brief explanation of how Colter had rescued him from serving time in a guardhouse. And while he regretted having to leave her before the colonel returned and made other arrangements, he was a soldier who had to follow orders.

"When do you report, Dobie?"

"Tomorrow. But if it's any help, I won't go until you return from work."

"Won't that cause trouble for you?"

"No, ma'am. And it will give you time to tell them at work. Maybe then we'll have heard from Naomi."

Elizabeth no longer held on to that hope, but Dobie didn't deserve to carry her burden. "You mustn't worry about us. I'll return to Emily's."

"Now, you know the colonel—"

"Dobie," she interrupted, "as you mentioned, the colonel isn't here. I cannot support myself and my child unless I work. We'll be safe. I know we will."

Elizabeth packed their belongings that night. Dobie promised to get a message to Josh to bring the wagon for them.

Elizabeth had one last chore to do. She sat down to pen two notes to Colter. But as she began to write, her fear and yearning to see him became an emotional outpouring that quickly covered several sheets of paper. When she was done, her hand was trembling, her fingers curled stiff around the steel pen, and she had nearly used up her ink supply.

Without reading it over, she tore the sheets into bits and began again, this time ordering her thoughts to be brief.

My dearest Colter, the extent of Andre's wounds are not known, but Naomi has gone somewhere to fetch him. I have returned to Emily, since Dobie is recalled to duty and I have had no word from Naomi. We have missed you.

There was temptation to add more, but in the end she merely signed her name.

She copied this onto a fresh sheet, folded them both and set one on the mantel in the drawing room, the other in her reticule to be delivered to his hotel room.

Morning came far too quickly, but she stole a bit of Nicole's excitement that they were going back to Miss Emily to carry her through the day.

Before she began to work, Elizabeth secured permission to leave early, thankful that Mrs. Marstand appeared far too distracted to question her. But she didn't forget to remind her that she would forfeit her pay.

Elizabeth worked quickly and quietly, constantly watching the slow crawling hands of the clock. Now that she had made her decision, she was anxious to have it done.

The cold bit through her cloak as she began her walk. Broadsides littered the streets, and while waiting for a lumbering wagon to pass so she could cross the street, she glanced down to read the glaring black headline proclaiming Freedom to Slaves! Across another, someone had scrawled Never! Elizabeth shivered more from the sentiment than the cold. Her family had not owned slaves; their small shipping concern had offered a comfortable support for all of them. After her father's death, her half-brothers had taken over the three cargo ships. One had been lost at sea, taking her brother's life, the other she believed had been confiscated by the Union forces, and the fate of the third had never been revealed to her.

Once again a series of shivers attacked her. Alma had seen to the disposition of the third ship, just as she had stepped in to sell their home. Caught by grief and forced to make hurried decisions, Elizabeth had never once questioned Alma after she agreed to marry James.

She walked around the outskirts of Capitol Square, where gentlemen were gathered in groups discussing the latest news from General Lee. Flour now being sold for almost seventy dollars. Voices rose in protest over scandalously high prices. Yet another group spoke loudly about the chance for profit in blockading or speculating in tobacco; one man bragged of his earning fifteen thousand dollars by margining a purchase of five thousand pounds.

Elizabeth took all this in but kept herself removed from the news.

Heated arguments erupted over President Davis's desire to be given the same powers that Lincoln had. He wanted the courts to grant him the right to suspend the writ of habeas corpus. But if the men who shouted about states' rights had their way, she knew he would never be granted this or any other power that could centralize his government.

With all this talk it surprised her to see women with their wide skirts taking a leisurely promenade, or little children being cared for by their nurses. Elizabeth continued on her way, avoiding the residential streets that had white banners flying to show there was smallpox.

When she finally reached the hotel, she straightened her shoulders, lifted her head high and stepped inside. She was thankful the lobby was empty, for she had not forgotten the curious looks she received as an unescorted woman. The clerk behind the counter was not the same man who had been there previously. When she approached him he was busy reading *The Richmond Dispatch.*

"I would like to leave a message for Colonel Saxton."

He held out his hand without glancing up from his paper.

"No, I do not wish this to be left in his box. I want his room number," Elizabeth explained.

"You and everyone else," he muttered in a bored voice. "Third floor, left hall, corner room."

Elizabeth puzzled over his remark. Who else had asked for Colter? She couldn't question him, but thought, strangely, of Jenna. "Is Mrs. Hugh Morgan's key still in her box?"

Annoyance marked his face as he closed the paper, a finger holding his place, to glance behind him. "Gone."

"Thank you." The words were sharp and curt, but she doubted that he heard her, for he was already engrossed in his reading as she headed for the stairs.

There was no one about but a maid on the third floor. Elizabeth saw the woman stop to watch her as she made her way down the hall to Colter's room.

She ignored her own embarrassment at what the woman likely thought. She knew she was not keeping an assignation. She took the folded note from her reticule and bent to slip it under the door. From inside, she heard the sound of a drawer close.

She froze for a moment, glancing back down the hall, but the maid was gone. Slowly she straightened, her breath trapped inside for a second then rushing out just as her heartbeat increased.

Had Colter returned? Was he inside the room?

She did not understand the sudden caution that beset her. Instead of calling out or knocking, she reached for the doorknob and turned it, lifting the inside latch. The tiny sound was loud to her ears and she knew, although she had yet to open the door, that whoever was inside was not Colter. All movement had ceased.

Thievery was not unheard of, and Colter had been away for weeks. She summoned enough courage to partially open the door.

The heavy draperies had been drawn tight across the windows, leaving the room in darkness. But the scent of a recently snuffed candle wafted out on a draft of air to her. She took a step through the doorway and stopped, allowing her vision time to adjust to the dark. A four-poster bed without a canopy took up the far wall. The vague outline of a large wardrobe against the wall to her right caught her attention for a moment. The doors were closed, but she eyed it suspiciously, thinking it would make an excellent hiding place, being one of Nicole's favorites when they played.

Elizabeth pushed the door to the room open slowly until it met the wall behind it. She sighed softly, thankful no one was hiding behind it to jump out at her. She took two small steps into the room and slowly made a turn, seeing a bureau and a writing desk, which was set between the windows. One of the drawers was partially opened.

Caution thrown aside, she went to the desk and opened the drawer. Someone had been searching. The papers were shoved in a haphazard manner that Colter, she knew as well as she knew herself, would never allow. Even the top of the desk was littered with post, some of it opened.

Anger replaced fear. Colter's mail should have been held in his box until he returned to claim it.

The thought of her own emotional outpouring, had she not torn it up and rewritten it, being read by a stranger brought a churn of nausea. With shaking fingers, she reached for the drapery behind the desk and yanked it open. Gray light filtered into the room.

The soft click of the latch closing behind her made her spin around.

Chapter Eighteen

"Jenna!" Elizabeth grabbed hold of the desk behind her for support. "What are you doing in here?"

"I might ask the same of you," she returned in a voice of utter calm, leaning against the door and watching Elizabeth.

"I've come to—" Elizabeth stopped herself from defending her reason for being here. She was unsettled by Jenna's unconcerned manner. "I do not believe I owe you an explanation." With an attempt to match the other woman's demeanor, Elizabeth walked to the opposite window and drew aside the heavy drapery, flooding the room with light. Turning once more to face Jenna, she gestured to the desk. "Why were you searching it?"

Jenna smiled, but there was no warmth in her eyes. "Like you, Elizabeth, I don't wish to explain. But you are forgetting the colonel is my husband's commanding officer."

"Jenna, I'm tired of your lies. If you think to play me for a fool, I beg you to reconsider the thought. You have no right to search this room, you have no right to be in it. And if you think I will not inform Colonel

Saxton of your being here when he returns, then it is you who plays the fool."

"My, my, the little mouse has courage."

Elizabeth curled her fingers tight to prevent her from giving in to the urge to slap her face silly. Jenna's soft laugh sent her blood up. "Perhaps you would like to explain your presence to one of the officers at the War Department."

"And you're catty, too." With a careless shrug, Jenna came away from the door. "Stop making idle threats to me. If I am questioned you can be sure I'll expose your part in all this."

"My part?" Elizabeth almost choked on the words but recalled Emily's warning of the very same. "Dear Lord, it is true. You're spying for the Yankees."

Jenna neither denied nor confirmed it as she prowled around the room.

"Where have you been, Jenna?"

"That's of no import to you." Coming to the desk, Jenna scattered papers until she found the one she wanted. Holding the folded missive, she turned to face Elizabeth.

"How did you manage to get Colter's mail?" she demanded of Jenna, thoroughly incensed.

"Colter, is it?" Jenna asked with a curious lift of her brow. "My, we are on friendly terms with the colonel, aren't we?"

"Stop it, Jenna. You're insulting. And attempting to distract me won't work. Now, tell me how you got hold of his mail."

"Hasn't anyone told you that scowling will age you, dear?" Jenna chided, but when Elizabeth stepped forward, she hastened to add, "Oh, very well. I merely flirted a bit with the clerk, and when he bent to pick up a dropped package, I removed the packet from his box." With a mocking look that swept Elizabeth from head to toe, she remarked, "Men are rather easy to manipulate, if you know how."

"I'm sure it is a skill you have perfected, Jenna. For myself, I have never cared to manipulate anyone. And I believe this conversation is going nowhere. You have no intention of telling me why you're here. I will draw my own conclusions and act accordingly."

Elizabeth started for the door and turned once more. "For your sake, I hope you are rid of those notes you stole. Mrs. Marstand is suspicious of you."

"Warning the enemy, Elizabeth? How charming of you. But you see, I've grown tired of all this Virginia politeness and being brave, along with having to work for a pittance. Don't worry your pretty little head over me."

"I am not concerned for you at all, Jenna. I was thinking of your husband risking his life, while you betray everything he is fighting for."

Elizabeth waited, hoping for a sign that Jenna felt some remorse. The woman began tapping the letter she held against her open palm, studying Elizabeth.

"Before you leave, you should read this, Mrs. Waring."

Elizabeth paled. In her confusion of hearing Jenna use her married name, she took the letter from her and turned blindly for the door.

"No, don't leave. Read it here, Elizabeth."

"Why?"

"Just read it."

Elizabeth unfolded the letter without looking at it. For a moment, she thought she spied compassion in Jenna's eyes, but knew she had been mistaken when a cold smile creased her lips. Elizabeth began to read the letter.

December 12, 1862

To Colonel Colter W. Saxton, C.S.A.
Richmond, Virginia
Please accept my apology for the delay in answering your request as to the whereabouts of James Waring. I have just this week returned to active duty after being wounded, and received post forwarded from the secretary.

Under the circumstances surrounding the losses at Shiloh, what you have asked might well have been an impossible task. Far too many of our soldiers lost their lives, but none haunts my memory as does James Waring.

I will not attempt to recall the details for you. On the night of April 5th, after day-long skirmishes between our forces under the command of General Albert Johnston against the Union forces led by Grant, James Waring proved himself to be that most detestable of men, a coward. By my own witness, he was shot down by men under his most immediate command when he attempted to run before the coming battle.

It grieves me to report this to you, since you have professed close friendship with this party. To further answer your query, I myself wrote to the family, notifying them of his death and asking what arrangements they wished to make. No reply was received. There is an unmarked grave in the tangled brush on a small hill; I believe his body is there. It also may interest you to know there is rumored to be a widow and child, but it is not my providence to verify this.

Very respectfully,
Your obedient servant,
Lieut. G. Beauregard, C.S.A.

"It's true, isn't it?" Jenna asked.

Elizabeth continued to stare at the letter she held, tears streaming down her face, unaware that she had cried out. James, poor James, to have lived beneath Alma's strong hand and now in death to be branded a coward.

"You had no idea that your husband was dead?"

Elizabeth glanced up and shook her head, feeling the wetness of her tears. She fumbled in her reticule for a linen hankie, turning away until she composed herself.

"What will you do, Elizabeth?"

"Do?" she repeated, facing Jenna. She couldn't seem to order her thoughts. A strange calm overtook her, one that left her blessedly numb.

Jenna moved to the wardrobe and opened the door. From the top shelf, she removed a decanter of bourbon and two glasses. "I don't know about you, but I am in need of a drink." She poured out full tumblers for each and handed one to Elizabeth. "Drink it down. You're as white as the bed linen."

With a tremoring hand, Elizabeth reached for the extended glass. She felt as if the blood had drained from her body. After her first sip of liquor, she felt a surging force, almost like a sudden storm, bringing flashes of Alma's grief-stricken face before her. The grief had been real, but the rest was lies...lies that had tormented her. All this time, Alma had known that James was dead.

Elizabeth closed her eyes, unable to bear her own thoughts, fighting now against the memories that were returning against her will to batter her.

"No. No!" she cried out, spilling the drink in her hand.

"Stop it," Jenna ordered, coming to her side and slapping her face. "Do you want every damn gray-coat in the place to come rushing in here?"

"You don't know," Elizabeth moaned, losing control. "You don't know what she did to me."

"And I don't want to."

"She nearly destroyed me. She tried to take away my child."

"A child?" Jenna repeated. With a shrewd look, she took the glass from Elizabeth and finished it herself. The burn of the liquor eased her pain. The loss of her child was not a lie. Jenna shook her head. She couldn't allow herself to get caught up in the past. Glancing around the room, she shrugged at the disarray and set the glass down on the desk. Tomorrow she had to leave Richmond. At the door, she turned back to look at Elizabeth.

"Come with me. We can't stay here any longer." But she had to go and take hold of her arm, since Elizabeth appeared to be incapable of moving on her own. Closing the door, Jenna saw the hallway was empty.

Elizabeth hung back. "Tell me, did you find that letter in Colter's desk or the packet of mail you stole?"

"I didn't steal his mail. Stealing implies the taking and not returning. I merely borrowed it for a short time. But the letter was in the packet," she snapped, stung by the accusation and unwilling to ask herself why she bothered to answer her. Voices coming from the direction of the stairwell alarmed her. "Come to my room, Elizabeth. We can't wait here."

"No. I must see Alma. She tried to have Nicole taken and she won't stop until she has her. But she has no right. I have proof of that now."

"Well, you can't go traipsing all over Richmond alone at night." Almost dragging Elizabeth down the hall with her, Jenna pushed open her door.

"Not Richmond. Petersburg. I've got to go to Petersburg."

"The Union forces are down there. Oh, damn you! Get inside. Why I should even think of helping you, I don't know."

Elizabeth went with her simply because she could not find the strength to argue.

"Give them the wagon and mules, Josh," Emily ordered.

"But Miz Elizabeth's waitin'—"

"And you heard Captain Halleck explain they have wounded men to transport." Emily glanced at the mounted patrol of Confederate soldiers. Four men rode double with the injured men held in an upright position in front of them.

"If you've blankets to spare, ma'am, they'd be mighty 'preciated."

Shivering beneath her light shawl, Emily turned to Rutha. "You heard the captain. Find all we can spare." Emily knew he was merely being polite by asking and would not hesitate to take what he needed for himself or his men.

Muttering to himself, Josh stalked off to the barn as a grumbling Rutha slipped back inside the house.

"Don't suppose you'd have a little something to warm a man's innards, ma'am?"

"Liquor, Captain?"

"Be fine, if you do." But he was sniffing the aroma that drifted out from the open kitchen door.

Emily thought of Colter's bottle of bourbon and swore silently to herself. She would give him the spirits, but that kettle of venison stew would have fed them for three days. No matter how small the portions, it would barely divide to feed all these men. But even as she turned to call out to Rutha to fetch the liquor, she thought of Colter stopping at some farm, hungry, and asking for something to eat while his stomach rumbled like the captain's.

"You and your men are welcome to share what little we have."

They refused to come inside, so Rutha continued her muttering under her breath while she filled bowls and cups with stew and carried them outside. Josh followed behind her, dispensing the last of their real coffee. But by the time they were done serving, they, too, remembered Colter, and wore smiles as praise was generously offered for the makeshift meal.

"I'll make sure your wagon and mules are returned, ma'am," the captain said, once they were mounted and his wounded men made comfortable in the wagon bed.

Emily doubted she would ever see them again. She dismissed the idea of telling him that they were the property of a colonel. Once the wagon and mules reached Richmond, someone would have need of them and likely not care who had owned them.

"You do that, Captain. And if I may ask a favor in return, could you give a message to my niece? She resides on Franklin Street and was coming for a visit."

"Be happy to, ma'am."

Emily made the message brief and wished them all well. Following Rutha and Josh into the kitchen, she latched the door and faced their reproachful stares.

"Now, you two know I had no choice. At least by giving them the wagon and mules and sharing food with them, they didn't take anything."

"An' Miz Elizabeth's waitin' for me," Josh reminded her.

"I know. I can only trust that the captain will keep his word and deliver the message to her. And as much as I dislike asking, Mister Josh, you'll have to walk to the city tomorrow. I should have asked them to take you with them."

"Be a heap glad you didn't. I wasn't 'bout to ride with them."

"An' he don't like bein' out in this dark, Miz Emily," Rutha stated.

"Well, then, it's settled," Emily answered in a brisk voice. "Tomorrow you'll leave at first light. And I pray that Elizabeth realizes something prevented you from fetching her."

"Miz Beth ain't no chil'. She ain't gonna do no fool thing an' risk hurtin' that sweet chil'," Rutha said, scraping the last of the stew from the kettle to fill three bowls.

"You're right, Rutha. Elizabeth is a sensible young woman."

Being sensible at this moment did not enter into Elizabeth's mind. Her whole being was consumed with confronting Alma Waring. It was the only thought she had in mind as she made her way home from the hotel. Her head ached from the constant questions she asked herself, and the lack of answers. Her control was hanging by a slim thread, and it almost broke when she walked into the house and saw Dobie's haversack near the door and no sign of Josh waiting for her.

Nicole rushed to her side, telling her what she already knew. Dobie had to leave and Josh wasn't here. But she was surprised that Dobie questioned where she had been.

"Working," she snapped. "We are shorthanded." But she couldn't look at him or understand why she lied.

"Can't rightly figure what happened to Josh. Know he got my message."

"How can you be sure?" she asked, managing to speak calmly.

"Farm up the road from Miss Emily's, 'bout four or five miles, raises hogs an' the corporal heading up the detail promised he'd see to it. Wasn't more than three or four hours ago that he stopped by."

"Maybe a mule went lame or he lost a wheel. Don't worry, Dobie."

"Can't help that, but I can't wait any longer."

She held out her hand and then flung her arms around his neck, giving him a quick hug. Stepping back, she warned him to take good care of himself.

"I will. And I'll try to come by and see you all."

"We'll miss you, Dobie," she said, holding Nicole at her side, knowing that she wouldn't be there if he did manage to come.

Dobie hunkered down before Nicole. "You won't be forgetting all I taught you, will you?"

"No," she said, shaking her head.

He caught her small chin with a gentle hold, ignoring the quiver of her lips. "You're a real brave girl, but I'll be needing a big smile to take with me."

Nicole tried but couldn't quite give him a real smile. She, too, flung her small arms around his neck, clinging tightly to him, until he removed her arms and stood up.

"Tell the colonel—"

"I'll explain," she cut in, anxious for him to go. "And don't worry about us."

He picked up his sack and with a curt nod, he left.

"Mama, we're all alone now."

Elizabeth stared down at her daughter but didn't see her. She knew what she had to do to buy peace and a future for her daughter, herself and Colter. What she had not counted on was having Nicole with her.

"Have you had your supper, Nicole?"

"Yes, Mama. Mister Dobie an' me together."

"Good. I want you to go to sleep because in the morning at first light we are going to take a trip."

"To Miss Emily's?"

"No, precious. We're going on the train. To see someone who..." Elizabeth stopped, shaking her head.

"It doesn't matter. But I need you to be very good for me."

"A train? I never had a ride on one."

"No. No, you never did." She rushed Nicole through her bedtime, impatient tonight, for she had to wait for Jenna and the passes she had promised to secure should the need arise for Elizabeth and Nicole to pass through the Yankee lines.

A fleeting thought crossed her mind that either Jenna was an excellent forger or the city of Richmond played host to more Northern spies than anyone was aware of.

She paced the length of the hall as she waited and finally considered the danger she was placing both herself and Nicole in. But a devil's voice nagged at her, promising that if she confronted Alma and all the lies of the past that had twisted her life, she would be free.

Free to love Colter without a hint of shame. Free to have him claim Nicole as his daughter. Free of the terrible guilt she carried for never having loved James, for she had finally come to understand that he had merely been Alma's pawn.

When Jenna arrived, she refused to come in. Their conversation was hushed. Elizabeth took the papers and before she had thanked Jenna or asked what she intended to do, the woman was gone.

Elizabeth closed the door, and knew that a mental door latched at the same time. If Jenna left Richmond, Elizabeth vowed to keep silent about what she knew.

Too restless to sleep, she packed a basket of food to see them through the day, for she had no intention of spending more time than she needed with Alma.

With this single-minded purpose driving her, she sat and waited for morning. In the pale dawn light, Elizabeth bundled up her sleepy child and left the house.

Under the same overcast sky, Josh, wrapped in the quilt Emily insisted he take to wear over his wool jacket, began his long walk into Richmond to get Elizabeth and Nicole.

Chapter Nineteen

At the northern edge of Richmond, a bone-weary Colter paused at a stream to let his exhausted hunter drink while he filled his tin cup and offered it first to Naomi and then to Andre. He took none for himself and glanced back to see that she held Andre secure before he started walking his horse into the city.

He blamed himself that Andre was wounded, for they had had no sleep for days, and then sleep had betrayed them.

He could hardly focus his mind on the day he had left Elizabeth, fully intending to return once he reported to the War Office. But the orders waiting left him without the chance to see her again. Andre and Brice were already in position by the time he joined them at Longstreet's headquarters on the left wing of General Lee's command on Marye's Hill.

All of the information they had gathered nearly six weeks before had proven true. Brice had filled him in on the positions of the Mississippi riflemen who had been posted in cellars, behind stone walls and at every point where a man could be sheltered on the south bank to pick off the Yankees that tried to lay the bridges that Burnside needed to make his crossing. As General Lee predicted, they hadn't been able to hold them off long, but it was noon before the bridges were completed. Burnside then bombarded the town of Fredericksburg, but the sharpshooters clung to their hiding places and when the Yankee engineers tried to resume their work on another set of bridges they were destroyed by their murderous fire.

The battle, as Brice retold it, saw wave after wave of Yankees shot down until the fields were littered with their bodies.

The cost totaled a little more than two Yankees for every Confederate soldier killed. But information was needed concerning what the Yankees intended to do next. The three donned Yankee uniforms and went across the river to gather what intelligence they could. A truce was declared to allow the Yankees to bury their dead, but the night was bitterly cold.

Tension ran high throughout the ranks, for the sky was lit with a stunning display of northern lights. Andre repeated to Colter and Brice what he had overheard the Confederate soldiers saying. They believed the skies were setting off fireworks to help them celebrate their victory, but then another claimed it couldn't be; they were northern lights, after all. Brice managed a laugh, but Colter could not. The sounds of dying soldiers seemed to rise up from woods and field and flay him with their moans. The useless slaughter of men sickened him.

He recalled General Lee's words when told of the Union losses along with his own. "It is well that war is so terrible, or we should grow too fond of it."

They made their way stealthily into the streets of Fredericksburg, and they listened as small groups of men milled about, paying no attention to the three Yankee infantrymen.

"It was the constant rattle of musketry that unsettled our troops."

"The Thirteenth New Hampshire regiment showed their mettle to those rebels. They crossed that railroad into a swamp down to Hazel Run—"

"Yes," another interrupted, "and the damn rebels opened fire when we came up out of the ravine till we could smell the powder from their muskets and had to fall back."

"Be thankful you lived to do so," Brice muttered to himself as they were safely past them.

Colter led them down to Caroline Street in the center of the city. Most of the houses lining the street were filled with wounded, for the residents had flown toward the Confederate forces for safety.

From a doorway, several Union officers appeared and Colter ducked into an alley with Brice and Andre close behind.

"I'd like to take one of them back with us," Colter murmured softly as they watched the five men.

"Any special rank, *mon ami?*"

"Don't joke, Andre."

"Never. Brice, guard our colonel," he whispered, and silently disappeared down the alley.

"Go after him," Colter ordered Brice, wishing that Hugh had not been sent to aid General Bragg in Kentucky. Andre was reckless, Hugh a sobering force who could sometimes control him.

Colter managed to make out the ranks of five men as they drew abreast of the alley where he hid. Colter thought the captain of an artillery regiment would serve his purpose.

As they walked past he flattened his body against the wall so that the shadows sheltered him. He had used the ploy of messenger with success before and had no reason to think it would fail him this time. Colter began to count, allowing the others time to get a ways up the street from him before he ran after them. He used the soot from the building brick to blacken his face and hands a bit, pulled the peak of his cap forward to shield his face and started to make his move.

Andre called out drunkenly from an opposite alley and charged into the group of men.

A few good-natured curses rose and then Brice, seemingly coming to rescue his drunken friend, who was offering a maudlin song, managed to isolate the very officer that Colter wanted. Praying for the few seconds' grace they needed to succeed, Colter slid free his knife and slipped up behind them.

He never knew what gave them away.

The captain shouted, "Rebels!" Shots were fired. Brice shoved the artillery captain at Colter, yelling for him to run, they would hold them off.

With his knife at the captain's throat, Colter jammed his knee in the man's back and got him moving. He had to force himself not to look back. He had to remember his mission took precedence over friendship. But another volley of shots rang out as he headed for the picket line stationed at the pontoon bridge farthest from the city.

Colter's luck held. He brought his prisoner back to the Confederate lines, but he didn't wait around to hear praise from Longstreet or Lee since the captain was carrying an order for the renewal of battle the next day. Colter went back for Brice and Andre in the captured captain's uniform.

He spent most of the night hearing varied recountings of the escapade. They had escaped. How, the Yankees didn't know, but he himself had been commandeered to help in a house-by-house search for the rebels. Dawn was about to break the night sky when Colter decided he had to get back or risk capture. Taking the opposite route of his earlier escape, he stumbled upon an ice house. If his senses had not been trained to detect the slightest sound, he would have missed finding Andre and Brice.

They were nearly frozen from an attempt to swim the river. Andre had the more serious wounds—a gash in his thigh and a miniball lodged in his shoulder. With a flesh wound in his side, Brice had managed to drag his friend to the ice house.

On the outskirts of Richmond, Colter stumbled along, yanking the reins of his horse when he almost fell. He tried not to think about the hours that had followed his finding Brice and Andre. All day they had remained hidden in the ice house, until details of Yankees came, trying to pry the frozen bodies of their fallen comrades for burial. By mingling with them, the three of them made good their escape.

But in the days that followed, Andre turned feverish, begging for Naomi, and Colter, securing permission from General Longstreet, had sent Brice to fetch her, since his wound was not serious. Colter almost envied him the chance to go to Richmond, but he had his own orders to carry dispatches to General Bragg in Kentucky.

And now he was finally able to bring Andre home and satisfy his own longing to see Elizabeth and his daughter. He rubbed the scraggly length of beard that covered his cheeks and chin, dragging forth a smile, thinking of what Elizabeth would say, wondering if she wore his Christmas gift.

At that moment, Elizabeth was hushing Nicole and thinking of Colter. She had accepted a ride on a dray wagon when carrying her daughter became impossible. As she glanced at the tall spires of the churches sharply etched against the ever-lightening sky, prayers for Colter's safety, wherever he was, formed in her mind.

The wagon turned toward the riverfront, and she sighed, longing to see the rail station. A water wagon carrying barrels rumbled alongside and the drivers exchanged greetings. She shivered to hear the water was going to Mr. Libby's warehouse, where most of the Yankee officers taken prisoner were housed. Others were held on Belle Isle in the river below.

If fate was cruel and Colter was ever taken prisoner by the Yankees, she hoped he would have more humane treatment than the men imprisoned within the walls of the Southern prisons.

"Fearsome sight, ain't it, ma'am," the driver stated as they rode passed the warehouse.

"Yes, yes, it is," she answered, shielding Nicole's eyes.

"Hear tell them Yankees don't dare go near the window. Sentries got a right to shoot them if they do. Fella was bragging a ways back that he got hisself a month's furlough for shooting one of them."

Elizabeth couldn't argue. She had heard similar stories. But she wanted him to stop talking about it and didn't know how to shut him up. She certainly didn't want to recall the well-known cruelty of Commissary-General Northrop, who told the captain in charge of supplying the prisoners' needs that he could throw them all into the James River.

Stacks of boxes were piled up outside the prison now, and Elizabeth turned away from the sight of Richmond's poor rifling through them while the sentries stood by and watched. She thought of herself as a loyal Southerner, but this sight disturbed her.

"Pity, ain't it. An' them warehouses down here are full up with flour an' no one can get to it, ma'am. Gonna be trouble over it for sure."

Elizabeth murmured, not really paying attention. Nicole was squirming, becoming restless, and she began to dread the coming train ride. Silently she urged the plodding horse to go faster.

At last they reached the train station, and Elizabeth thanked the man for the ride. She hurried to purchase her ticket, daunted by the crowd. So many soldiers milled about, many of them wounded, helped by their fellow soldiers or hovering family members.

She was thankful they didn't have to wait too long, for Nicole, eyes wide, was asking questions that embarrassed Elizabeth.

"Where's his leg, Mama?" she asked as one soldier hobbled by on a pair of crutches.

"Yeah, Johnny-reb," someone good-naturedly teased, "tell us where it is."

Mortified, Elizabeth watched as the man stopped and began to maneuver himself around so that he faced them. She didn't even realize that she had pulled Nicole close and placed a protective arm around her shoulders until the soldier spoke to her.

"Ain't no need, ma'am. As for you, little darlin', I lost it to a Yankee."

"That's silly. He can't use three legs," Nicole answered, smiling up at him.

Guffaws and softer laughter from the women greeted this remark, and several of the soldiers burst into a song as several harmonicas played "Dixie's Land." Elizabeth always found it strange that a minstrel song written by a Northerner was the South's anthem of choice.

The Richmond & Petersburg engine pulled in, giving off great white clouds of steam due to the cold. Several of the soldiers helped Elizabeth up the steps the conductor lowered, and then made sure she and Nicole had seats.

Excited by her first train ride, Nicole was bouncing up and down. Elizabeth tried to calm her but gave up until two dour-faced matrons sat opposite them.

Fumbling from nerves, Elizabeth withdrew a small piece of corn bread and a napkin, giving them to Nicole, hoping that after she ate she would nap. The stench of the train crowded with soldiers made her stomach churn. The men tramped up and down the aisles, shouting, drinking and spitting on the floors. Officers looked the other way.

As the train picked up speed, she closed her eyes, for she had never been at ease travelling by rail. They seemed to rush across the countryside, threading the miles over a shaky timber trestle past land where no life could be seen.

The closer the train came to Petersburg, the more her nerves felt frayed. Was she doing the right thing? What if Alma wasn't at Twin Pines? No, she chided herself a moment later, she would be there. Until her last breath, Alma Waring would remain on her precious land and in her home. She would be there, as always. Waiting.

Nearly twenty-two miles away in Richmond, Colter's thoughts almost echoed those same words. Elizabeth would be waiting for him. But within minutes of gaining access to the house she had shared with Naomi, he knew she was not there. The rooms held a strange emptiness, and once he had settled Andre in bed, he searched the house until he found her note.

His vague feeling of unease vanished. He told Naomi that Elizabeth had had to return to Emily's. "As soon as I purchase whatever you need, I'll ride out to see her."

"Rest first," Naomi urged. "Stay here with Andre, and I will go out."

Colter caught a glimpse of himself in the bureau mirror. He looked as though he had been indulging himself in a drunken revel for more than a few days. He smelled like it, too. With a rueful grin, he nodded. "All right, you go, Naomi."

Once she left, he started fires in all the rooms, for the house was cold. Certain that Andre rested, he crossed the yard to the kitchen and began a fire there. Drawing water from the well, he filled the kettle and paced as he waited for it to come to a boil. The pantry yielded little to tempt him, and he once again trekked back to the house to check on Andre. When he returned and found the water still had not heated, he wondered how a woman ever got anything done having to wait like this. His solution was to add more wood to the fire.

It was on his third trip back to the kitchen that he saw Josh opening the back gate. He called out, startling the old man.

"That you, Colonel?" Josh asked, not recognizing him.

Colter met him halfway across the barren yard. "What are you doing back here? I just arrived and found Elizabeth's note that she had returned to Miss Emily."

"She did?" Josh stared at him with a puzzled look.

"You did come to fetch her, didn't you?" Colter felt the unease return and grow.

"Yes, suh. See, the captain, he took—"

"What captain?"

"Captain...uh...Halleck. That's it. He come by jus' when I was fixin' to come an' fetch Miz Elizabeth. Says he needs the wagon 'cause he's got wounded men. An' Miz Emily, well she says give him the wagon an' mules."

"Then where is Elizabeth?"

"If she ain't here, Colonel, don't reckon I know."

Angry, Colter plowed his fingers through his hair. He was about to vent that anger on Josh when he stopped himself. The old man was shivering and had obviously walked all this way.

"Come into the kitchen, Josh. There's a fire and sure to be something else to warm you."

"But Miz Elizabeth—"

"We'll talk inside."

Once Josh recounted what had happened, Colter was at a loss to understand where she and Nicole could be. He knew she would never attempt to walk with the child all the way to Emily's. With Dobie gone, she had no one to leave Nicole with, and he was certain she did not take the child to work with her.

"Josh, Lieutenant Colonel Laurent is in the house. He's been wounded and needs someone to stay with him until his..." What the devil was he going to call Naomi? His mistress? Lady? "There is a woman who will be here to care for him, but I can't wait. I must search for Elizabeth."

Colter did not attempt to take his hunter. The poor beast rested in a three-legged doze, and he could not demand more than the horse had already given him. He set out on foot, realizing his unkempt appearance was garnering stares. If Elizabeth was at work, he couldn't very well go barging in there, demanding to see her, looking like a madman.

Going a few blocks out of his way, he headed for his hotel.

Finding a duplicate of Elizabeth's note under his door made unease dissipate and fear replace it. The disordered contents of his desk caught his attention, and at first, he merely thought the bait he left had finally been taken. He almost didn't notice the two glasses and decanter as a knock on the door distracted him. Colter took the hot water he had ordered in the lobby, but set it aside.

He started to unbutton his tunic, when he stared at the glasses. In spite of his urge to hurry, Colter was drawn to the desk. He began to look at the papers scattered across the top, noticing the dates.

These were mostly letters pertaining to business that should have been waiting for him in his box at the hotel counter.

It made no sense that someone would have gone to the trouble to remove his post, bring it up here to his room, obviously read it and then make no attempt to cover up what they had done.

Unless this had been left in so deliberate a manner for him to find it, and draw the conclusion that was now fighting its way into his mind.

Had Elizabeth stumbled into his room while his desk was being searched? And if she did, what had happened to her?

Filled with a chilling rage, Colter forced himself to be calm and think this through. The other scene he envisioned was that Elizabeth gained entry to his room, left her note, but no, he stopped himself. Elizabeth would never read his mail. No, *she* would never do that.

Grabbing his hat, Colter ran for the door. He knew exactly who had been in his room. And the Union army couldn't save that hide if Elizabeth was hurt.

Elizabeth offered a prayer that no one would recognize her as the train began to slow before pulling into the station.

She shook off her sudden misgivings, woke Nicole and waited until the soldiers and the two matrons had departed before she carried her daughter off the train.

Carriages and wagons that had come to meet passengers were soon filled with baggage, and she sought out a public conveyance to take them from Pocahontas to the beginning of the Jerusalem Plank Road. Twin Pines lay fifteen miles southeast of Petersburg, between the Norfolk and Petersburg railroad and the Petersburg and Weldon rail line. The idea of walking all that way brought home to her how reckless her journey was.

The air held the warning of snow. She murmured comforting reassurances to Nicole that she would soon be warm, and knew she had to find them transportation.

In the end, Elizabeth decided to approach an elderly Negro couple with a farm cart. They didn't question her, for which she was grateful, nor did they think her strange for asking to be dropped off a ways from Twin Pines. She was afraid and wished she could blame the couple's telling her about the Yankee bands foraging in the area, stealing whatever they wanted, but she knew her fear came from her own growing dread to see that house again, with all its horrid memories.

She cradled Nicole against the jarring of the wagon and took courage for what was to come by remembering her promise to Nicole that no one would take her, no one would harm her.

She had to find the strength to face the woman who, in her eyes, personified all that was evil.

Chapter Twenty

Colter raced down the hallway and around the corner to Jenna's room. He didn't bother to knock. He kicked the door open. At first, he thought he was too late, that she was gone, for the bureau top was stripped clean and the wardrobe doors gaped open, revealing it was empty. It wasn't until he stepped into the room that he found her portmanteau behind the door. He released a breath that he didn't realize he had been holding.

There was nothing he could do about the splintered door molding, but he did manage to close the door to wait for her. He hoped for Jenna's sake that she did not keep him waiting too long.

It was nearly an hour later when he heard her voice in the hallway. His patience had been stretched to its limit.

Jenna, so attentive to details, noticed the door frame and turned quickly to the porter following her. "Please wait in the hall for me, I won't be a moment." The man nodded and she took a deep breath, released it and walked inside, closing the door behind her.

"Colonel, I did not expect to find you here."

"No games, Jenna." But he had to admire her calm, collected manner, for as he continued to gaze at her, he realized that she was really not at all surprised to find him here.

"Games, Colonel? I don't quite understand your meaning."

Colter allowed himself a bitter laugh. "My dear, there is no need to ply your charm on me. It would be wasted. I'm not Hugh."

"No, you are not my husband, but he is your dear friend. I believe he once mentioned that you valued your honor above all things. I have often wondered if that were true."

Colter stared back at her. He could almost see the sharp working of her mind, and sensed that each calculated remark was setting him up for something.

"Where is Elizabeth, Jenna? I know she was here in the hotel."

Her lashes lowered. "Why would you think I would know? Perhaps, she came here to visit another gentleman."

Anger surged through him. He wanted to shake her and had to restrain himself from crossing the room.

"I warned you, no games, madam. I know she was here and it was not to see anyone. She left a note in my room. I believe she interrupted someone who was searching it."

"Are you accusing me, Colonel?" she asked in a honeyed voice.

"No, Jenna, I'm not accusing you. I'm telling you what happened. But it is unnecessary for me to say more, isn't it? You were there. Fact, not accusation.

Fact, you have been steadily supplying information to the—"

"You go too far, Colonel. I would suggest that you think carefully before you say another word. My husband would call you out if I told him what you have dared. Breaking into my room and making these—"

"Do you believe that your empty threats are going to stop me, Jenna?" Colter stepped toward her, satisfied to see her visibly shaken. "I want to know where Elizabeth is. If she has come to any harm, I will see that you pay for it. You and your Yankee lover."

She paled and shrank back against the solid wood of the door.

Colter smiled. "Surely you will forgive me for not acting the gentleman, but I haven't time to waste. You will tell me."

"And in return?"

"Ever the whore, Jenna?"

She tossed her head, her chin angled defiantly and her eyes blazing at him. "What would you know? I was forced to marry a man I didn't love. Never once did he come to see me after I lost our child. What right have you to judge me?"

"Hugh couldn't come to you. War had been declared and he was needed. You knew that. He wrote to you. And I don't care why you've become a traitor. Do you understand?" he asked, coming closer and closer to her, until he was mere inches from her.

"I know exactly what you've been doing all this time. I have made sure that you were kept properly supplied with false information. You worked for us, against the Yankees, Jenna."

"That's how much you know," she stated with a last show of bravado.

"Tell me about Elizabeth. I know you had something to do with her disappearance."

"I won't say a word unless you are willing to bargain with me."

He assessed her with a frank scrutiny that should have made her blush. She met his gaze unflinchingly.

"Do we have a bargain, Colonel?"

"Tell me your terms, Jenna," he said, smiling coldly, "but remember, I am not Hugh, so don't count on my being a gentleman."

"Get me a pass to Washington. That is all I want. No, wait." She glanced around the room, avoiding his penetrating gaze. "You must think of something to tell Hugh so he won't ever come after me."

"A high price. Where is Elizabeth?"

"You'll agree?"

"It will be my pleasure to rid my friend of you."

Jenna trembled under the hardness of his voice and his eyes that suddenly appeared devoid of emotion. She tried inching away, but his arm entrapped her on one side and she stilled.

"There was a letter in your post about James Waring. Elizabeth read it. She's gone to Petersburg to confront her mother-in-law."

"Sweet Christ!" Colter closed his eyes. Whatever he thought, whatever he had expected, this had not entered his mind. "When?" he demanded, pinning Jenna with his fierce gaze once more.

"She was to leave at first light. And now, my terms."

Colter spun around and walked away from her. He couldn't bear to be near her any longer. What was he going to tell Hugh? The man loved her, loved her just as much as Colter loved Elizabeth. Raking his fingers through his hair, Colter paused before the desk.

"Have you paper and ink?"

"The top drawer," she answered, afraid to move from the door. She watched as he hurriedly wrote out a few lines and turned to her, folding it.

"Take this to the War Office. You'll get your pass. They know my signature, so you shouldn't have any trouble."

"And Hugh?" she asked, taking the proffered note and unfolding it to read.

"Don't you trust me?"

"No, Colonel, I do not. This is my life that I have risked. For nothing, so you tell me. But there are a few things I have managed that I am sure you are unaware of."

"Bragging now that you have what you want?"

"No. I am not. I've stolen notes from the Treasury Department. I must say, my forgeries were quite good."

"Why are you telling me, Jenna?" he inquired with impatience stamped across his features.

"I want to make sure that you don't change your mind. You see, Elizabeth helped me."

"You bitch!" Colter started for her and barely stopped himself.

"Not really, Colonel. I know about it, and now you do. I just wanted to warn you that any revelations you make regarding this will implicate Elizabeth." Jenna refolded the note and smiled. "You are going after her, aren't you?"

"As soon as I rid myself of you," he stated coldly, clenching his hands to his sides. Her laughter was mocking.

"Make sure that Hugh doesn't follow, Colonel. My *Yankee lover* is quite jealous. He would likely enjoy killing him."

"Stand aside." The words came from between his gritted teeth.

With a sweep of her skirt, Jenna did just that. But as Colter opened the door, she added, "By the way, Colonel, it's been reported that Yankee bands have been raiding the countryside around Petersburg. I would suggest that you hurry."

Colter refused to answer her goad. He didn't even slam the door closed. But at least he could justify to himself the lie he would tell Hugh about Jenna's death. The man deserved better than Jenna.

Jenna watched his rigid back recede down the hall. Her ploy had worked but left her with a bitter taste. Colter's Southern honor would force him to hold to their bargain. He would find a way to tell Hugh that she was dead and she would be finally free.

The cart had long since turned off the main road, and Elizabeth felt every jolt as the wagon dipped and swayed. She knew they were approaching the lane that would lead up to Twin Pines, for through the trees she had caught glimpses of half-hidden homes, set well back from the road. Fear had settled into a cold, hard knot inside her belly. And when they turned into a smaller lane lined with pine and hickory trees, she knew only minutes remained before she and Nicole would be set down.

It came too soon. She thanked the couple for the ride, listened to their warnings to be on watch for the Yankee patrols, and, with arms that ached from the strain, she lifted Nicole and began to walk.

There was a desolate air that slowly seeped into her, forcing her to examine her surroundings. The day had grown overcast and the entwined branches, laced into a canopy overhead, seemed to whisper warnings in their play of shadows. Elizabeth shivered and held Nicole tighter. She stumbled and Nicole cried out, hushed quickly by Elizabeth's murmured voice.

The road curved and Elizabeth stopped for a moment to shift her daughter's weight. The air had warmed and she could almost smell the damp coming of snow. The woodlands, where she once had sought refuge, no longer offered security. Elizabeth felt as if an unseen menace watched them.

From inside herself she dragged up the courage to continue.

The house emerged from a tall stand of pines and once again Elizabeth stopped. The house was of wood, with squared pillars ascending from the ground to the roof to support the wide verandas on both levels. She gazed around and frowned that there was no sign of life. The quarters and work buildings were beyond a small rise, close to the creek, and directly behind the house were the smokehouse and kitchen, along with the cabins that housed the servants. But all seemed empty.

"Mama, I'm hungry."

"Yes, love, I know you are. And I promise you'll soon be fed and warm." But even as she offered these reassurances to her child, Elizabeth began to wonder if Alma was there. She started forward, noticing the gaping stable doors, half-torn from their bracings, and other signs of neglect. Fences, once neatly white-washed, were either missing or had broken gaps in them. Coming up around the curve of the driveway, she saw the peeling paint on the house itself, the shrubs and vines that had once graced the lower veranda ripped from the ground.

Elizabeth could not take another step, no longer afraid of confronting Alma but of what she would find behind the closed doors. She set Nicole down and took firm hold of her small hand, dropping the basket she had carried.

Nicole made no sound, but when Elizabeth looked down at her daughter, she knew she had to brave whatever waited and get Nicole out of the damp.

Together then they climbed the wide steps and approached the door. Elizabeth knocked, waited and then knocked again.

"Mama, no one's here. I wanna go home."

Elizabeth didn't answer. She gripped the door latch and to her surprise it wasn't locked. Pushing open the door, she led Nicole inside with her and trembled at the rush of memories that took hold.

The lofty arched hallway was just as she remembered, with its fluted pilasters and carved paneling. The wide curving stairs that led up to the room where she had been held prisoner brought one shiver after another, until she visibly shook.

"Alma," she called out. There was no answer. The doors to the drawing room were closed, and Elizabeth hesitated a moment before she opened them. The room was exactly as she remembered—the marble mantel crowded with figurines, the wallpaper from England, the richly shadowed portraits, the damask coverings on the windows, the ornate carvings on the furniture. The room oppressed her, but there was wood in the box and she hurried to get a fire started.

Once the kindling caught, Elizabeth settled Nicole with her quilt in a large wing chair and dragged it close to the blaze. She forced herself to smile, added small logs to the fire and began to talk to dispel the gloomy silence.

"Now, you be a good girl for Mama, and stay right here while I find us something to eat. We'll have a cozy supper here where it's nice and warm."

"It's a bad house, Mama."

"No. This is not a bad house, Nicole. Mama wouldn't—"

"I 'member this. You cried."

Elizabeth couldn't face her daughter. She closed her eyes, wondering if Alma was right and she was insane. All the reasons she had given herself to come here no longer mattered.

"Mama—"

"No. No, Nicole. I'll show you this house isn't bad. There is nothing here that can hurt us. Not anymore. Now, wait right here for Mama."

Elizabeth searched each room on the lower floor. She couldn't find anything out of place, yet there was a sense that no one had used these rooms for some time. It wasn't the covering of dust on the furniture, just a deserted air that she could almost breathe. She stood in the hall once more, staring up the stairway, but nothing, no force could make her climb them. With a firm step, she headed to the back of the house, outside and across to the kitchen.

The smoldering coals in the massive fireplace first lent hope that someone was here. A few crumbs littered the wood table, but the pantry revealed bare shelves.

She called out for Alma repeatedly but received no answer. Drawing a bucket of water from the well, she set it to heat in the kettle and went around back of the building to the root cellar. The thick wooden slab took all of her strength to open it, and a rank smell that made her gag came rushing out.

Elizabeth peered down the few steps into the blackness below. She felt the hairs on the back of her neck prickle and thought of returning to the kitchen to get a candle to light her way. Only the thought of Nicole being hungry drove her to make the descent in the dark.

The smell of something rotting overpowered her. She lifted her skirt and covered her mouth and nose, trying not to breathe deeply. The light, overcast as the sky was, did not penetrate the cellar. She turned to the shelves built into the dirt wall and searched blindly with one hand.

The first few feet of shelving proved empty and she stepped deeper into the blackness, cautiously feeling her way. She nearly cried out when she touched the edge of a burlap sack and dropped her skirt to use both hands to lift it free. Tucking it under one arm, Elizabeth knew she had either dried beans or rice, but once again reached out along the shelves, ignoring the brush of webs that caught in her hand.

With every breath she took, nausea roiled until she couldn't stand it. The rank damp chilled her and she spun around, losing her balance and falling.

Elizabeth dropped the sack, grabbed hold of a shelf and felt the wood splinter into her palms. She cried out as she hit not the hard-packed earth of the root cellar floor, but a large, tough object that bowed her back.

For a moment she lay stunned, her breath knocked from her. Elizabeth lifted her head, drawing air into her lungs at the same moment. Her eyes widened as her hand felt the shape of the thing beneath her.

A scream welled up but her throat closed, refusing to allow her terror free.

The icy chill of a bony hand met her searching fingers. She rolled to her side, unable to control the heaves that emptied her stomach. A body! She had fallen on a body. Her legs wouldn't hold her, so Elizabeth crawled. Every move to free herself of this sickening grave shoved the wood splinters deeper into her palms. But she didn't feel the pain. She frantically clawed the earthen floor to put distance between herself and the corpse.

She had to get out of there. Staggering, Elizabeth managed to find the stairs and climbed them. Outside, she collapsed onto the ground as heaves once again racked her body.

On her hands and knees, head bowed, Elizabeth refused to think about the body in the cellar. She wiped her mouth with the back of her hand, knowing that she had to reach Nicole.

Her daughter had been right. This was a *bad house.* And she was truly mad to have come back here.

Swallowing the bile that rose again, she stood up and dragged fresh air into her lungs, then ran back to the house. She threw open the door, pain slicing her again as the pressure drove the wood so deep her palms bled.

"Nicole! Nicole!" she screamed, driven now by the unnamed menace that she had sensed and so foolishly ignored.

The hall seemed to have lengthened in the few minutes—or was it hours—since she had deserted her child. Or were her own legs refusing to carry her forward?

Elizabeth came to a sudden stop. The drawing room doors were open. "Nicole," she whispered. Not a sound answered.

"Dear Lord, no! No! Answer me, Nicole. Answer me!"

She slowly turned toward the stairway and tried to swallow the bile that coated her mouth. There was no moisture to aid her. For a moment she swayed, resisting her mind's command for her to climb those stairs.

It was only the thought that Nicole might be up there, frightened, needing her, that gave her strength to overcome the remembered horror the rooms above held for her.

"Mama is coming," she whispered, more to reassure herself.

"She cannot hear you, Elizabeth."

"Alma." Elizabeth barely mouthed the name. She stilled. The fear that almost paralyzed her crumbled into fragments. She held on to the one thought she could never deny: Alma would not harm Nicole. A strange calm seeped through her body and she turned to face her.

Elizabeth felt as if she were meeting Alma for the first time again, seeing her through a haze. The woman's bearing was regal. Her stately height, her slender figure, every angular feature perfectly proportioned, all lent great presence, although she was no beauty. Her milk white skin, protected from the sun at all cost, took years off her age, as did the white blondness of her hair, pinned into a chignon.

Ice. Cold, chilling, ice. Just like the diamond earrings that flashed as she tilted her head, staring with eyes that were so pale a blue that they almost appeared devoid of color.

"Join me. I have been kept waiting far too long."

Elizabeth watched Alma retreat into the drawing room. The order lingered, replaying its insidious command in her mind like so many others before it.

This is what you came here for, she reminded herself. Believe that Nicole is safe. Yet, she didn't move.

She glanced down at her hands and saw them as if from a great distance. Slowly turning them over, she viewed her red, swollen flesh, unable to stop the trembling that overtook her body.

Coward. Coward. The litany of fear that she had often sung to herself, which had held her a prisoner here as much as the lock on the door, repeated its chanting now.

No. She was not a coward, but she would be a fool to underestimate Alma. The woman was evil. Even as the thought came to her, Elizabeth walked forward and entered the room.

She searched for a sign of Nicole. "Where is she, Alma?"

"Resting. I put her in your old room."

She ignored Alma's gesture to sit before the fire. Nicole was upstairs and likely locked in. Elizabeth cast off the far too familiar role of victim that Alma enjoyed seeing her play.

"Tell me, Alma, have you truly enjoyed your little game of power? I know about James. I know how he died. A coward, they called him. Shot by his own men when he ran from battle." Elizabeth paused. Every word she spoke filled her with a sense of power, of freedom. Her voice was firm, lashing out again at the woman who watched her, unrepentant for the destruction she had caused.

"Lies, all of it," she continued. "From the very first you twisted all of us—me, James, Colter and my daughter. How do you live with yourself? Did you truly grieve for your son? Or was all that a lie, too?"

"James was not worthy of my grief."

"Dear Lord, you unfeeling witch! He loved you. James did everything to please you." Elizabeth stepped nearer, staring at Alma, hoping for a sign, a small crack in the icy demeanor. There was none. "Did you really think I would allow you to mold my daughter in an image of yourself? I would die first."

"You may well do just that, Elizabeth." Alma lifted the hand concealed by the drape of her skirt. She smiled, then raised the long barrel of the pistol she held. "I believe you should retire, my dear. You have had a long journey."

"Whose body is in the cellar, Alma?"

"That need not concern you."

"Whose body is in the cellar?" Elizabeth repeated on a rising note, desperate now to keep her wits about her.

Alma gracefully stood up and, still holding the gun, began walking toward her. Elizabeth had no choice but to back up.

"Where are all the servants, Alma?"

"Run off with that Yankee trash that came 'round with promises of freedom. What would they know? Freedom carries responsibilities."

"Yes, yes, you're right." Elizabeth reached the hall and thought of running, but Alma quickened her pace and was right there with her.

"You are going to be obedient, are you not, Elizabeth?"

"Yes. Yes, I will."

"Good. I am pleased to hear that."

Elizabeth couldn't take her eyes off the pistol. She measured Alma, gauging how strong she was, and wondered if she would have a chance if she made a grab for the weapon.

As if she had read her mind, Alma cocked the hammer. "Go upstairs, Elizabeth. I have already used this and found I am quite good. It only took three shots to finish Billings off."

"Billings?" Elizabeth questioned, hating the quiver of her voice. Her heel hit the bottom step, and without turning, she lifted her skirt, wincing as her hands closed over the cloth, and began to back up the stairway. For a moment she thought Alma had forgotten her. The woman's eyes held a glazed look. With a slight shake of her head, she directed her attention to Elizabeth.

"Billings is the man I hired to bring Nicole back where she belongs."

"You . . . you killed him?" Elizabeth knew then that Alma was insane. Not just driven to keep what she believed was hers, but truly mad.

"He failed me, my dear. I cannot tolerate failure from anyone. It was just as well that James died. He failed me, too."

"James loved you, Alma. Remember how he would bring you presents when he returned from a trip? You loved his gifts. You—"

"You were jealous."

The underlying hate that crackled in her voice made Elizabeth hesitate. She didn't know if she should agree. How was she going to keep Alma stable? How was she going to get Nicole and herself away from here?

"How did James fail you?" she asked, hoping to distract her.

"The fool exposed himself to mumps. He recovered but lost the only useful ability he had. James could not father a child. But then, we found you. A weak, tedious, witless fool. You were so ready to believe that Colter betrayed you. But even then, I had to convince James to offer marriage. The dolt had scruples. With all that was at stake, he dared to put his friendship with Colter before me. James would have seen me cast from my home. I am glad that he is dead, do you hear me? I am glad that I will not have to rid myself of that weakling like I did his father."

Elizabeth was speechless.

Alma began to laugh.

The sound sent fingers of dread down Elizabeth's spine. She turned and ran. She finally knew why James had lied about Colter.

A shot splintered the wall above Elizabeth's head.

A shot that caused the Union captain leading his patrol to halt on the curving driveway that led to Twin Pines.

Chapter Twenty-One

Colter rode south, passing Williams Wood and the Sturdivant's Mill, testing the endurance of himself and the stallion he had stolen. It was dusk when he was forced to veer off the Plank Road, for the thick wet snow had left the road soft and wagons were cutting deeper ruts until they became mired in the mud.

He tried to remain alert, cutting across the roads, passing houses with lighted windows. Warren, Avery, Gwynn, he named each family's land, trying to stop his thoughts from wandering, trying to stop the weariness from overtaking him. Brown, Rowland, Ambree. He forced himself to recall a family's crops, the best of their horses or the last time he had seen a family member, anything to keep himself awake.

Veering south, he splashed through creeks and found little-used trails, letting the big stallion choose his own firm footing, guiding him around Lee's home and then the mill. Heading across Pigeon Creek, Colter ignored the icy splash of water, giving the stallion his head up the bank and back through the forest.

He rode with his head bowed, so that his hat brim offered some protection against the pelt of snow, and he hoped that Elizabeth was warm at Twin Pines. Of her safety, he did not dare to think.

Between his knees he felt the muscles of his mount slide and tense and relax, and knew the animal had great strength held in careful reserve, ready at a touch to be freed.

Colter wondered at his own strength. Did he, too, have reserves left to be drawn upon?

Snow melted on his tiered greatcoat until its wet weight hindered his movements. It disappeared, too, as the flakes touched the sweating flanks of the horse. Still, Colter drove him.

Questions he dared not ask himself before suddenly loomed in his mind. But he had no answer to the most important ones. Why had Elizabeth decided to confront Alma on her own? What had there been about James in the letter she read that would have driven her to risk coming down here with Nicole?

The stallion's snort warned him of riders coming, and he barely managed to conceal himself behind a small stand of saplings. Colter felt his head droop forward, his body heavy and tired, and he pushed himself to lean down, whispering and covering the stallion's nose so he wouldn't give away their presence.

The damp velvet neck was warm against his cheek and he closed his eyes, wanting to rest. But the horse's spirit was not nearly as downtrodden as his own and its restive moves jerked Colter awake.

He urged him at a walk now, picking his way through the forest, damning himself for not sighting the riders so he would know if they were friend or enemy.

Twin Pines would not be far ahead, he was sure. He could sleep there and be rid of the soaked cloth that burdened him.

He wondered if the stallion had somehow read his thoughts, for his ears pricked alertly and his step was short and springy.

"Guess you'd like warm mush and a thick bed of straw," Colter whispered. Through the thinning trees, Colter sighted the lane, and yet something held him back from letting the stallion take the curving driveway up to Twin Pines at a full canter.

Until he heard the shooting. Then nothing could stop him. He raced the blooded beast full out, with a demand for all he had, uncaring of the ruts, the mud, or the dark that sent him blindly into fire.

Elizabeth and Nicole were his only thought. And Colter had an answer to his own question. He did have reserves of strength to call upon.

"Fire!" Captain Michael Thorton ordered his small Union patrol. Their bullets raked across the lower floor of the house, shattering the windowpanes. Silence. He raised his hand slowly for his men to hold their fire.

"These damn rebs are all crazy," one of his soldiers muttered.

The captain was inclined to agree. When he had heard that first shot, he ordered his men to fan out and approach the house from the woods and the cleared fields, using whatever they could find for cover. He assumed that someone had been on watch, for they had barely broken cover when they were fired upon. Yet, what struck him as truly strange, were the fires that were lit in each of the front rooms. He used his field glasses to search the lower floor, hoping to catch sight of a shadow that would alert them to where the shooter was located.

There was no sign of anyone. He could smell the thick smoke that poured from the massive brick chimneys and thought of the shelter they had sought only to find themselves embroiled in a skirmish with another staunch rebel.

"Think we hit him, Cap?"

"Odds tell me we should have, but instinct warns me I'd be wrong. Take two men and circle 'round back." He waited, thought of the warmth that his cold, tired men needed and wondered if the rebel who shot at them was at all rational. Those fires warned him, but of what he could not even begin to guess.

And into that tense quiet came the frightened cry of a child.

A short volley of shots came from the far right window.

"Fire!"

Elizabeth heard the order again and clutched Nicole tight. They were huddled in the far corner of what once had been her prison. Fleeing from Alma, Elizabeth barely had time to realize that the furniture had been stripped from the room, so she had nothing to use to bar the door, when she heard the first shots and the return fire.

If Alma had not screamed "Yankees!" she wouldn't know who was out there. Nor could she think of them as enemies. They were keeping Alma away from her and Nicole.

Once again Nicole cried out, and the bullets flew, shattering what was left of the windowpanes onto the floor below. Elizabeth buried her own scream. She heard a few shots, thought they were from Alma and then there was a thick, waiting silence.

What if Alma decided to climb up here? What if she was mad enough to fire at the Yankees from these windows?

"Mama, I'm scared."

"I know, love, I know." Elizabeth couldn't risk her child any longer. "Listen to me. We are going to play a game that will take us away from here. Just follow me, precious, don't talk, just move."

She cast aside the quilt she had wrapped around Nicole and, laying herself flat, waited until Nicole followed suit. Elizabeth felt the heat of the thick wooden floorboards against her stinging palms and cheek but paid no attention to it as she crawled along the floor.

"That's it, Nicole. We'll pretend we are little snakes wiggling our way home."

"I don't wanna be a snake. I'm a worm."

"Anything, love, be anything you want, just keep your head down." Elizabeth ignored the sporadic shots. She was almost to the window. "Keep down and wait for Mama." With her body prone, she raised one hand to feel along the sill. She prayed as her fingers inched across the wood, hoping she would not find the small slivers of wood that were shaved and hammered between frame and window to seal it shut.

The Lord was not listening. Halfway across the sill she found the first one. With a sob of despair she dropped her hand. Utter defeat swamped her.

"Hot, Mama. The floor's hot."

Elizabeth dragged her head up. She smelled smoke. And heard the echo of Alma's prideful voice. "The entire house was constructed from wood cut and cured in our forests."

Nicole crawled over to her and Elizabeth lifted her to her lap. The resinous heart-pine floors and walls would burn until they were consumed in the flames.

The windows! She had to break out the window. With one hand shielding Nicole's face against her shoulder, she crooked her elbow and slammed it against one of the small panes. The chill night air rushed in, and she turned her child's face so she could breathe it.

"You'll never set foot in my home!" Alma screamed from below, torching the draperies in the drawing room.

Flames shooting from the lower floor windows was the sight that greeted Colter as he reached the house. He sawed on the reins and the stallion reared.

"Cap, it's a damn reb!"

"Hold your fire," Thorton ordered.

"Elizabeth!" Colter shouted, aware and uncaring of the enemy at his back.

Hearing Colter below, Elizabeth set Nicole down. She stood before the window, and with her hand wrapped in the hem of her skirt, began to break out each of the panes of glass, calling his name.

Captain Thorton ran in a crouch, yelling for the reb to get under cover. Shots whizzed over his head and he dove flat out for the ground.

"Get down, you fool. There's a crazy man inside."

"A woman," Colter yelled, trying to control the near-crazed stallion. The horse reared repeatedly, his high steps and side swings making them an impossible target.

The fire was spreading, a huge ruddy glow that lit the yard with wavering shadows. For a few minutes both men stared and then Colter turned to the Yankee.

"Can your men give me cover? That's my wife and child up there."

"Sweet Lord! And who is shooting at us?"

"A crazy woman," Colter snapped, looking above. "Elizabeth, kick out the window! Use something to break the wood."

"I can't. There's nothing here."

"Hold my horse," Colter ordered, tossing down the reins. He whispered to the stallion, calming him with soothing pats even as he kneed the horse closer to the veranda.

Thorton grabbed the reins and ordered his men to cover them. Crawling alongside the wicked hoofs of the stallion, he issued a warning. "You can't hope to climb the support. There's no purchase, reb."

Colter didn't answer as he threw off his hat and rid himself of his greatcoat and tunic. Kicking his feet free of the stirrups, trying not to listen to the repeated splintering of wood that Elizabeth made above him, he braced his hands flat on the saddle.

"Steady him good, Yank."

He could feel the trembling that rippled over the stallion's body and slowly lifted his right leg until his boot found purchase on the saddle. A shot breezed by his shoulder and he crouched down, barely keeping his balance.

"Order your men to keep up a steady barrage of fire, Yank!"

Under other circumstances Thorton may have smiled at the imperious tone of the rebel giving him orders.

But he had heard the rising cry of a child, and pity moved him to give that order. He watched as the reb once again began to raise himself to stand on the saddle and he too issued soothing commands to keep the stallion still.

Elizabeth had no strength left. She had kicked out a small hole in the wooden frames that held forty-eight panes of glass. She knew she was as crazed as Alma for remembering how she counted each pane when the loneliness and despair of this room drove her to it in days past.

"Nicole, come here and let me lift you free. Colter is waiting for you, precious. He'll get you down."

"No, Mama, no. I don't wanna leave you."

"I'll be right with you." The smoke was getting thick. She could feel the intensity of the heat coming up through the floor, and with it, she heard Alma's wild laughter coming closer.

"Hurry, Nicole." There was no time to be sure that the glass and wood wouldn't hurt her child. She lifted and shoved her out onto the veranda.

Elizabeth had long since closed her mind to the pain that ripped through her hands. She gripped the wood frame with both hands on one side, bowed her head and swung her shoulders against the half-shattered frames. The wood held.

"Elizabeth. Elizabeth, where are you?" Alma crooned in a singsong voice.

Colter lost his breath, staring up at the frightened face of his daughter. His fingertips barely reached the edge of the veranda floor. Heat rose as the inferno below raged out of control. He could hear the shouts of the men in the yard and realized that more than one were holding the stallion still.

"Can you climb over the rail, Nicole?" He heard the desperation in his voice and felt his gut clench into a twisted knot when she shook her head.

"Hurry, Elizabeth, hurry," he urged, as one of the soldiers yelled a warning that flames were starting to lick the underside of the second-story veranda.

Elizabeth heaved her body again, and again, until the wood broke and she fell free.

Snatching Nicole up, she lifted her above the rail, lowering her and tossing wild looks over her shoulder.

She could see the flames shooting up the staircase, and within the doorway was the shadowed figure of Alma.

"You cannot leave, Elizabeth. You will never be free, never."

"I've got her," Colter yelled, handing Nicole down to waiting hands. "Hurry, love, come over the rail," he begged Elizabeth.

"It's Alma. I can't leave her to burn, Colter."

With a cry torn from his soul, Colter saw her turn away from the rail. "No! Leave her!" He listened to the snapping crackle of fire eating into wood. The whole left side of the house was blazing. "Elizabeth!"

"Mama! Mama!" Nicole screamed from below as one of the soldiers carried her away from the house. He tried to shield her from the sight, but she fought him, and he could barely keep his hold on her.

Elizabeth stepped toward the window. "Alma," she called softly. "Come to safety with me. No one is going to hurt you. But hurry, the flames—"

"No. I must find James."

"James is dead, Alma. He's dead!"

"No!" Alma screamed. "I will never leave my home. Never." The gun dropped from her hand with a clatter. "Useless James," she muttered. "Weakling. Where are you?"

"Alma, don't," Elizabeth cried as she watched Alma turn back toward the blaze in the hall. "Alma?"

There was a roaring blast and the stairway collapsed. Elizabeth backed against the veranda rail, shielding her face from the intensity of the heat and scorched smell that seemed to smother her. She felt a tug on her hem and turned.

"Colter...oh, God, Colter, she went back."

"Come to me, love. Just come to me." He tried to heave his body up, but his hand slipped.

Elizabeth bit through her lip at the lancing pain in her hands as she braced her body and climbed over the rail.

She couldn't jump and Colter couldn't grab hold of her.

"Turn around," he ordered, sweat blinding him, his heart missing a beat at the way she froze. "Turn, damn you! Trust me!"

In blind obedience, she turned, lowering her legs.

Colter took firm hold of her weight.

Blood welled from her palms. She couldn't keep her grip on the rail. A silent scream tore from her raw throat as she plunged free.

Her sudden fall threw Colter off balance. He barely managed to lock his arm around her waist, twisting his own body to break their fall.

But the Union soldiers closed tight and their strong shoulders bore the impact of Colter's and Elizabeth's bodies. There was a scramble until they were able to stand, and all of them turned to run, Colter dragging Elizabeth by the hand.

She fell to her knees, tearing free of his hold, cradling her wounded hands against her chest. Colter came to kneel beside her, unable to speak but offering her the shelter of his arms.

"Nicole," she whispered.

"Right here, ma'am," a soldier answered, setting the child down beside them.

Elizabeth was beyond crying, just as Colter felt his throat close so tight he could not utter a sound. He opened his arms and snuggled his child tight to him.

"What do we do with the reb, Captain?"

Thorton didn't answer immediately. He glanced behind him. The house was a blazing inferno. He had seen other fires, some he himself had been ordered to set, and knew of blazes that had consumed homes of those loyal to the Union. The losses were costly on both sides in property and human lives. He gazed again at the couple kneeling in the sodden earth with their child between them and wondered if they offered prayers of thanksgiving.

Colter lifted his head at that moment and met the direct gaze of the young Union captain. "If you will give me a few minutes with my family, sir, I will accompany you. I only beg that you allow me to first see them to shelter."

"We could all use that, sir," the captain returned. "Corporal Beck, find and secure a building as far from this hell as you can. We will offer our guests whatever there is to share."

"Thank you, Captain," Colter said with simple gratitude. "I will not forget your kindness or your help."

"And I, sir, hope this war will never let me forget my own code of honor to the point that I need make prisoners of a woman and child. And that is who I have offered my protection to this night."

Colter realized that the Union officer was going to ignore his presence and allow him to go free.

Colter slowly raised his hand and extended it to the Union officer. After a moment, Thorton shook it.

"Colter," Elizabeth whispered, "Alma killed the man she sent after Nicole. "He's . . . his body is in the root cellar. She was mad. Not even a bit of grief for James. She called him a weakling, and useless."

He thought to hush her and realized that he could not. She needed to talk, and he, he needed to listen. He learned of his once-best friend's death, of the shame his mother cast on James for his inability to father a child, of the lies that had separated them and the horror that Elizabeth had lived with.

When she was done, Elizabeth rested her head against his shoulder, and he found that he could only press a kiss to her temple. Colter knew then that the reserves of strength a man could have were not only the physical but from the heart, as well. He urged her to stand and held Nicole's small hand with his, sliding his other arm around Elizabeth's shoulders.

"My love," he murmured, his voice husky with emotion. "If you remember the story of Lot's wife, you know she was warned not to look back. To look back is to give the past power. Come with me," he coaxed. "Lot's wife was offered a promise of paradise. Until the war is over, I have nothing to offer you but a small corner of heaven." With a catch in his husky voice, he added softly, "Just as you and our child have given to sustain me."

Elizabeth lifted her tear-bright eyes to meet his imploring gaze. She raised her hand and traced the line of his lips with her fingertips. There was no need for her to turn around, for the flames of the burning house were reflected for a moment in his eyes.

And then, those flames were dimmed by the blazing glory of love and all its promise that shone down on her in the look he bestowed.

"I love you, Colter," she whispered.

"An' me," Nicole cried, tugging on his hand. "I love you the bestest, too."

* * * * *